For a long time Rose had believed she hated this place.

Now…maybe not. The memories had faded, even the worst of them. At least to a livable degree.

She'd learned not to expect more than adequacy from her life.

Rose straightened, folding the edge of her sweater over and holding the awkward bundle of tomatoes to her abdomen. She walked to the back door, feeling nearly as unwieldy as a pregnant lady.

Unexpectedly, the comparison made her smile. She'd pushed the pregnancy to the back of her mind for many years, but returning to her hometown had brought it all up again. There were times she had to consciously work to keep her feelings to herself. Aside from a small circle of people—her nonsupportive family, the despicable Lindstroms, Pastor Mike—it was still a secret to Alouette that she'd once been pregnant.

She didn't suppose that the townspeople would be too surprised to learn the truth. They'd always believed the worst of Wild Rose.

Dear Reader,

The residents of Michigan's Upper Peninsula—Yoopers—pride themselves on being hardy, independent people. (Ya, you betcha! Surviving five months of winter takes fortitude.) After her thorny appearances in the previous NORTH COUNTRY STORIES, Wild Rose Robbin was an interesting character to embrace. Evan Grant—who is caring, patient and very normal—turned out to be the perfect hero to tame this wild woman. But it's his shy daughter, Lucy, who needs Rose the most and teaches her how to open her heart.

This time around, I had fun writing about a few of the Yoopers' favorite winter pastimes—high school basketball, Christmas shopping, sledding and…snow shoveling. Although winter passes much too quickly in this book, Wild Rose does get to fulfill her dream of having A *Family Christmas*.

Happy holidays!

Carrie

P.S. To learn more about the NORTH COUNTRY STORIES miniseries, visit my Web site at www.carriealexander.com and sign up for the Get Carried Away e-newsletter.

A Family Christmas
Carrie Alexander

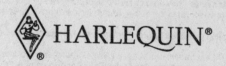

HARLEQUIN®

TORONTO • NEW YORK • LONDON
AMSTERDAM • PARIS • SYDNEY • HAMBURG
STOCKHOLM • ATHENS • TOKYO • MILAN • MADRID
PRAGUE • WARSAW • BUDAPEST • AUCKLAND

ISBN 0-373-71239-1

A FAMILY CHRISTMAS

Copyright © 2004 by Carrie Antilla.

www.eHarlequin.com

Printed in U.S.A.

Books by Carrie Alexander

HARLEQUIN SUPERROMANCE
1042—THE MAVERICK
1102—NORTH COUNTRY MAN*
1186—THREE LITTLE WORDS*

*North Country Stories

Don't miss any of our special offers. Write to us at the
following address for information on our newest releases.

Harlequin Reader Service
U.S.: 3010 Walden Ave., P.O. Box 1325, Buffalo, NY 14269
Canadian: P.O. Box 609, Fort Erie, Ont. L2A 5X3

CHAPTER ONE

THE WOMAN WAS THERE AGAIN, sitting cross-legged in the grass at the edge of the high-school sports field. At a distance, so that she might have been passed off as a loiterer, not an observer. But Evan Grant had been keeping his eye on her for many months—ever since the previous basketball season.

She was called Wild Rose.

And she *was* watching. Always watching.

Evan ambled past the long-jump pit. Two boys were stalling nearby, tightening the laces on their running shoes. He stopped to get them up and running. With loud groans, they joined the team members who were already jogging around the track that circled the field.

Evan was in sweatpants and sneakers himself, so he followed the group for half a lap, hectoring them like a drill sergeant until they were moving at a faster clip. The boys showered him with a chorus of complaints. They'd rather be in the gym, shooting baskets.

Calling encouragement to the stragglers, Evan peeled off at a jog and gradually slowed to a stop. He was now near the watcher, within speaking distance.

He didn't look directly at her. He surveyed the field. It was early September, the weather was warm and the new school year had just begun, but already some of the trees showed tinges of rusty color. His basketball team was not in top shape after a lazy summer. But this was only their first practice and before fall had really arrived he'd have built up their endurance.

In Evan's peripheral vision, the woman called Wild Rose hunched over a sketch pad. Disheveled hair as black as a crow's wing blew across her face. Her hands made quick, furtive movements. Slashes of the pencil, a scrub with the eraser, nervous fingers brushing aside crumbs that reminded him of the strawberry-flecked crusts his pouting daughter had crushed into her eggs that morning.

He drew closer. "You're Rose Robbin."

The name was odd. It brought to mind storybook illustrations—a mother robin in a kerchief, plump with feathers, brooding over a nest—accompanied by bouncy lyrics about bob-bob-bobbin' in the springtime.

At his voice, Rose bolted like a thoroughbred at the starting gate, but she didn't go far. Guilt was stamped across her face.

The guilt was what bothered Evan.

He was responsible for these kids. While he couldn't imagine the woman approaching any of them, she *did* have a certain reputation, so the question remained.

What interest did she have here?

He might have asked that outright, except there was a hint of vulnerability in her expression that made him want to treat her gently.

Rose flung back her head. Storm-cloud-blue eyes glared beneath the swoop of dark hair she impatiently pushed aside. "Yeah, I'm Rose Robbin. So what?"

Evan squinted. Being of fair mind, he'd tried to overlook what townspeople said about her. But there was no denying she was one of the hardscrabble Robbin family—supposed tough nuts and bad characters, all of them. She could handle herself. Perhaps he'd imagined the vulnerability out of a penchant for helping others—wounded females especially.

"You're interested in athletics?" he said.

Her mouth pulled into a sour pucker. "Not much."

"Oh. I've been counting you as one of our biggest fans."

She shook her head. "Don't think so."

"You went to all the home games last year."

After a hesitation, she shrugged. "Not much else to do in Alouette, is there?"

Evan scratched behind his ear. He'd been living in the small northern town on the shore of Lake Superior for nearly three years and had never been bothered by the remote location and lack of city-style amenities. The unspoiled countryside offered a wealth of activity—hunting, fishing, biking, hiking, skiing, swimming. "I seem to think of plenty to do."

"Bravo for you."

The stonewalling didn't exasperate Evan. Even though Rose must be in her early thirties, she wasn't so different from a sulky adolescent who had to show how little she cared before she could allow herself to soften. In his years as a teacher and coach, he'd had plenty of practice at probing beneath the veneer of stubborn independence. With teenagers, the trick was not to come on too strong—at first.

But this was an adult woman and he only needed answers, not involvement.

He cleared his throat. "Then it's coincidence that you're here at our first team practice of the season?"

Rose held the sketchbook to her chest beneath crossed arms. "Yeah," she snapped, still belligerent even though her quick indrawn breath told him there was more to her being there.

Not what he wanted to discover.

"It's a free country," she added.

He held up his palms. "Sure."

She glowered.

"You're an artist?"

Her arms tightened on the sketchpad. "No."

He said nothing, but raised an eyebrow. That usually worked.

She tossed her hair again. "I'm a clerk at the Buck Stop, as if you didn't know." Alouette was small—most faces were familiar, even if there'd been no formal introduction.

"Of course." The Buck Stop was a run-down convenience store a couple miles outside of town. Evan had stopped there now and then for gas, but it wasn't a particularly welcoming place. Not unlike Rose. "That wouldn't stop you from being an artist."

She gave a grudging hitch of one shoulder. "I draw a little."

"Can I see?"

She shook her head.

"Why not?" He wondered what she drew. Figures, perhaps. She might be using his team as unknowing models. That was all right, he supposed. If potentially creepy.

"My drawings are none of your business."

"As long as you don't bother my team."

Her eyes darkened. Color stained her cheeks. "Are you accusing me?"

"No. Warning you, maybe."

"I haven't done anything wrong!"

"I realize that. I didn't mean to insinuate—" He made a conciliatory gesture, stepping toward her.

She backed away one step. "Yes, you did mean to insinuate."

Caught. He moved forward again. "Maybe so. But I'm sorry if that seemed insulting—"

"It was." Another step back.

If his arms had been around her, they'd have been dancing.

He tried again. "Look, all I wanted was to be sure that your interest in my team wasn't—uhh—"

Her eyes shot sparks. "Wasn't what?"

"Improper."

She snorted. "Obviously you have no idea who I am. Do I look like a proper lady?" She glanced down to indicate her flannel shirt, bleached, frayed jeans and chunky sandals with worn-down soles.

Her toenails weren't painted. But they were clean. Small enough to appear delicate. Almost…provocative.

What she was, Evan thought as he quickly returned his gaze to her hard face, was a curious character. He knew very little about her, but she appeared to be a solitary soul who existed on the fringes of Alouette society. If she had friends—or boyfriends—it wasn't in public. In private might be another matter. Some men smirked at the mention of her name. Evan wouldn't normally jump to conclusions based on town gossip, but with her surly, unapproachable personality she gave no other evidence to go on.

"You know what I mean," he said.

Her chin lifted. "Uh-huh. Well, you have nothing to worry about. I've never spoken to any of your players unless they've come into the Buck Stop to try and cadge a beer." Her gaze darted over the ragged clutch of boys jogging around the track. "I couldn't care less about them."

"Then why are you here?" And why did she come to every basketball game and sit at the top of the bleachers, tucked into a little knot with her arms hugging her knees and her eyes fixed on the court, rarely speaking to the other fans, never letting out a cheer that he'd noticed?

"No reason," she said.

"Fine."

"Then stay off my back." She frowned. "And I'll…" The edge in her voice softened as she moved farther away. "I'll cause no trouble."

He was within his rights to tell her to stay off school property altogether, but he didn't think that was necessary. It wouldn't surprise him if she ran off like a wild creature of the woods and never came around again.

What did surprise him was that he cared. Just a bit.

Good reason to back off. He didn't need complications in his life just now. Already to his credit was one mistaken marriage that had lasted only because he'd hung on until he was exhausted, various friends and students whose problems had become his own, and especially his own troubled daughter who needed more than he had to give.

Enough, already.

Wild Rose Robbin was one paradox that he would leave on her own without trying to solve. She could, after all, take care of herself. Right?

"You're welcome to attend any of our games," he said as she strode away.

She flipped a hand in token acknowledgment, but didn't bother to reply. Or say goodbye.

Evan returned his attention to the straggling runners. The woman had no social graces, but for once that wasn't *his* problem.

AFTER THE HUMILIATING INCIDENT with the coach, Rose had every intention of staying away. She couldn't blame the guy for calling her on the frequent appearances. Had to look weird, her hanging around basketball practice like a groupie.

She tried to stop. Her life became work, eat, work, sleep. Mornings were spent on paperwork and upkeep at the rental cabins her mother owned—Maxine's Cottages, thirty bucks per night—afternoons and evenings at the Buck Stop. When Rose couldn't bear to wash another sheet or sell another pack of cigarettes, she escaped to the woods with her sketchbook and watercolors for a few stolen hours.

The days continued warm, clear and bright—Indian summer. Rose knew she should be enjoying every drop of sunshine before the long winter came. Too often autumn rains shortened the season.

She managed to keep away for a week. After all, for most of the summer she'd had only glimpses of Danny—at the car wash, biking along Vine Street, hanging with his friends at the Berry Dairy ice-cream stand. She told herself that she should be able to wait another month for the basketball season to begin, when she could watch him to her heart's content. No one but the coach would notice her at the games.

Except Danny's adoptive parents—who had far more reason than the coach to be suspicious of her motives.

The thought of *them* asking her to keep away from their son sent a shiver through Rose. She had made no demands. No self-serving explanations, or attempts to meet Danny. No contact at all, even when they'd reluctantly approached her. She only wanted to see him from a distance now and then and know that he was happy.

Rose despised the skulking, but she was used to it. She'd been raised to skulk. Her father, Black Jack Robbin, had been a dominant personality with a loud voice and a mean streak. Her two rowdy older brothers and shrill, fractious mother had taken the household noise level even higher, making Rose the silent, forgotten one of the family. Until she'd grown up, fallen in love and all the troubles had begun....

Escape, Rose thought as she worked her way through the trees that ringed the school field. She'd done it once before. But in the end it hadn't worked. She'd never stopped remembering. And now she was back home, freed of her father but just as stuck with her mother. The one light in her life was being able to see Danny—

"What are you doing?" said a small voice.

Rose let go of the branch she'd been bending out of the way so she could scan the track. It snapped back, into her face, swatting her in the eye.

"Ouch." She pressed the heel of her palm against her stinging eyeball.

The small blond child who'd startled Rose came closer to stare up at her. "Say zipperzap."

"What?"

The girl smiled slightly. "Saying 'zipperzap' makes it stop hurting."

Oh, I want to stop hurting. Tears were leaking down her cheek. She rubbed at her eye.

"I say it all the time," the girl encouraged.

"Does it work?"

Her face puckered doubtfully.

Rose blurted, "Zipperzap."

"Better?"

"Yeah." She blinked the tears away. "It worked."

"Princess Ella Umbrella Pumpkinella Fantabuzella says zipperzap to make her wishes come true."

Rose didn't get children. "Uh. Sure."

The girl came closer, stepping off the mown field into the underbrush. "It's a very good story. You should read it."

"Maybe I will."

"The liberry has all the Princess Ella books." The girl stared. "You go to the liberry?"

"Yeah, I do."

"I saw you there. But I'm not allowed to talk to strangers." The girl came closer, though she stayed on the other side of the sapling that had struck Rose. She was thin and pale and seemed very delicate, almost weightless. An unzipped pink windbreaker flapped on her small body and her pants had cartoon characters on them. She wore frilled anklets under her pink jelly sandals. Clean, tidy and quiet. Not much like the boisterous kids who came tearing into the Buck Stop, the only type of youngsters Rose usually encountered. Families didn't stay at Maxine's Cottages.

"My name is Rose."

The girl's eyes were blue marbles. "Lucy," she said in a whisper.

"Hi, Lucy. Nice to meet you. But you'd better go back where you came from now."

"My dad said I could play in the woods if I wanted."

"Then I'll go." Rose looked through the screen of yellowing poplar leaves as runners approached. The boys of the basketball team wouldn't be running outdoors much longer. Soon all their time would be spent in the gym, where watching Danny was impossible for her.

Rose faded back. "Is your father nearby?" she asked Lucy.

Lucy nodded and pointed toward the open field. "Coach Grant."

Of course. Rose remembered that she'd seen him with a little girl. She just hadn't paid a lot of attention to faces or names, tending to be occupied with her own concerns whenever he was around.

Rose winced to herself. Lucy would tell Evan about her encounter with the woman in the woods. Asking the girl not to say anything would make the situation even worse.

She *had* come here with a cover story—the usual, sketching in the outdoors, which wasn't even a lie. But it was best to leave immediately, even if she hadn't managed to get a long look at Danny. She could wait. Good training for the years ahead, when she'd be plunged back into the void of no contact at all.

Sneakered feet pounded the track. Rose drew deeper into the woods. Above the heavy breathing of the laboring runners, she heard Evan Grant's voice, urging them to keep up the pace. He was a good coach, even-tempered, disciplined, encouraging, yet still intense enough to rally the team at game time.

"Where's your mom?" Rose asked Lucy after the runners had gone by. She couldn't remember there being a Mrs. Grant at the games. A proper citizen recognized every face in small-town Alouette, but Rose kept to herself.

And skulked.

Lucy had caught at her bottom lip with a row of small white baby teeth. One gap. Her narrow shoulders sloped. "My mom's in heaven."

Rose gulped. "Sorry."

Lucy's shiny lip pooched out a little. "She's there for a very long time. Daddy says she won't ever come back."

There was a pause between them, awkward on Rose's side.

"No, she won't." Rose had no talent for talking to children. She hoped it was okay to tell the girl the truth. "My dad is in heaven, too." Most folks would say Black Jack had gone straight to hell, but even Rose knew that Lucy didn't need to hear that particular truth.

"Then he could be an angel, like my mom."

Rose smiled at the thought of Black Jack in flowing white robes. She'd never seen him wear anything but worn work clothes topped by a smelly fishing vest and hat. Soap couldn't touch his grime. A halo was out of the question.

Lucy had followed Rose deeper into the trees. She pointed. "What's that?"

"My sketchbook."

"I have one, too. But it's in my backpack. I left it in the car. My baby-sitter is getting a root canal. That's an operation on a tooth."

"Oh."

Lucy's head tilted. "Do you draw nice pictures?"

"I guess so."

The girl exhaled expectantly, looking at Rose with her shining eyes.

Rose knelt near a fallen log so old it had gone all soft and mossy. She put her sketchbook on it and opened to the first page. "Would you like to see?"

"Yes, please." Lucy came close, standing beside Rose as she flipped through the pages. The book contained ink drawings, pencil sketches and small watercolors of outdoor scenes. She'd made a number of detailed studies of leaves, flowers, birds, clouds. Amateur stuff.

No princesses or flying dragons to delight a child. Rose's dreams were as mundane as her reality, but she'd captured on paper the only beauty she knew. The only goodness that was everlasting.

"Pretty," Lucy said, stopping Rose at a watercolor of the climbing rose vines that blanketed one side of her little stone house. "I like pink flowers."

"They're roses." The painting did have a fairy-tale quality, she realized. Misleading as that was.

"Like your name."

"Yes. Wild roses." They clung to the stones, somehow surviving the harsh winters to return each spring. She'd painted the cottage scene just last week, knowing the roses wouldn't last much longer. On impulse, she tore the page from the book. "Would you like to have it?"

Lucy made a small sound of pleasure. "Thank you very much."

"Put it in your pocket so you don't lose it." Rose

helped Lucy slide the small watercolor into the kangaroo pocket of her windbreaker, thinking too late about her father's reaction. Well, he'd have to live with it. She'd done nothing wrong.

"I wish I could draw like you," Lucy said.

"Keep practicing." That sounded about right, like something a wise adult would say to a child. "And try this—" Rose pulled a pen out of her pocket and flipped the sketchbook to a clean page. "I always work from nature." She plucked a leaf from a maple sapling and laid it on the paper, then gave Lucy the pen. "Trace the leaf."

Lucy dropped to her knees in the mulch. Leaning over the book with a look of utter concentration, she carefully drew around the leaf. "Is that right?"

"That's a tracing. But now your fingers know what to do and you can draw the leaf on your own." Rose tapped an empty space on the page. "Go ahead and try it."

Lucy put the pen nib to the paper, squinting hard at the leaf.

"Uh-uh. Not that way." Rose covered the leaf and the tracing with one hand. "Draw it from the picture of a leaf in your head. Your fingers will know how."

Lucy was doubtful. With her small face all scrunched up, she drew a fair approximation of the leaf. She studied the lopsided sketch. "It's not as good as the other one."

"It's better. Draw another, only faster. Don't try to be perfect. Make your pen race. Let it go all squiggly if you want."

Lucy smiled and drew a second leaf, glancing at Rose for approval.

"Make more of them," she said. "One on top of the other. Faster. Faster."

Lucy laughed as she drew, her ink line becoming loose and free. The first careful leaf became a scribbled pile.

"There, you see?" Rose showed the girl the real leaf again, green mottled with a soft rusty red. "You've made your own kind of leaf. But you should color your drawing in. And, see, if you study the pattern of the veins—"

A man's voice interrupted them. "Luce, where are you?"

Lucy's head came up. "That's my dad."

"Lucy?" With a crackle of branches, Evan Grant pushed through the underbrush. "I heard you laughing—" He saw Rose and stopped. *"You."*

She met his eyes. "Me."

A stiff nod. "Hello."

"Hello."

Evan said, "Time to go, Lucy," in a calm voice, but he stared at Rose, his expression severe.

A blush stained her cheeks. She was furious that he'd made her feel guilty. In spite of her reputation, she was *not* a criminal.

Lucy went to her father, head down as she tugged at the zipper of her jacket. He put his hand on her shoulder and asked softly, "Why did you run off, Luce?"

"You said I could play in the woods."

Evan's gaze returned to Rose. "Yes, I did." He shrugged. "I didn't expect her to do it, though."

Rose realized that he wasn't accusing her. He was merely…surprised. Surprised at Lucy, for some reason. That put her off-kilter.

"I was drawing leafs, Daddy," Lucy said. "Rose showed me how!"

"That was kind of her. Did you say thank you?"

Lucy's solemn little face transformed into sweetness and light when she smiled. "Thank you."

Rose's voice came out so rough-hewn it might have been hacked with an ax. "Err...welcome." She stood, hurriedly tucking the sketchbook under her arm. An explanation poured out of her, despite the raw throat. "I was walking in the woods. Lucy came across me. It wasn't— I didn't intend—" She gritted her teeth. *Damn.* Always on the defensive.

Evan shook his head, telling her he didn't want a justification. "Lucy, do you want to go on over to the car now? I'll follow you in just a sec."

"All right." The girl threw Rose another shy smile and turned away, her pale hair lifting off her neck as she reached the field and started to run.

Rose stretched her neck to see past the branches. Practice was over; the boys had departed. She tucked in her bottom lip and swallowed.

"Thank you," Evan said.

Rose blinked. "What for?"

"You made Lucy laugh. She doesn't do that a lot."

Rose didn't reply. She wasn't accustomed to handling sincerity and appreciation.

Evan spoke haltingly. "Her mother died. Less than two years ago. She's been very quiet and shy since. Easily frightened." He looked down, crossed his arms over his chest, kicked up leaves with the toe of one running shoe. "I try to encourage her. But she always wants to stay near me. I didn't think she'd actually go into the woods. She says the creaking of the trees scares her. You know, as if they're alive."

He looked up to the forest canopy. The sun had

lowered in the sky. What remained of the filtered, dusky light dappled his face and inside Rose there was a stirring…an attraction. So unfamiliar it startled her.

Logically, she could see that Evan Grant was a handsome man. He had short brown hair that matched his eyes, and an open, friendly, intelligent face. Very clean-cut and vigorous, with his workout clothes and healthy air.

On the surface, he wasn't the type to look twice at a woman with Rose's reputation, but she knew that what men said in public and did in private were often very different things. Sixteen years ago, no one had believed that Rick Lindstrom, star athlete and the most popular boy of the senior class, could possibly be interested in awkward, unsophisticated Wild Rose Robbin.

She pushed the thoughts away. Flying under the radar was the only way to survive.

"Well, you know…" She coughed. "The trees *are* alive."

Evan laughed, carving grooves into his cheeks. "Please don't tell Lucy that. I had to cut a branch off the oak beside our house. It was scratching her windowpane."

"She has imagination."

"Too much, I think."

"Uh." Rose was feeling all choppy again. "Nice kid, anyway. I guess."

Evan glanced over his shoulder. "I should leave."

Rose couldn't believe he wasn't going to get on her about spying on the practice.

"I promised Lucy we'd go to the diner to pick up some takeout and have our dinner at the picnic tables by the harbor. Maybe you want to come with us?"

Rose had been ready to take off. Instead she froze. The man had to be kidding. Or he was a kindly soul throwing her a pity invitation. She got them occasionally, from the motherly owner of Bay House B and B, or Pastor Mike's do-gooding wife. Rose almost always said no.

"No," she croaked, not looking at Evan. "No, thanks. I have work soon. Night shift at the Buck Stop."

"But don't you have to eat before you go on?"

"I get something at the store."

"Shrink-wrapped burritos. Twinkies. That stuff doesn't make a good dinner." He smiled at himself. "Listen to me. Lecturing you like you're my daughter. Who is sure to insist on deep-fried, unidentifiable chicken bits and Mountain Dew."

Rose was too unnerved to play along. "Do I look like a health nut?"

He was too nice a guy to take the opportunity to check out her boobs in a tank top that had shrunk in the dryer. His gaze stayed on her face, but that was bad enough. She had to meet his eyes. And he had warm, charismatic eyes—not confrontational. Not judgmental.

Which was confusing to Rose. She had little experience in being affable. Her fringe role in the community was established. Nothing much was expected from her, and she liked it that way. If feelings of desolation began creeping in, she always had Roxy Whitaker, who could be called a friend in a casual way. They'd gone berry-picking just a month ago.

"Next time," Evan said with a shrug. He turned to go.

Rose exhaled. "Yeah."

Tickled with shivers, she untied the hooded jacket from around her waist and pulled it on. There wouldn't be a next time if she could help it.

CHAPTER TWO

"DADDY? DADDY..."

Lucy's high-pitched voice woke Evan from a light doze. He reacted before his brain was at full speed, lurching up from the easy chair and stumbling over the ottoman that had skidded out from beneath his feet. The yammer and glitz of a familiar late-night talk show filled the room. Around midnight, then.

Evan shook his bleary head, coming awake enough to stop and listen, hoping that Lucy would settle on her own. As much as he wanted to reassure his daughter's every fear, the clinginess and anxieties hadn't abated as he'd been told they would. Her mother, Krissa, had been gone for a year and a half. More. Nineteen months. Roughly a third of Lucy's life.

Nineteen months and the worry that his fumbling efforts were hurting Lucy more than helping her still sat in Evan's gut like a leaden weight. With a tired exhale, he found the remote control and *Sports Illustrated* he'd dropped when he stood, then clicked off the TV.

Lucy's call escalated to a panicky howl. *"Dad-deee!"*

Evan's foot crunched down on a bag of pretzels as he hurried from the living room. But he didn't stop. "Coming, Lucy."

Her bedroom door was directly across from his in the modest single-story house. Butterfly night-lights were plugged into outlets in the hall and in Lucy's room. They'd helped some, but she continued to wake during the night, frightened of dreams, of shadows, of trees, of thunderstorms, of being alone.

Lucy was a small, huddled shape in the bed. Tears glistened in her eyes. Although Evan's heart went out to her, he kept his tone matter-of-fact. "What's up, honey? You're supposed to be sleeping."

"There's a m-m-monster in the corner."

And in the closet. Under the bed. At the window.

"You know monsters aren't real. Why didn't you turn on your lamp to see?"

Lucy drew in a shuddery breath. "I was too scared to move. The monster would eat me."

"Go ahead and do it now." According to the book he'd found in the library, *Comforting the Timid Child*, he should try to get Lucy to take her own proactive steps to combat the fears.

Reassured by his presence, she pushed aside her covers and leaned over to reach the bedside lamp. He'd bought her a new one recently, easy to turn on by a switch in the base.

Click. Light flooded the room.

"See there?" Evan said. "It's just a lump on the chair from the extra blanket and your jacket. Hey, little girl! Weren't you supposed to hang that up?" Lucy was usually orderly. Too much so, he thought. He'd like to see her noisy and laughing, barreling around the house, even breaking things.

But that was how he'd grown up, with three brothers and parents who only threw up their hands in cheerful surrender as they rounded up their sons like bumptious sheep. Raising a little girl like Lucy was a different matter. There were times he felt that he'd never get it right.

"I'll do it just this once," he said heartily, taking the jacket to her closet. Lucy watched with big eyes, probably thinking a witch would jump out when he opened the door.

As Evan put the jacket onto a hanger, he felt something in the pocket. He pulled out a piece of stiff paper. "What's this?"

Lucy held out her hands, suddenly smiling and happy. "My picture!"

He glanced at the small painting, finding it innocuous enough. Yet it had made Lucy forget her fears, at least for the moment.

"Rose gave it to me. She painted it."

"Ah." Evan approached the bed, studying the picture more closely in the lamplight. He'd have expected Rose's artwork to be bold and graphic. This was soft, romantic. She'd painted a stone house, covered with climbing vines and pink flowers, surrounded by trees.

Lucy took the painting. "It's a fairy-tale house."

"Did Rose tell you that?"

"I just knowed."

Evan sat on the bed beside Lucy, putting an arm around her. "And does a princess live there?"

She nodded. "Uh-huh. Tell me a story about her, Daddy."

He could have handled swashbuckling pirates or even a talking skunk that wore a beret, but princesses and other girly things? He didn't have that much imagination.

"You tell me," he urged. "What's the princess's name?"

After some thought, Lucy said, "Princess Kristina," and Evan's heart gave a thump. The choice, so close to her mother's name, had to hold significance, even if it was only a subconscious wish.

Lucy went on, unperturbed. "A wicked fairy god-mother put a spell on her."

"What kind of spell?"

"Princess Kristina has to live in the enchanted forest forever. Or a big ogre will chop her head off."

"Ouch."

"He's twenty-ten feet tall. He's green all over and he has stinky breath." Lucy giggled. "Like me when I kiss you good morning."

"Pee-ew! That's bad."

"Really bad."

"Is the princess scared of the ogre?" Lucy's favorite movie was *Shrek,* so the story might go the other way.

"Oh, yeah. Really scared. 'Cause he's gonna chop her head off, 'member?"

"Right. But maybe the ogre is a nice guy inside."

"No, Dad. He's mean. Very, very, very mean." Lucy made a growling noise. "He scares the princess so much she has to stay in her house all the time. She never gets to go home to see the king and queen."

"They must miss her a lot."

Lucy nodded over the painting.

Evan decided it was time to quit. The story wasn't heading in a direction conducive to sleep. "There has to be a way to break the spell. Do you think that maybe a prince will come to defeat the ogre?" No, better to encourage her by having the princess rescue herself.

"Or maybe the princess will find a way to become the ogre's friend. But for now, the princess is safe inside her house." He took the picture and propped it up on Lucy's table lamp. "You can tell me more of the story tomorrow night, Luce. I want you to get some sleep."

She breathed a quiet sigh. "Okay."

"Slide down."

She burrowed deeper under the covers and he gave her a snuggle before rising from the bed. He checked the curtains—they had to overlap so no monsters could peek in—and went around to peck Lucy's forehead before shutting off the lamp.

Her voice stopped him at the door. "Daddy?"

"Yes?"

"I like Rose. She can draw real good and—and—"

Evan waited. Lucy's fingers clutched the edge of the blanket. Her pale hair lay across the pillow, as fine as any princess's. His heart swelled, and he vowed once again to protect her from as many ogres as he could.

"Rose isn't afraid of the woods," she said.

"No, she certainly isn't." He thought of Wild Rose Robbin, lurking in the forest shadows. An ogre or a princess? Time to find out for sure, with his daughter's interest so captured.

"We were going to color in the leafs…" Lucy's voice was fading.

"Shh, now." Evan left the door halfway open. "Sweet dreams."

ROSE CLOSED the Buck Stop at midnight, exiting through the back door where she'd left her bike against the tar-paper wall. Although she used her mother's car during the winter and bad weather, the bike was her favorite transportation. The autumn months were particularly precious for her, with the crisp air and falling leaves and the need to hold on to each day for as long as possible. She was old enough to regret how often she'd wished her life away. Particularly a certain nine-month span of time…

In retrospect, it was hurtful to remember how slowly she'd believed the days of her pregnancy had passed, and how fiercely she'd longed for it to be over and done with so she could escape her pain. She'd had no clue.

But she'd been barely seventeen. So confused, and raw with the horror of what had happened to her. She hadn't known how her perceptions would be altered by the baby boy she was sure she didn't want.

Rose wheeled the bike past the rutted gravel of the convenience store parking lot, onto the paved road. There wasn't much traffic at this time of night. She had a headlamp and reflector patches, so she was safe to ride on the road, even in the dark. In fact, she preferred it. She was never as free as when she coasted along in the darkness with no eyes upon her except the glowing circles belonging to the porcupines and raccoons staring at her from the trees. She could breathe. She could fly. The couple of miles to town sped by.

Usually she tried to keep her mind blank during her bike rides. On this night, she found herself thinking about Evan and Lucy Grant. She knew very little about him—*them*. What she'd learned now that she was paying attention had only roused her curiosity further, but she couldn't see herself asking around to learn more. That would be obvious and embarrassing.

Her older brothers, Jake and Gary, had laughed and teased mercilessly when they found out she had a crush on Rick Lindstrom of the hotsy-totsy Bay Road Lindstroms. Later, in private, when she'd been spotted in Rick's convertible and the gossips were slurring her name, sure that Rick was only interested in one thing, Jake had warned her away. He'd said that Rick was playing her.

She hadn't listened. And look where that had gotten her—alone and brokenhearted.

Evan Grant would be another mistake. He wasn't as far out of her league, but he was an upstanding citizen, in a position of influence, expected to hold to high moral standards. Regardless of the pity invite, he must have some idea of her reputation. Even if *he* was willing to buck expectations, she wasn't.

She always learned her lessons the first time. Her father had only had to hit her once before she knew to keep quiet and out of his way. And that one horrid encounter in the woods near the cottages had been enough to send her away from home for more than fifteen years....

Her head filled with bad memories, Rose reached town before she knew it. The streets were vacant and quiet. The only businesses open at this time of night were the bars, thriving even without her father's patronage. Black Jack had closed them down on frequent occasions before coming home to roar at his wife and children.

Rose pedaled faster and faster, until she reached Blackbear Road, a country lane that led north out of town. A few farmhouses and newer ranch homes dotted the landscape. A big dog rushed down a driveway, barking as Rose whizzed by.

The road sloped down toward the river. Finally she

slowed and turned onto the driveway of her home, such as it was. The sign announcing Maxine's Cottages was faded and worn, as it had been for as long as she could remember. There wasn't much reason to replace it. Very soon the business would fold.

Almost nothing would make Rose happier. Her mother could call her ungrateful all she wanted, but Rose had been anticipating the day as a righteous reprisal ever since she'd moved home.

For now, she did as her mother wanted, and Maxine refused to close the cottages. Business had slowed to a trickle even before Black Jack's death; now it came one drop at a time. These days, even the type of rough-and-tumble sportsmen they catered to expected more comfort and conveniences than the spartan stone cottages offered. While Rose did what she could, little money had been put into upkeep over the years and the place had deteriorated into a shabbiness that was a painful contrast to the natural beauty of the peaceful river setting.

Maxine's Cottages consisted of a central home and office surrounded by eight one- and two-room cabins perched along the Blackbear River. Rose lived in the farthest cottage, all her worldly possessions contained in its one room, with space to spare.

Before going home, she stopped at the main house to check on her mother. It was a duty she bore with equal parts of exasperation and sympathy. Maxine Robbin had led a hard life—married to a hell-raiser at sixteen, often in bad health, scraping by for a living, putting up with Black Jack's temper. The only break she'd ever had was when an uncle had died and left her the cottages.

The door was unlocked. Rose scraped her shoes on the rubber welcome mat before entering. The Robbins' house was not much bigger than the rentals—two bedrooms, a kitchen and an L-shaped combination living/dining area, with the cubbyhole office at the front. Rose's brothers had shared the second bedroom. She, the youngest and reportedly an unexpected mistake, had been given a daybed in a curtained-off corner of the living area. Small wonder that as a girl she'd spent all her daylight hours outdoors—and even the nighttime ones whenever she was able to sneak out.

At the sound of the door, Maxine's querulous voice rose from the back bedroom. "Is that you, Rose? I dropped my clicker and I can't find it. I've been lying here in misery, with nothing to do but stare at the ceiling. Why you had to pile my bed with all these extra blankets and pillows is beyond me."

Because if I hadn't you'd be calling me back to complain about the hard mattress or the cold draft. Rose stopped outside the bedroom door and took a deep breath, wishing for the patience needed to deal with her mother.

Black Jack's dominating personality had turned Maxine into a mealy-mouthed complainer. Her voice was like a mosquito—an annoying high-pitched whine that went on and on for so long a body began hoping for the sting that would end it. Remembering that Maxine had been swatted down more often than any person should have to be was how Rose made it through each long day.

Rustling sounds came from the bedroom. The mattress creaked. "Ohhh. It hurts so much I can't get out of bed. My arthritis is acting up."

"I'm here." Rose slipped into the bedroom and began straightening the blankets and picking up pillows. She found the remote control in the folds of the comforter and set it on the bedside table. "How was your evening, Mom? Did Alice stop by?"

"She brought a store-bought coffee cake that tasted like gravel. Came carrying tales, of course. You know Alice." Maxine shrugged bony shoulders. She'd always been a petite woman, but illness and worry had shrunk her to a wizened, sallow shadow. At fifty-six, she was old before her time.

She droned on about Alice's gossip, finishing with, "As if I give two hoots what the ladies of the book club or the guests at Bay House have gotten up to."

Rose smiled to herself as she continued straightening the room. One of her mother's remaining pleasures was a good gab with Alice Sjoholm, who was kind enough to look in on Maxine when Rose was at work. But it simply wasn't in Maxine's makeup to admit to any enjoyment.

"At least Alice is someone to talk to," Maxine said. "I get zilch outta you."

"I have nothing to talk about. You know that not much happens at the Buck Stop. It's a drudge job."

Maxine snorted. "That scarred hermit Noah Saari was coming into the store and you never said a word until I heard from Alice that he was courting some fancy gal at Bay House." Maxine tilted her head, eyes narrowing at Rose. "You always were a Miss Butter-Won't-Melt-in-Her-Mouth. Such a sneaky child, running off into the woods and keeping secrets."

"I wonder why," Rose muttered.

"Eh? What's that?"

Rose sniffed the air. The ashtray on the bureau was wiped clean, but when she checked beneath the tissues in the wastebasket she found black residue and several stubbed-out cigarettes.

"Mom." Rose let out a big sigh. "You've been smoking again."

Maxine went into instant-whine mode. "I'm all alone. I get nervous at night."

"You know you can't smoke with the oxygen tank in the room. You'll blow yourself to smithereens!"

"Then take it out of here." Maxine gave the tank beside the bed a disdainful glance before she drooped into a familiar, imploring pose. "Don't yell at me, Rose. Shouldn't I be able to do what I please, now that your father is gone? Bless his soul."

Rose knew quite well that her mother was using emotional blackmail. Even so, she couldn't seem to stop the rush of pity that often became capitulation.

Maxine had an advanced stage of emphysema. She could still get around, though she often preferred not to, and her doctors had said that with vigilant care she might have years to live. A stronger person would have become determined to enjoy their remaining time, but Maxine was too cowed to fight. And she'd soon realized that the illness was a surefire way to keep hold of her only daughter and manipulate Rose to her bidding.

Maxine's wants were simple enough, if wearing, so Rose usually found herself complying. She believed that her mother deserved some happiness. Even if it was a twisted, bitter sort.

"I'm not yelling, Mom. I'm worried."

Maxine smiled. "What goes around comes around."

Avoiding *that,* Rose found the pack of cigarettes hidden under her mother's pillow and stuck them in her jacket pocket. "It's the cigs or the oxygen," she said, overriding Maxine's complaints. She glanced around the room, which had changed little in twenty years. Same with the entire house. Black Jack's boots were still parked under the bed and his fishing hat hung on the back door. She itched to get rid of them, but her mother refused that, too. Any sane person would have wanted to shed herself of reminders of a sorry life, but not Maxine.

"Should I help you to the bathroom before I go?" Rose asked.

"I suppose."

Rose gave Maxine her arm and escorted the woman to the adjoining bath. She was quite capable of getting there on her own, but Rose had learned it was easier to help out now than be called on in the middle of the night.

After her mother was resettled in bed, Rose put a brisk tone in her voice. "All right, then. I'm leaving. Are you all set for the night?"

Maxine fussed with the bedclothes. "Can't think of anything I need. But I can always ring."

Rose stifled a groan. She had no telephone in her cottage, but there was an old farmhouse bell hanging at the front door, put there so arriving guests could ring for help when no one was in the office to check them in. Maxine seemed to take pleasure in rousing Rose at least once a night with the clanging.

"It's after midnight," Rose said. "I need a good night's sleep." For a change.

"So do I." Maxine shifted in bed. "I can hardly get an hour's sleep without waking up wheezing and coughing. But you don't hear me complaining."

Yeah, right. Rose plumped the pillows, smoothed back her mother's hair, once black as her daughter's but now heavily laced with steel-gray, and dropped a kiss on her forehead. "Night, Mom."

"Night, Rose." Maxine patted her arm. "You're a good daughter. I don't know what I'd do without you."

The praise was perfunctory. Yet it worked. Rose had been given so little praise in her life that even crumbs seemed worthwhile. Her chest tightened as she pulled away.

She paused at the door, wanting to speak from her heart but not knowing how.

And of course Maxine couldn't leave well enough alone. "Your brothers never call," she moaned. "And you could run away again at any time. What would I do then? I'm so afraid of being left on my own."

"That's not going to happen, Mom. I've promised to stay. Now go to sleep." Rose flicked off the light and hurried away before her mother saw the tears of frustration welling in her eyes.

She dashed them away, swearing at herself as she left the house and grabbed her bike by the handlebars. When would she learn?

She was the one who was on her own.

"And I like it that way," Rose said out loud to the whispering pines and the black rushing water.

But for the first time in a long while, she wondered if she was lying to herself.

THE NEXT DAY, Evan had no practice scheduled and was able to pick Lucy up from her sitter's early. They decided to make a trip to the library, one of Lucy's favorite places in Alouette. Not being a big reader himself, Evan worried that his daughter was spending too much time with books when she should be outdoors in the fresh air. But he couldn't argue with the benefits, or the pleasure it gave her.

The biggest bonus was that visiting with Tess Bucek always made Lucy happy.

Tess was the librarian. She and Evan had dated for a short while, earlier that year. Although the relationship hadn't progressed very far, he'd considered asking her to marry him simply because Lucy had been so hungry for Tess's motherly touch.

He'd backed off when he realized that making a wrong marriage would be worse for Lucy in the end. Tess was now a good friend, and happily engaged to a newcomer to Alouette, a writer named Connor Reed who lived in the keeper's cottage of the Gull Rock lighthouse.

Lucy ran ahead, pushing open the door to the rainbow-hued Victorian house that had been converted into a small library. Evan followed her through the entryway, thinking how good it was to see Lucy so enthusiastic.

She raced into the library proper. He heard her voice, very bright. "Hi!"

After a pause the answer came, and it wasn't Tess. "'Lo."

A moment later, Tess chimed in, greeting Lucy with her usual perky cheer.

Evan arrived, his senses already heightened. Wild Rose Robbin looked at him, smiled and then hurriedly looked away, tucking her lips inward as if to keep the smile from escaping. She edged a stack of books across the checkout desk, toward Tess.

"You know Rose, right, Evan?" Tess was saying, looking from Lucy to Evan to Rose with a bright-eyed interest.

Evan cleared his throat. "We've met."

"She showed me how to draw leafs in the woods," Lucy said. She was staring up at Rose with an awe that approached reverence. One step closer and she'd be hanging off the woman's sweater, begging for attention. Normally she was shy to the point of invisibility, especially around new people.

"Have you practiced?" When she looked into Lucy's face, Rose's mouth curved into a smile that was as natural and pretty as a daisy dancing in the breeze.

"I *tried* to." Lucy put her hands on her hips, acting almost belligerent. She bobbed her head. "But my teacher said I was scribbling!"

Evan blinked in surprise. This was a new Lucy. Or, rather, the Lucy his daughter had started out to be, before the loss of her mother.

"I bet she wanted you to make a perfect leaf." Rose held up one hand and drew a maple leaf in the air.

"Uh-huh," Lucy breathed. She raised her own hand in imitation.

Rose shook her head. "Your teacher hasn't really looked at the autumn leaves, then, has she?"

"Nope. They're all, like, curly and nibbled on and— and—" Lucy scrunched her hand into a fist.

"So that's how you should draw them," Rose said. "Right?"

Even while she processed the books, Tess hadn't missed an inflection of the conversation. She threw a significant look at Evan.

He shrugged, although the interaction was pretty amazing. Even with Tess, Lucy hadn't come out of her shell so quickly.

"How are you, Rose?" he asked.

"Going to work." She looked down at her books, a reflex to fill the awkward silence.

He followed her gaze. She'd checked out a large tome of Audubon bird prints, a hardcover he couldn't see the title of and two paperbacks that featured embracing couples with flowing hair and ample cleavage. Hard to tell which was the male and which was the female.

Rose saw him looking and gathered up the books. "For my mother."

"I loved *Passionate Impulse,*" Tess said. Her eyes danced.

Evan was sorry he'd noticed. "Uh, sure. Listen, Rose, I was thinking—"

"I have to go," she interrupted. She made for the doorway, ducking past him with her rumpled hair falling across her forehead into her face. "G'bye, Lucy."

Lucy followed the woman's departure with beseeching eyes. "Bye."

"Go on, Lucy, find yourself a few books," Evan said when the door had clanged shut and she still hadn't moved. The children's room was adjacent to the main area, a space filled with light, plants, craft projects and colorful decorations. Throughout the summer he'd brought his daughter to story hour twice a week, but now that she'd started kindergarten and he was busy with basketball practice after school, their visits would be less frequent.

Lucy trotted off obediently. Evan stared after her,

not yet willing to face Tess's curiosity. He could feel it rolling off her, ripe with questions.

"The sequel, *Passionate Embrace,* wasn't quite as good," Tess finally said with a laugh in her voice.

"You women." Evan had to grin. "All that romance gives you barmy ideas."

"Sure, blame us if it makes you feel better." Tess was petite, with short coppery hair and a warm personality—the kind of person who was a pillar of the community, with her penchant for running charity tag sales and Scrabble tournaments. "Got something besides romance on your mind, Evan?"

He shrugged. What the hell. In for a penny...

"Don't read anything into this," he said.

The librarian made an agreeable sound that he didn't believe for a second.

"But..."

Tess made an impatient gesture. "C'mon. Out with it, man."

He gave in. "Tell me about Wild Rose."

CHAPTER THREE

TESS FROWNED INSTEAD of continuing to tease him. "Like what?"

"How she got her name, for starters."

"She's had it forever, it seems. I couldn't say."

"You could say. If you wanted to. She's about your age, right? You must have gone to school together."

"She was a grade behind me."

"It's a small school system. I'm sure you knew her."

"Yes, but we didn't hang out. Rose was…"

"Wild?"

Tess shook her head. "Not then. I mean, when we were younger. Maybe a little—she grew up with two older brothers. It wasn't until later that…" She shrugged.

"So you *do* know how and when she got the nickname."

"Evan, why don't you just go by what she is now? I've been the subject of town gossip myself, so I'm not that eager to repeat tales about another person. Especially when it's old talk. And who knows what's truth and what's exaggeration?"

"I'm not looking for reasons to condemn the woman, I promise."

"Then why?"

"You saw Lucy with her. She really came out of her shell. So I was thinking I could hire Rose to give Luce drawing lessons. But there's the woman's reputation to consider." And the reason she continued to lurk at his practices and games. Unless…

What if Rose had a crush on him?

Heat crawled up his neck. He wasn't so conceited he thought every woman was after him. But it had been known to happen. After Krissa had died and a decent interval had passed, a number of single ladies had approached him with casseroles and come-ons, both as subtle hints and open-ended invitations. The principal's secretary had mooned over him for months until he'd spelled out his disinterest. Even though she was going out with one of the bus drivers, she still gave him the occasional lingering glance. And there were some of the high-school girls, who were far too bold.

"Do you think—" The question stuck in his throat. He couldn't ask Tess. She might think he was condescending to Rose, especially after he'd been nosing around her reputation.

"It's a great idea!" Tess leaned over the checkout desk and gave his arm a squeeze. "From what I just saw, art lessons will really make Lucy blossom. And they might be good for Rose as well." Tess smiled like a pixie, lifting her brows a little.

"Don't get any ideas," he warned. *I'm already having enough for both of us.*

She batted her lashes. "Like what?"

"I only have a professional interest."

"Aw, that's no fun." Tess's mouth straightened. "Rose could use a friend."

"Doesn't she have any? How about you?"

"I try. I chat her up as much as I can and I've invited her places and encouraged her to come to community events. But she's not very interested. And then, there's her mother." Tess leaned forward with her palms on the desk. "She has a sick mother at home."

"And Rose takes care of her on her own?" Evan adjusted his thinking on the woman one more time. Apparently Rose wasn't out partying with the rough crowd who bought their liquor at the Buck Stop.

Tess nodded. "Rose came back to Alouette for her father's funeral. I guess it was, hmm, maybe two years ago already."

Around the time of Krissa's illness, Evan thought. No wonder he hadn't noticed.

"Her mother's health was deteriorating and she couldn't handle the family business on her own," Tess continued. "So Rose stayed in town."

The family business. Evan thought of the quaint but run-down cottages off Blackbear Road. He hadn't realized they were still operational. Couldn't be turning much of a profit. "No other family members offered to help?"

"Her brothers didn't return for the funeral. Bad blood, there, I hear. One of them went off to join the Army years ago and the other's in prison."

Evan's alert flag went up. "Prison?"

Tess scrunched her nose, as if she'd said too much. "Held up a liquor store at gunpoint. Don't judge Rose by that, okay?"

"Hard not to," he murmured.

The librarian straightened and struck a scolding tone. "Look at her actions—judge those. She runs the rental cabins, she takes care of her mother, she works late hours at the Buck Stop. I'd say Rose is practically a saint."

Evan grinned. "Go ahead. Shake your finger at me. I can tell you want to."

With a muffled snort, Tess wagged an index finger under his nose. "Don't make me laugh when I'm lecturing you."

"Oh, I'm listening, Marian." Whenever Tess got too librarian-ish, he used the nickname on her.

"You'd better. Rose deserves a break."

"Yeah," he said, but he was thinking that it didn't have to come from him. Arranging the drawing lessons would lead to getting involved, to some degree, and he had already decided not to go down that path.

"In a small town like this, where people have known each other forever, it's not easy for someone like Rose to make a fresh start. But with you…" Tess cocked her head. "You have the ability to see her as she is, not through the filter of her past mistakes."

"You're not going to fill me in, are you?"

Tess hesitated. "I can tell you some of it. Do you promise to be fair?"

He gave her a look. She should know him well enough by now.

"All right," she conceded. "You're as good a judge of character as anyone I know."

"Except when it came to Connor." Evan had bristled when he'd first met Tess's fiancé, but then even *she* had suspected the man of skullduggery.

Tess rolled her eyes. "Pah. *That* was a territorial pissing contest. Metaphorically, of course."

Evan laughed. "Well, you know men—we're animals. Connor had to prove himself before I trusted him with you."

"You think Rose hasn't proved herself?"

"Questions remain." The lurking, primarily. The rest was his own curiosity.

Tess walked to the doorway to the children's room, checking on Lucy's progress. She motioned to Evan to wait and disappeared into the room, where he could hear her discussing books with his daughter. He moved off, glancing around the main room to be sure there were no eavesdroppers, then took a chair at one of the more secluded study tables.

Objectively, his interest in Rose should be curtailed, not fed. But there was his daughter's welfare to consider, and Lucy had taken to Rose like no other. He'd risk his own involvement in the woman's life if that meant helping Lucy. Although his heart went out to Rose now that he knew more of her situation, her troubles would have to remain secondary.

The arousal of his male interest—that was unsettling. The veritable monkey wrench in his plan.

Especially if Rose was equally attracted to him.

"Why the scowl?" Tess pulled over a chair and sat beside him. She crossed one leg over the other, tugging on her short red skirt when it rode up.

"Hmph." The librarian had great legs, but Evan found himself wondering what Rose would look like in a dress or skirt. She might be pretty if she tried. Not that he expected women to keep themselves turned out like Barbie dolls. There was a certain appeal to Rose's rakish independence. The intense blue of her eyes, how her wild, wavy hair framed her face...

Tess put her elbow on the table and tucked her fist

beneath her chin. Her shoulders relaxed with a sigh. "Lucy's rereading one of the Princess Ella books. She never gets tired of them."

"Tell me about it. Every night, she wants one as a bedtime story. I know them by heart."

"No offense, but you two need a woman in your lives."

"We're doing fine."

"Then why the interest in Rose, hmm?"

"That's, uh—" Evan slid his spine lower in the chair. "Don't come at me from a different direction, hoping for a slip-up. I already explained. She's good for Luce."

Tess patted his thigh. "Keep telling yourself that, hon."

He glowered, but he wasn't as miffed with Tess as he pretended. She was only asking the same questions he'd asked himself. She'd probably guessed that he was feeling oddly uncertain.

Tess had her own fix-it streak and would gladly be the one to push him over the edge into unwelcome territory. For his own good, she'd say. With a twinkle in her eye.

"So," he said in a low voice. "Spill the beans."

She sighed again. "Most of this is rumor."

"I'll take it with a grain of salt."

"You'd be better off talking with Rose herself."

"I don't know that the Spanish Inquisition could make her talk."

"She's not that bad!"

"Bad enough."

"Why do I feel we should have theme music?" Tess said. "The song about not giving a damn about your bad reputation would do. That's Rose, all right."

"You're wrong. She does care."

Tess turned her head on its side, still propped on her fist. She narrowed her eyes at him. "You've looked that closely?"

He wondered how much he'd given away. "Get on with it, Marian."

"What I remember…" Tess looked off across the library. "Rose was a different sort of kid when we were in grade school. Shy and quiet, but also stubborn. Rebellious at times. She didn't take well to authority, like her older brothers. But it was as if the teachers expected no better. The Robbins were that sort of family."

"What sort?"

"Not…admired," came the careful answer. "The father was a hunting and fishing guide. Something of a blowhard. A big drinker, arrested at least once for illegal poaching. I don't know a lot about Maxine, Rose's mother, except that she stayed close to home. The brothers were hellions."

"And Rose?"

"She wasn't too friendly, but then she didn't get much of a chance to be, either. All the 'good' mothers warned their kids away from playing with the Robbins. Let's just say, we sure weren't having picnics or slumber parties out at Blackbear Road." Tess ducked her head to press her knuckles beneath her nose. "In retrospect, I feel pretty awful about that. Rose must have been lonely, even if she acted like she didn't care."

Evan pushed down his rising empathy. "If she was this lonely outcast you say, how did she get the reputation?"

"This is where the rumors begin." Tess took her

voice down another notch. "When we got older, like fifteen, sixteen, the boys started paying more attention to Rose. She was striking—black hair to her waist, slim, tanned. The snobbier girls dismissed her because she didn't have the right clothes or social graces. But of course the boys didn't care about that."

Evan's mind drifted, imagining Rose at sixteen. He could see her—a wild rose of the forest, hardy but also beautiful and so fragile.

Damn. Where was the poetry coming from? Somebody ought to slap him in tights and call him Romeo.

Tess continued with a shrug. "What mattered to the boys was that she didn't have a curfew. Or many other rules. The Robbins kids basically ran wild."

"I see."

"Supposedly, Rose had a few temporary…alliances. And the boys talked. Bragged. You know. So she got this reputation. Wouldn't surprise me if it was overblown, knowing how gossip balloons in this town."

Evan was familiar with the concept. His first year as head coach, he'd suspended several of the team members for drinking and breaking curfew. The incident had expanded into a brouhaha that took over a school board meeting. Some of the more belligerent parents had wanted *him* reprimanded for overly harsh discipline, but he'd remained calm and kept a firm stance, and wiser heads had prevailed.

Tess had fallen silent. He prodded her. "And then?"

"Rose started hanging with a bad crowd. They got into trouble—underage drinking, petty vandalism, that kind of thing. People said she was just like her brothers. Then, I don't know, there was an incident that was hushed up pretty fast, except that people whispered about it for a long time. They said there was some kind of confrontation between Black Jack Robbin and the Lindstroms. The rumor was that Rose had become involved with Rick Lindstrom—led him into temptation, according to his parents."

"Or vice versa."

"All I know for sure is that the Lindstroms wouldn't want their son associating with someone like Rose. Rick's gone now, died in a forest fire out west, but I remember him well. The golden-boy type—handsome, charming, spoiled and arrogant. I seriously doubt that Rose was the instigator, in whatever happened between them."

Evan's stomach dropped. "Do you think it was only a sexual thing?"

"Probably. That's what my classmates assumed." Tess aimed a "sorry" look at him, as if he had a personal stake in Rose Robbin's love life. "But there was also a rumor about ill-gotten money, stolen maybe, or a payoff. The cops were supposedly called in, and suddenly Rose went away. Some said she ran away, some said she was sent to juvenile detention. After a while, it was clear that she was gone for good. She didn't come back, even for a visit, not until her father's funeral."

"Did you ever ask her what she'd been doing, all those years away?"

"Sure. She said she'd been working here and there. Never got married, never had kids."

Evan mulled that over for a minute or two, counting up the years. He hadn't been able to imagine what Rose would find interesting about his basketball team—good kids, all of them, but just an ordinary group of teenage boys, fascinating only to their girl-friends and their...

Parents.

Suddenly the explanation was obvious. Though times had long changed since the days when a girl in trouble was sent away in shame to spare the family embarrassment, the epidemic of pregnant teenage run-aways remained. He knew well, having put in a work-study course at a shelter and a runaway hotline during his college years. It was astounding that no one else in Alouette had come to the same conclusion.

On the other hand, he could be way off base.

"Hold on," he said when Tess started to rise. "You're sure Rose said that, in so many words?"

"What—the marriage and kids part? I don't remem-ber her exact words. But it's obvious, isn't it?" Tess slid sideways in her chair, eyeing him doubtfully. "Evan. What are you suggesting?"

"Nothing," he said quickly. Rose's business was her own, as long as she didn't make trouble.

"Be nice," Tess warned as she stood.

"Of course." He glanced up. "When haven't I been?"

"Oh, every now and then. Like whenever you see wrongdoing." Tess looked worried. "I shouldn't have spoken out of turn. You're thinking that there's some-thing *wrong* with Rose."

"No, I'm not. Honestly." Evan rose, towering over the petite librarian by nearly a foot. He tapped her under the chin. "I'll give the woman a fair chance."

"Does that mean Lucy will get the lessons?"

"Maybe. We'll see what Rose thinks. She might not be willing."

"Turn on that charm of yours." Tess tossed a saucy grin over her shoulder as she walked back to the main desk, reminding him why he liked her so much. Connor Reed was a lucky guy to have won her heart.

"What charm?" He considered himself to be a standard-issue, salt-of-the-earth type. A good guy. He worked hard, loved his daughter, paid his bills, did what was right. Solid, but nothing spectacular. Krissa had married him for that, and six years later asked for a divorce for the same reasons.

Tess only shook her head fondly. "Ack. You're such a guy."

There was nothing he could say to that, so he went to collect his pink, sparkly, princess-loving daughter, who at times still seemed like a foreign species to him.

"AHEM. I hope I'm not interrupting."

Rose opened her eyes, recognizing the voice with a flip of her stomach. "Evan," she said. Her throat rasped. "Uh—" She scrambled to set aside the mop and cleaning supplies she'd cradled in her arms while she sat on the stone step outside her cottage to savor the last of the afternoon sun.

"Let me." Evan took the mop while she dropped the dust rags into the scrub bucket she'd emptied nearby. "Fall cleaning?"

"We had guests in two of the cottages—bird hunters. They left this morning, so I was cleaning up the—" She stopped and shrugged, aware that she was giving away more information than necessary. That wasn't like her, but Evan made her nervous. "Y'know."

It had been more than a week since she'd run into Evan and Lucy in the library. Seeing him on her home territory was strange, particularly when he'd been on her mind so frequently. She might have believed that she'd conjured him up if he didn't seem so solid and strong and real. He wore a jacket over a blue Alouette Gale Storm sweatshirt, dark jeans and running shoes. His hair was so neat, his jaw so cleanly shaved, the whites of his eyes so bright that she felt grungy and dowdy by comparison. Which she was. That hadn't bothered her before. Much.

"Deer season next month," he said, handing her the mop. "You'll be full up, I suppose."

"We have several bookings, but it's not like the heyday when my dad was here to be the guide." She wouldn't have been able to stay if that had been the case. Even their occasional guests were a trial for her. She was wary of all men, but especially strangers, and was on constant alert until they were gone. A lesson learned the hard way.

"That's a shame." Evan scanned the woods. Fragrant pine boughs swayed in the breeze. "It's a picturesque location. Great piece of property."

Maxine's Cottages overlooked a particularly nice, secluded section of the Blackbear River—a wide S-curve bubbling with rapids, with a steep slope to the water's edge, mature forest and no other homes in sight.

"Yeah." Although her mother had entertained several generous offers, none of them involved keeping the cottages open for rent. Maxine still expected that one of her boys would come home to take over. Rose, under no such delusion, had collected business cards from Realtors and land developers in anticipation of the day her mother saw reason. She did have an attachment to her cottage and the riverside setting, but she'd sacrifice them in a heartbeat if given the opportunity to get out of Dodge.

She stated the obvious. "The place hasn't been kept up, unfortunately." All that she could manage was keeping the rooms clean and the grounds trimmed. Paint was peeling off the wood trim, shingles were missing, the faulty plumbing was a constant trial. There wasn't the money to hire pros, so she tackled the bigger jobs as she could. Her friend and handywoman Roxy had offered to help out, but Rose was uneasy about accepting handouts.

Evan barely glanced at the slipshod maintenance before he turned his gaze on her. His eyes were brilliant, the color of a mug of icy root beer shot with sunlight. Under his perusal, the skin on her cheeks became warm and tight.

"Do you have any plans for the business?"

Rose shook her head. "I'd shut down tomorrow if my mother would allow it. She's the one in charge."

"Ahh." He nodded. "I just met Maxine, over at the main house. She said it would be okay if I came out here to find you. I called the other day, but I guess you didn't get the message?"

"Sorry." Rose looked down and mumbled. "My mother must have forgotten to tell me."

"No problem. I was curious to see your place close up anyway. Never stopped before, even though I've driven by a number of times." His gaze went to her little stone house. "This is the one from the painting you gave to Lucy, isn't it?"

"Yes. My quarters, for now."

"Lucy calls it a fairy-tale house. I can see why."

Rose turned to look at the cottage. While there was nothing fancy about the humble place, it had charm. The stone walls were thick and covered in moss and ivy. Along the side that had a southern exposure, climbing roses grew, dressed for autumn in yellowed, curled leaves and the hard red globes of rose hips. Soon the remaining leaves would fall, revealing the twist of thorny vines. Inside, Rose would build a fire in the woodstove and huddle under layers of wool blankets, hibernating for the winter.

"You're probably wondering why I'm here," Evan said.

She half laughed. "Yeah, well, I don't get many visitors." Suddenly she winced, realizing she'd fallen down as a host. "Shi—er, sugar. Pardon my manners. I should have asked you to sit. We can go—" No, not inside. "Can I get you a drink?"

"No, thanks. Let's just sit out here." Evan didn't look around for a chair. He lowered his tall frame onto the step where'd she'd parked earlier, then glanced up expectantly.

Of course. She couldn't remain where she was, standing in front of him. But the step was small and she didn't like to get too close to strange men, or any men at all, for that matter.

She plopped into the grass, crossing her legs in front of her.

He smiled. "You'll get cold, sitting on the ground."

"I'm used to it."

"All right." He had an easy manner that smoothed out some of her hackles. "This won't take long."

She said nothing, waiting. She hoped he wasn't going to suggest dinner again. Even though, all week, she'd wondered what might have happened if she'd said yes.

In the end, she'd decided that the only sure outcome was that at least one well-meaning meddler would have made it a mission to warn Evan away from her, and that was too humiliating to contemplate for long. Rejecting his overtures—all overtures—was the only way to stay aloof and protect herself.

"I have a job for you," he said.

"Oh." A job. That's all. She stared down at her lap, where her fingers were tightly braided.

"If you're interested."

"I'm pretty busy, but…" Might as well admit what he must be thinking. "I could always use the money." She made minimum wage at the Buck Stop, and her mother's disability checks were only enough to sustain her. Medical expenses unpaid by her meager insurance coverage were mounting. The cottages brought in the bare minimum it took to pay their utilities and taxes.

"This job isn't so much about the money. It's more of a favor, to help me out. But I will pay, of course. Whatever you think. Fifty per session—does that sound good?"

Rose froze inside, even though a part of her knew that Evan could not be saying what it sounded like. She turned an icy glare on him, the same look that worked on the creeps who came into the Buck Stop thinking she was up for grabs. "Fifty bucks for what?"

He was momentarily rattled. "Wha'd'you—" He winced. "Sorry—I should have explained up front." He laughed at himself, a little awkwardly. "I'm talking about art lessons for Lucy."

Rose wanted to cringe with embarrassment. Instead she leaned forward and tore out handfuls of grass. Rip, rip. *You're an idiot.* Rip. *As if a guy like Evan Grant needs you.*

"What do you think?"

"Uh, I don't have any training for that kind of…thing." Her voice was like rust, corroding her throat. She had no social skills at all. A total loser.

"I've seen you in action. You're a natural."

"That was only—" Rip, rip. "Off the cuff."

"Exactly. That's what Lucy needs. See, she doesn't react well to the pressure of a structured environment. She's in kindergarten now, but already her teacher is telling me she's intimidated by the classroom and the other students." Evan stopped and boyishly scrubbed a hand through his short brown hair. His forehead had pleated with worry.

Torn blades of grass fell from Rose's fingers. "But she's only just started. She'll be more comfortable when she gets used to the other kids."

Rose remembered her own experiences in the classroom. After the freedom at home, where she'd been left to her own amusement most of the time, she'd been ill-prepared for school. The first months had been frightening—the teachers, the children, the strict rules and expectations.

Although she'd never learned to fit in, she had adjusted. In her own way. Lucy was lucky—she was much more socialized than Rose had been.

"That's what I'm hoping," Evan said. "Except that when I saw her with you, and then saw how excited she was to get home and try drawing, it occurred to me that if she had something special to give her confidence, something she's really good at, that would help her overall, you know?"

He took a deep breath, his shoulders rising and falling. "She's a bright girl, but she doesn't know how to shine. Not since her mother passed away."

Rose picked at the green flecks on her palms. "I'm sorry for your loss."

"Thank you." She felt Evan's direct gaze on her, like a hot ray of sunshine. "But Krissa's death was mainly Lucy's loss. My wife had left me and we were in the middle of divorce proceedings when she found out she had a brain tumor. When the prognosis wasn't good, she came back home to spend all the time with Lucy that she could."

"Still, I'm sure you—you must have been—" Rose shrugged when the words stalled again. She wasn't articulate. Too many years on her own.

"I'm doing okay. It's Lucy I worry about."

"She seems like a normal kid."

"Around you, she is."

Why me? Rose was truly baffled. She wasn't even remotely similar to Tess Bucek, whom children flocked to like chicks to a mother hen. The kids that came in the Buck Stop acted as if Rose was a wicked witch who'd seize them for her stew pot if they got too close.

If she'd ever had them, and her situation made *that* doubtful, her motherly instincts had withered and died long ago. Wild Rose Robbin was the last person Evan should want near his daughter.

"I can't do it," she blurted.

"Why not? I mean, if you don't want to, there's nothing I can say. I won't push." He paused. "But I might beg. For Lucy. She really needs this."

"I can't," Rose repeated miserably. Part of her wanted to. She identified with Lucy's fears.

"Give it a try," Evan pleaded. "One lesson." He put out a hand and touched Rose, his strong fingers gripping her shoulder.

Startled, she pulled away, heart in mouth. She had to stop herself from bolting to prove she wasn't a total freak. She could deal with normal touching—handshakes, pats, rubbing shoulders in a busy supermarket. It was an unexpected male touch that made her adrenaline pump, even when it was a friendly gesture like Evan's.

He had withdrawn immediately. "Sorry."

She scrambled to her feet and busied herself with brushing off her jeans, shedding grass like an Easter basket. "Not your problem."

He got up. "Excuse me if I've been an imposition—"

"No, you weren't," she said, an unexpected rush of compassion making her want to overcome her fears to reach out. For his daughter, if not for him. "I wish I could help."

She tipped up her chin. Read the look in his eyes.

He didn't have to say it. She already knew. She *could* help, if she really wanted to.

Be generous, she thought. *The good karma might come back to you.*

Danny's face flashed in her mind's eye. Was it possible to develop the motherly instincts she lacked?

She blinked. "All right. Okay. I'll give it a shot. One time, to see how it goes. But don't expect me to know what I'm doing." She rubbed her palms on her jeans, sweating with nervousness at the mere prospect.

"Let's not even call it a lesson. That sounds as if I'd have to come with a plan. Lucy and I can just get together—"

"Thank you." Impulsively, Evan started to reach out to hug her, but he stopped with his large hands hanging in midair. After a moment of hesitation, he thrust one toward her. "I appreciate this."

She swallowed thickly and shook his hand, pumping vigorously to show him again that she wasn't a complete coward. "I make no promises."

"I do." Evan looked at her with more confidence and belief than she'd accumulated in her entire lifetime. "I promise you won't regret this."

Rose had to turn away from such a bright, bold faith. It left her feeling so empty. "Yeah, well, let's hope—" She choked off her words. *Let's hope you don't, either.*

"Hope for the best," Evan said.

Rose nodded.

CHAPTER FOUR

"CAN I BORROW your phone, Mom?"

"Sure." Maxine sat at the dining table, laying out a hand of solitaire. When Rose had wiped down the table minutes before, she'd seen her mother surreptitiously stick an ashtray and book of matches on the seat of one of the chairs, hidden by the vinyl tablecloth. "Who you calling?"

"Just a friend." Rose had put the last dish away, squeezed out the sponge, stowed the leftovers. She couldn't stall any longer. It had been several days, and Evan was expecting her to set up a date for the drawing lesson.

"What kind of friend?"

"That's my business."

"My phone." Maxine's lips curled into a smug *so-there.*

Rose might have pointed out that she'd just cooked dinner and cleaned up, in addition to the rest of her daily chores. But she didn't. She swallowed her tongue the way her mother had been forced to when Black Jack was in one of his moods.

Get me out of here, she thought, taking the cordless phone outside to the dusky backyard, as far as the range allowed. Behind her, the window near the dining table opened with a screech of the sash. Her mother must have had a burst of strength to go along with her nosiness.

Rose's exhale was visible in the cold air. Frost tonight. She wrapped her sweater tighter and punched out Evan's number—memorized. He'd written it on the back of a scrap of paper from his wallet and asked her to call as soon as she was certain of her work schedule. She hadn't told him that she was in charge at the Buck Stop and could arrange any hours she liked as long as the time was covered by the store's only other employee, a grumpy retiree aptly named Cross who worked to pick up extra income to supplement his social security.

The phone was ringing. "Hullo," Evan said, harried but cheerful. "Grant residence."

A match flared inside the house. Rose realized she should have called from work, but all she'd been thinking was to get it over with already.

"Hello?"

It was strange, hearing Evan's voice on the phone. Familiar, but not. Slightly thrilling.

"Anyone there?"

"Hello," she finally said. She cleared her throat. "It's Rose. Robbin. Rose Robbin."

"Rose. Good to hear from you. Lucy's been asking about the lesson every day—she's very excited."

"I, uh, the store's been busy lately."

"I hope you're not backing out."

"No. I can be free any afternoon the rest of this week."

"Well, let's see. Lucy gets out of school at three and usually goes to her baby-sitter's house while I have basketball practice. I could probably take time off to run her out to your place—"

"Not my place." Rose thought frantically, struck by the notion that if she worked it right, she might be able to catch sight of a few minutes of the basketball practice. "I could come to the school, and stay with Lucy while you ran the practice. That way you won't need the baby-sitter at all."

The grade school and the high school were separate buildings on the same property, linked by covered walkways that led to a common structure that served both schools. The gymnasium was part of the central building, and surely that's where they'd meet. Rose held her breath, pressing the phone so tightly to her ear that it hurt.

"I suppose I might ask for a favor and have the art room opened," Evan said.

"Oh, don't bother. I'd rather take Lucy outdoors. If that's all right with you."

"Nature sketching?"

"Yes."

"If the weather's bad—"

"We'll figure something out."

"That works for me. I'll be sure that Lucy dresses warmly."

"Great. Tomorrow okay?"

"Sure. You're more eager than I expected."

Rose felt guilty. She swallowed that, too. "Uh, yeah. I guess maybe it'll be okay."

Evan laughed. "There's the Rose I know."

He thought he knew her? He'd barely scratched the surface.

"Okay, then," she said. "Bye."

His startled "Bye," came as she was pressing the Off button.

Rose stuck the phone in the pocket of her cardigan and absently rubbed her stinging ear. She supposed she'd been too abrupt. Talking on the phone with "boys" was another social skill she'd never developed properly. None of her boyfriends—if they could be called that—had ever called for her at home. She hadn't had real dates, either. Just met them at the bridge or the beach. Sometimes she'd been picked up at the side of the road.

She kicked at a pinecone embedded in the stretch of dirt and brittle pine needles that was the backyard. God, she'd been dumb. And naive, even though she'd thought she was tough.

"Rose?" came her mother's voice, carrying out the window. "Are you finished with the phone?"

"Shut the window, Mom. I'll be there in a minute."

She went over to the small garden she'd put in that spring. Nothing much to speak of, just a few rows of carrots, squash, cucumbers and lettuce. Several old rusty barrels contained the tomato plants and she bent over them, searching through the cold leaves for the remaining green fruits. More of the tomatoes remained on the vines than she'd expected and she cradled the pile of hard globes in her sweater, her fingertips gone numb with cold.

The wind was sharp and brisk. Beyond the darkness, the river rushed and gurgled, a sound so familiar it had taken moving away for her to miss the soothing constant.

For a long time, she'd believed she hated this place. Now…maybe not. The memories had faded, even the worst of them. At least to a livable degree.

She'd learned not to expect more than adequacy from her life.

Rose straightened, folding the edge of her sweater over and holding the awkward bundle to her abdomen. She walked to the back door, feeling nearly as unwieldy as a pregnant lady.

Unexpectedly, the comparison made her smile. She'd pushed the pregnancy to the back of her mind for many years, but returning to her hometown had brought it all up again. There were times she had to consciously work to keep her feelings to herself. Aside from a small circle of people—her nonsupportive family, the despicable Lindstroms, Pastor Mike—it was still a secret to Alouette that she'd once been pregnant.

She didn't suppose that the townspeople would be too surprised to learn the truth. They'd always believed the worst of Wild Rose.

AFTER AN HOUR OUTDOORS in the quiet, shaded woods, stepping into the school gym was an assault on the senses. The intense illumination from the banks of overhead lights bounced off the varnished floor and white cement-block walls. The sight, sound and fury of the basketball players was overwhelming—running, flying, crashing bodies, shouts and animal grunts, the constant tattoo of the basketball on the floor and the backboard. Evan's shouts and the shrill pierce of his whistle added to the cacophony.

Although Lucy should have been somewhat accustomed to the raucous scene, Rose wasn't surprised that the girl remained by the door, staring at the scrimmage in progress with wide eyes. Rose took Lucy's hand and they walked into the gym, past the rows of blue metal bleachers.

Evan saw them and waved. He said something to his team and then ran across the floor, all bouncy energy and squeaking sneakers. He wore a sleeveless T-shirt with sweatpants, his face and arms glistening with perspiration. "Hey! Lesson over?"

Rose stepped back, her nostrils flared. So much testosterone. Muscles. Male. "We came inside to warm up." Her tongue was thick in her mouth. "Is that okay?"

"Sure it is. Go ahead and take a seat." Evan glanced at his watch. "I've got another twenty minutes of practice. You're welcome to stay, but if you'd rather leave…"

"I'll stay." Rose was trying not to stare at the boys, but only one thought was running through her head: *Danny's there, Danny's there.*

"Great." Evan jogged away, turning on nimble feet to continue backward as he added, "There are vending machines in—"

Rose waved him on. "We're set." She'd stuck a Thermos of hot chocolate and a few cookies in her backpack.

He saluted and returned to the practice.

She squeezed Lucy's gloved hand. "Come on. Let's sit in the bleachers."

"Can we go all the way to the top?"

"I guess so." Rose would have liked the close-up view from a courtside seat, but it was probably better if she didn't draw attention to herself. At Rose's request, Danny's adoptive parents had never told him his birth mother's identity.

Also by Rose's choice, the contact between her and

Ken and Alana Swanson had been kept to a minimum. They were childless and in their forties at the time of the adoption, which would put them in their mid-fifties now. She'd kept her eyes and ears open since returning to Alouette, and by all accounts the Swansons lived a quiet, respectable life. Fifteen years ago, they had offered to share information with Rose, to keep her up-to-date on Danny's life, even arrange face-to-face visits. She'd thought that knowing him would make her feel worse, so the contact had been limited to photos and cards that were her greatest treasures.

Since her return, she'd daydreamed about what would happen if she changed her mind and asked to be included in their daily life. Not that she'd actually follow through. The last thing she wanted to do was cause trouble for the Swansons, who'd given Danny an exemplary home.

Rose threw glances at the court as she and Lucy climbed to the top row of the bleachers. Danny was a good player, a sophomore who was expected to be a starting guard this year.

"Still feeling cold?" she asked Lucy, who nodded and shivered. Rose slung her backpack around and set it on the bleacher in front of them. "I brought hot chocolate and cookies. Do you like Chips Ahoy?"

Lucy nodded again.

Rose took out the sketchbooks, then dug in the bottom of the pack for the Thermos. Her gaze remained on the court, watching the players race up and down the floor. Danny wasn't the tallest, but he stood out, at least to her. He had gleaming black hair and a quick smile. He was skinny but not gangly, more the wiry, compact, athletic type. Like Rose, though she'd gained a little weight over the years and had become sturdy instead of lithe.

Lucy piped up. "Rose?"

"Oh. Right." She gave herself a mental shake. *Don't stare so hard. You'll look like a stalker.*

"Hot chocolate and cookies, coming right up," she said, pouring out a cup for Lucy. She reached into the backpack for the packet of cookies. "These may be sort of crushed. But you can pick out the biggest pieces."

Lucy seemed satisfied by the inelegant refreshments. She had peeled off her gloves and unzipped her jacket. Her pale face was dotted with rosy color—even the tip of her nose. She sat back on the far edge of the bleacher, alternating between sipping and munching, mindlessly swinging her feet so her heels and toes tapped the metal seat with a rattling rhythmic beat.

"You've probably been to practice before," Rose said. Danny was dribbling the ball, so capable and grown-up her heart ached at the visual reminder of the years she'd missed.

"Sometimes," Lucy said.

"Do you know the players?"

"Uh-huh." The girl pointed her cookie. "That one's Steve, that one's Brad, and that big one's Jeremy. I call him Germy 'cause he teases me."

Rose managed to get a chuckle past the lump in her throat.

"The boy with red hair is Corey…."

"And that one, with the basketball?" Senseless, Rose knew, but she wanted to hear her son's name. To talk about him, even if it was only to a five-year-old.

"Danny. He's nice." Lucy bit into the cookie.

"He's a good player."

Lucy shrugged.

"What does your dad say?"

"'Bout what?"

Does he like Danny? Is Danny his favorite? Is Danny happy? Does he get good grades, does he have a girlfriend? Does he ever wonder who his birth mother is?

Rose gritted her teeth to keep all that back. "Does your dad think he has a good team this year?"

"I dunno. If he yells at them a lot and blows the whistle too much, that means they are being bad." Lucy giggled. "My dad says he wishes he had a whistle to stop me when I'm being bad."

Rose pretended to be shocked. "Don't tell me you're ever bad?"

The girl quickly shook her head, her eyes gone wide as if she expected a scolding. "Not very much."

"That's okay if you are, you know. I mean—" Rose held up two fingers "—just a smidgen."

Lucy still looked doubtful. "What's a smidgen?"

Rose smiled, bringing her fingers within an inch of each other. "About this much."

Lucy brushed her fingers off on her jeans and replicated the gesture with a look of dawning shrewdness. Rose hoped she hadn't stepped out of bounds, giving allowances where she had no business. During their art lesson outdoors, she'd been struck again by Lucy's timid obedience. It hadn't seemed like a good thing, although some parents might beg to differ. Not Evan, judging by what he'd said the other day. He'd welcome a more emboldened Lucy.

Out on the court, the scrimmage had ended. Evan gave the players a breather, then lined up a row of bas-

ketballs along the center line and had the boys perform
a drill in which they ran a complicated pattern, picking up balls as they went.

Light and quick on his feet, Danny finished first and
ran off for the dressing room. Rose's eyes followed
him hungrily, even though Evan was climbing the
bleachers toward her and Lucy and might notice her
preoccupation. At the moment, that didn't matter. She
literally couldn't tear her gaze away.

Evan paused several steps below them, one foot
propped on a bleacher seat. "How's everything up here?"

"Rose bringed Chips Ahoy," Lucy said as she
picked through the remaining crumbs.

The locker room door swung back and forth as the
other players entered. A few stragglers took their time,
but soon the gym had emptied. Rose focused on Evan's
face and saw he was watching her. Damn. "Is that
okay? I didn't mean to ruin her supper."

"It's fine. She usually has a snack after school."

"MaryAnn makes me eat icky food." Lucy screwed
up her face. "Like wrinkly fruit and crab cake."

Rose raised her brows. "Crab cake?"

"Carob cake," Evan said with a smile. "Lucy's baby-
sitter is a health-food nut. I mean a health-food enthu-
siast."

"I should have checked with you." Rose winced.
What a lousy caregiver she'd make. Might as well have
poured raw sucrose down Lucy's throat. No wonder
the girl seemed so happy—know-nothing Rose had
doped her up on sugar.

"Doesn't matter. She'll live. It's better than the burnt
charcoal I give her at home."

"Huh?"

"I'm a lousy cook." Evan leaned closer to Lucy, propping his elbows on his upraised knee. "I can see that you two had a good time." He smoothed his daughter's hair. "Right, Luce?"

She nodded happily. "Yeah, Dad."

His eyes went to Rose. "Thanks." He straightened. "Are you willing to wait a few more minutes? I have to run into the locker room to check on the boys and get my wallet. I'll be right back."

Rose nodded, filling with renewed anticipation. She might see Danny again when he came back out after showering. Maybe up close this time, if she hustled Lucy out of the bleachers.

Evan's low voice cut through her inner turmoil. "What is it? You're radiant."

Radiant? She was unaccustomed to compliments. She drew back, feeling so shy it was as if he'd touched her with the same gentle care he'd shown Lucy. Or not the same. Maybe…more.

He'd asked a question. *What is it?* She couldn't answer that—no way.

Instead she cleared her throat, prepared to prevaricate. "Must've been the cold air."

"Yes. It put roses in your cheeks."

Lucy had twisted around to stare. Softly, she sing-songed, "Roses in Rose's cheeks."

"Yeah, and yours, too, ladybug." Though Evan spoke to Lucy while he backed down a few rows, he continued looking up at Rose.

Her face wasn't cold. It was flaming. If not for the second chance at Danny, Evan's admiring appraisal would have sent her scurrying out the door. No man had looked at her like that since…since…

She couldn't remember. Maybe never.

And he probably thought nothing of it. He was only being nice.

Rose bit her lip, closed her eyes. She was not a normal woman. Couldn't even respond to a guy's offhand compliment without making it a big freakin' deal.

"Five minutes," Evan said, and descended the remaining bleachers in big strides that made them rattle and clang.

Rose rubbed her forearms, where goose bumps had risen despite the warm layers of her sweater and jacket. "Okay, Lucy. Let's pack up." She screwed the cap onto the Thermos.

"You forgot the cup."

"Run down to the water fountain and rinse it out for me, okay?"

"Okay." Lucy carefully made her way down the bleachers on her bottom. By the time she reached the gym floor, Rose had repacked and zipped up, leaving out Lucy's sketchbook. She grabbed it and trailed the girl to the water fountain, set into a niche in the wall between the doors that led to the boys' and girls' locker rooms.

Lucy rinsed the cup, the tip of her tongue protruding between her lips as she concentrated. "Okay?" she said, shaking it dry.

Rose exchanged the cup for the sketchbook. "You can take this home and show your dad what you drew today." She wanted Evan to see that she'd given him good value, even though she wasn't a trained artist or teacher. Lucy had been an eager and talented student, forgetting her inhibitions as she became absorbed in capturing various items and scenes. Before the cold

October air had driven them inside, they'd drawn leaves, pine cones, ferns, and turned twig tracings into animal shapes.

Lucy clasped the sketchbook. "What will we draw next time, Rose?"

"I don't know. We'll see if your father wants you to have another lesson."

Lucy nodded with some confidence. "If I say so."

"Oh? Are you the boss?"

The girl nodded, pursing her lips into a mischievous smile. "Daddy says I'm getting spoiled."

"Spoiled, huh?" Rose put on a show of looking Lucy over, squeezing her arms and legs to make her double over in giggles. "I hope he doesn't have to throw you in the trash like a mushy banana."

Rose heard the door to the locker room open behind her. "What's going on here?" Evan said.

She straightened with a snap.

A limp Lucy dropped to the floor. "I'm a banana-nana, Daddy. I'm covered in squishy black spots."

Evan approached, holding his wallet. He opened it and withdrew several bills, handing the money to Rose. "What did the ape say to the banana?"

She hoped she wasn't supposed to answer.

He bent over Lucy, sliding his hands under her arms to hoist her onto her feet. His face was near hers. "You're so a-peeling," he said, and smacked a kiss on her forehead.

He straightened, looking at Rose with a shrug. "You see where my level of humor has fallen."

"Uh-huh. That was pretty bad." She looked at the bills in her hand. Two twenties and a ten. More than she made for an eight-hour minimum wage shift at the

Buck Stop, after taxes had been taken out. "This is too much."

"I offered fifty per lesson."

"I thought it was twenty-five per hour," she bluffed.

"Either way. Doesn't matter to me."

"Yes, but…has it been two hours?" Although he was better off than she, a schoolteacher's wages weren't making him rich, either. She doubted he could keep up the lessons for long at that rate. And she wanted to continue. Not only because of Danny.

"Close enough."

"Except that I could have left earlier. I didn't expect you to pay me for the extra time." She held out one of the twenties.

He wouldn't take it. "Keep it."

"Please," she said, feeling wooden as she pressed it on him. She wasn't a charity case. "I insist."

"A compromise." He took her hands and exchanged the twenty for the ten, squeezing her fingers over the remaining bills. He gave her knuckles a friendly tap. "I'll pay you forty per session, no matter the length."

Rose silently vowed to make sure that each lesson lasted for at least ninety minutes, if not longer. She put her head down and nodded, pleating the bills with nervous fingers before she looked up at him. Her stomach was doing flip-flops again. "Then you want to continue?"

"How does once a week sound?"

Lucy let out a cheer. "Yay!"

Rose smiled at her, admiring an enthusiasm that was uncomplicated by money, secrets or strange tingly attractions that were mostly just a nuisance to work around. "That sounds wonderful."

"Wonderful?" Evan tilted his head to catch Rose's eye. He grinned. "Whaddaya know. We've stepped up from *fine* to *wonderful*." The grin became a laugh—one that was on her, but he did it with such charm that she had to join in. The lightening of the weight she carried around felt…

Wonderful.

Really, truly wonderful.

"You have roses in your cheeks again," Lucy pointed out. Her solemn blue eyes seemed to take in everything around her. Including emotions Rose wanted to keep private and unspoken.

"I should go." She grabbed the backpack she'd dropped on the polished floor. "I have work."

"Need a ride?" Evan said. "We're leaving, too."

"No. Thanks. I have a bike."

"A bike? It's too cold for a bike."

The locker room door opened, momentarily distracting Rose when a group of boys in blue letter jackets came out.

"Rose?" Evan said.

"It's okay. I ride the bike until we have snow." She moved toward the wall, hoping that he would just let her go. One of his players spoke to him, engaging his attention long enough for her to surreptitiously search the faces. Danny wasn't among them.

The first group of teenage boys left, but others emerged from the locker room. Some had a few words for Lucy and she responded with a shy smile. There were several curious glances thrown Rose's way, but she'd shut down her expression, willing herself into wallflower invisibility. Many of the boys had been in the Buck Stop for gas or snacks, but even if they recognized her face or knew her as Wild Rose, she was a nobody to them—just an older woman of no great beauty or personality.

She clutched the pack to her chest and waited for her chance to escape. Now that she had the perfect opportunity, the idea of actually seeing Danny up close, maybe even meeting him, was absolutely terrifying. She wanted to run, but she was frozen.

And then it happened. Danny exited the locker room with another boy.

Rose's eyes went immediately to her son's face and then slammed shut before he could feel her staring. She clamped her arms and held the backpack tight to her body, thinking she could contain her runaway heartbeat.

"Everybody out?" she heard Evan ask, as casual as if this was any other day.

Danny said, "Yeah, I think so." His reedy voice sent a thrill through Rose. She cracked her lids. Despite the wiry, hard-muscled body, he was still young. His cheeks were rounded and flushed pink; his mouth was soft, cherubic. The bulky athletic jacket seemed two sizes too big.

She wanted to hug him, cover his boyish face in kisses. Crazy impulse. Too late for that. *Years* too late.

"I'll check. Wait for me, Luce." Evan disappeared into the locker room.

Rose pushed her spine into the hard cement wall.

"Hi, Danny." Lucy twirled a lock of hair. "Hi, *Germy.*"

"Look who's here," said the other boy. "It's little Lucy Goosey. Hiya, Lucy Goosey." He was taller than Danny by eight inches and outweighed him by upwards of fifty pounds. Rose recognized him as the team's center, Jeremy Kevanen, a friendly guy with a snub nose and bad skin. She knew his mother. Gloria was a plump chatterbox who exuded rah-rah school spirit and community pride like the aging cheerleader she was.

Rose gave Gloria a wide berth. For several reasons.

"Whatcha got, Lucy Goosey?" Jeremy asked.

Lucy swung her shoulders from side to side. "My sketchbook."

Jeremy reached for it. "You gonna lemme see?"

"Nuh-uh."

"Aw, c'mon."

Lucy glanced back at Rose.

Rose swallowed as if she was forcing down a brick. "Go ahead."

Both boys looked at her. A vise squeezed her lungs so she couldn't breathe. "Show them what you drew," she said through unmoving lips. It was an effort not to stare at Danny. She fixed her eyes on Lucy instead.

The pressure relieved slightly when Danny got down on one knee to look at the book the girl opened. His jacket gaped at the back of his bare neck, where the fringe of his dark hair was still damp. "Are you an artist?" he asked Lucy.

"Rose said I'm gonna be."

"Cool. I like to draw, too."

"Can you draw a picture of me?" Jeremy said. He showed his profile, lifting an arm to flex his biceps. "Ain't I pretty?"

"No way!" Lucy shouted with glee, then bashfully held the sketchbook over the lower half of her face.

The boys laughed and moved on, loping across the

gym floor with swinging arms and bobbing heads. Jeremy waved. "See ya, Lucy Goosey."

Danny looked back and nodded at Rose, who was staring again. She held her frozen position until the door banged shut behind them, and then she exhaled, loosening her hold on the backpack so it slid to the floor. She would have followed it if her knees hadn't locked in place.

Evan came out, securing the door behind him. "All clear. Did the boys leave? Let's go, then. Sure you don't want a ride, Rose? I could put your bike in the trunk, no problem."

She couldn't face his easy cheer, but the casual chatter was a blessing. "No, thank you."

He retrieved her book bag and took her gently by the elbow. "Did you meet Jeremy and Danny?"

"N-not really."

Lucy capered ahead of them. "Danny thinks I'm an artist!"

Rose let Evan walk her to the door even though she wanted to shake off his hand. He must have noticed her distress. Deliberately, she made her heart into a stone. *Pull it together. He's already suspicious.*

"Jeremy asked me to paint him!"

Evan chuckled, watching his daughter twirl. "Lucy seems enthused."

Deflect attention. "She did well." Rose gathered herself, walking with more purpose so that Evan had to let go. "She has talent." She probably should have elaborated, but every word was a struggle.

They left the school building. The wind scattered crisp leaves across a cement courtyard outlined by brick pavers. Many of the upper branches were already stripped bare. Fall had flown by while Rose was obsessing over her lost son. She was wasting her life, but her other regrets were worse.

Evan tried again at the bike rack. "Let me give you a ride."

"No. I don't want to be a bother."

"It won't take ten minutes to run you out to the Buck Stop."

Lucy was already waiting at Evan's car, a blue Honda, one of few vehicles remaining in the parking lot. "C'mon, Dad! I'm hungry!"

Rose shook her head emphatically. "I'm fine on my own," she insisted through clenched teeth.

"So you say." Evan paused, waiting, then finally set down her pack and turned to walk away. "At least the lesson was a success. Next week, then?"

She made a nominally agreeable sound, keeping her eyes focused on the distance. *Leave already. Just leave.* Her rigid spine was melting. She felt herself sinking. *Please leave.*

Lucy called goodbye. The car doors slammed, the engine fired. Rose lifted a hand to wave, and that was the end of her strength. She dropped to her knees beside the bicycle, barely retaining enough presence of mind to pretend to check the gears as Evan drove slowly away, looking back at her with a worried frown.

Finally he was gone and she let herself crumple. One dry sob escaped before she covered her face with her hands. *Danny,* she thought with utter despair. He'd looked at her like a stranger.

Why had she expected anything more?

CHAPTER FIVE

IN THE UPPER PENINSULA of Michigan, winter often arrived by early November, long before the calendar said it had. It seemed to Rose that the final warm weeks of autumn passed more quickly than ever before. One day the sun was shining and the trees were dressed in rustling skirts of color and the next the landscape was barren, whistling with wintry winds. The weather suited her gray mood. Instead of feeling blessed for having some meager contact with her son, her heart was chilled. Coming within touching distance of Danny had made her know, without a doubt, that giving him up had been the worst mistake of her life.

Logically, the decision still made sense. She'd had no prospects to provide for him—monetary or emotional. Even as scared and alone as she'd been during her pregnancy, she'd expected to have some feelings of motherly love for the baby inside her. She hadn't. Not really. Certainly not in any of the acceptable, sentimental, soft-focus Hallmark card ways.

After the birth, she'd waited for a burst of whatever emotion other mothers experienced that made them go all googly and tender at the sight of their caterwauling infant, but that hadn't come, either. At most, amid the pain and exhaustion, she'd been drawn to her baby with a kind of appalled fascination. The small red wrinkled creature had terrified her.

Surely, she'd thought, that wasn't natural. She was wounded. Abnormal. Very confused. There was only one resolution. The best she could do for her child was to give it to a couple who already knew how to love.

Nothing had happened since then to prove otherwise. She became ill at the thought of what kind of warped life a traumatized seventeen-year-old who'd shrunk from human contact would have given to a child.

Rose gripped the steering wheel of her mother's car, staring blankly at the streets of Alouette as she drove toward the high school. Her mind was back in time, trying to remember how the teenage version of herself had thought. Primarily, she'd wanted to run away from her problems. The baby had seemed to be an encumbrance. A constant reminder of her broken heart and the terrible events that had followed. She hadn't realized that learning to love and care for Danny might have helped her heal.

But that wouldn't have been fair, keeping Danny for her own selfish reasons. He truly was better off with the Swansons.

Even if she had to continue to pay the price for the rest of her life.

Traffic picked up around the school and she slowed the car, looking for a parking spot. The days had shortened so much that the old-fashioned streetlights were on already, honey-colored globes glowing in the shadowed dusk. All the spots on the street were taken, so she drove to the parking lot behind the school. It was nearly filled, even though this was a Tuesday night game. The first basketball game of the season was a major event.

Rose parked. Loud laughter and voices rang across the flat expanse as fans hurried into the gym. She wrapped her scarf once more around her neck, pulled a knit hat lower over her forehead. Armor. She would soon get lost in the crowd, but the first minutes of exposure to the boisterous deluge of humanity was always a shock when her days were framed in solitude and an unchanging set of responsibilities.

Except for Lucy. Rose left the car and trotted across the cold pavement toward the school. They'd had two more drawing lessons, and Rose had begun to anticipate her time with the girl. When Lucy came out of her shell, she was delightfully bright and inquisitive. Each skill Rose demonstrated was greeted with wonder, bolstering Rose's confidence as equally as the girl's. Perhaps it was a pitiful thing, to draw your self-esteem from a five-year-old's admiration, but Rose didn't care. She liked Lucy and her innocent, nonjudgmental enjoyment of their time together. They made up stories to go with their illustrations and chatted about nothing more important than favorite foods and TV shows. Lucy was a friend.

Evan was another matter. Afraid that she'd revealed too much on the day she'd encountered Danny, Rose had kept her distance from her son's observant coach. She greeted Evan's friendly overtures with cool, clipped answers that discouraged further conversation. Sometimes that made her feel despicable, but he'd been obliging. Aside from the necessary contact concerning Lucy's lessons, he'd left her alone.

Rose told herself she was relieved, even when he

hadn't bothered to mention his team's first home game. Why should he? She'd been a scowling ingrate. She wouldn't blame him if he couldn't care less if she came to watch.

She paid for a ticket and pushed past a group clustered near the doors. The lights, action and noise inside the gym was always a shock, even though she was prepared for it. A piercing buzzer went off and the floor thundered with running bodies. The junior varsity team was already playing the first game of the evening.

Hovering near the bleacher railing, she waited a few minutes for the crowd to be absorbed in the game before slipping toward a seat in the upper stands. A few people greeted her. She returned the hellos with silent nods, moving on quickly until she'd found an open space near a younger group who gave her arrival scant notice.

She scanned the gym. Danny would be in the locker room, preparing for the varsity game. But Evan was there, down front, acting as assistant coach for the young male teacher who ran the junior squad. His back was to her, so she let her gaze linger. His hair looked freshly clipped. He wore a bright blue tie with a white shirt and a dark suit that emphasized his broad shoulders. He exuded authority.

Wow. She clutched her hands between her knees. Evan's manner was so natural that she sometimes forgot how handsome and in-charge he was. Once upon a time, she'd preferred athletic, confident—even cocky—men, like Rick Lindstrom. That was before Rick had dumped her and then another man had harmed her irreparably. After that, all men had intimidated her, and it had been years before she'd made a fumbling attempt to be normal.

So far, though, Evan was different. His confidence was tempered with kindness. He gave her breathing space without giving up on her.

A knot had grown in Rose's throat. Disgusted, she rolled her eyes upward, staring at the ceiling until the unwanted palpitations and welling tear ducts had subsided. When she was back under control, she tried to watch the game, but her gaze kept drifting to Evan.

For distraction, she picked out Lucy's head instead, several rows from the front, sitting between Tess Bucek and her fiancé, Connor Reed. Lucy ate popcorn, looking back and forth between the couple as they chatted and cheered. A different kind of feeling prickled at Rose's composure. Envy? Longing? Regret?

She didn't know, except that a part of herself—a small part, maybe one percent, five percent—wanted to be down front, sitting beside Lucy, belonging with Evan.

The revelation wasn't as startling as it might have been, yet Rose was shaken. How had that happened? Mushy feelings had sneaked up on her when she wasn't looking.

The buzzer sounded to end the game. The crowd applauded. She checked the scoreboard, realizing she'd missed the entire fourth quarter with her meandering thoughts. The Gale Storm had lost to the visiting team, forty-eight to thirty-nine. The bleachers began emptying out as fans took advantage of the break to visit the refreshment stands and rest rooms. Rose stayed put. In minutes, the varsity team would emerge from the locker room for warm-ups. She didn't want to miss that.

"Hey, Wild. Figured I'd find you here."

Rose looked up. Roxy Whitaker stood over her, tipping a half-full bag of popcorn into her mouth. Roxy was the handyperson at Bay House, a local bed-and-breakfast. Tall, strong and direct, she usually wore her sandy hair pulled back into a ponytail that suited her makeup-free face. She was the most un-girly girl Rose had ever encountered, aside from herself.

"Hey, Rox. You decided to become a b-ball fan?"

"Not really. Nothing else to do tonight." Roxy sat and offered her snack to Rose. "Popcorn?"

She took a small handful.

"Haven't seen you lately," Roxy said after a while. Rose was nibbling popcorn and surveying the crowd, trying to maintain her cool. "Been busy?"

"Same as usual."

"Oh? I heard you're giving art lessons to ·Evan Grant's daughter."

"Where'd you hear that?"

"Around." Roxy shrugged. "You know."

"Gossip." Rose had known that, sooner or later, the talk would start. She groaned.

"It's not good gossip until it's salacious. Is there anything salacious going on between you two?"

"Of course not!"

"I didn't think so." But Roxy's sidelong glance wasn't convinced.

Cheeks afire, Rose busily brushed popcorn flecks off her jeans. "We barely speak. I spend the lesson time with Lucy, not him. Tell that to the curious cats at Bay House, why don't you?"

"Hmm, but he's a hottie, right? I'd buff his basketballs."

Rose hushed her with an elbow to the ribs. "You would not."

The other woman laughed. "Nope. I don't bounce that way."

"Well, I don't bounce at all."

"Who's to say you can't start?"

The team exited the locker room and ran across the floor in their blue warm-ups, putting on a show as they moved in sync for a drill, sending balls swishing through the hoop one after the other. Rose edged forward. Danny dribbled, spun and unerringly sank a basket before returning to the line. She started to clap, then caught herself and steepled her hands beneath her chin. As if anyone would notice or care who she applauded.

Except Roxy. She winked, then gave Rose a nudge for good measure. "There's the coach."

"Uh-huh."

"You didn't even look at him. So much for the gossip."

"Told you."

"Shame," Roxy said with a sigh.

Rose's eyes followed Danny as the team went into another formation. Evan stood beneath the basket, jacket unbuttoned, one hand holding his tie flat as he caught the bouncing balls with the other and tossed them back onto the floor. His quiet assurance was appealing. Every female in the stands must have noticed. Rose told herself that she had no shot with him. He tolerated her only for Lucy's sake.

Roxy emptied the remains of the popcorn into her mouth, balled up the bag and tossed it away. She munched for a while, then spit out a hard kernel. "Has he tried anything?"

"God, no."

"What would you do if he did?"

"He's not going to."

"But if he did?"

Rose ran a hand through her hair. One finger caught on a snarl. "You mean, because he's heard I'm wild?" Which translated to *easy*.

"I've got news for ya, hon. You've been a nun for way too long to keep the reputation active. You're only called Wild Rose these days because nicknames stick in this town. It'd be more accurate to call you *Mild* Rose."

Rose made a wry smile. "Do me a favor. Pass the word."

"Sure."

The bleachers had refilled while the teams finished warm-ups. Rose caught sight of two familiar faces across the floor. Danny's parents. They were a quiet, conservative couple, not boisterous boosters who waved foam fingers and yelled at the ref. But it was clear how proud they were of their son. They never missed a game.

The past basketball season, Rose had often wondered if they'd noticed her presence and worried about her motives. She would have liked to reassure them, but after she'd rebuffed their initial overture and seen how relieved they'd been to keep her out of their son's life, it had seemed less disruptive to simply continue to keep her distance. The few times their paths might have crossed, she'd switched course to avoid what would have to be an uncomfortable meeting.

The teams had gathered around their coaches. The high school pep band tootled experimentally and an announcement was made, asking the crowd to rise for the national anthem.

"*If* he did," Roxy said as she stood, the shuffle of the crowd sounding like distant thunder. "Just say he asked you out. Would you go?"

The anthem began, saving Rose from a quick answer. Her gaze strayed away from the large American flag hanging in the rafters to Danny, and then Evan, both standing with shoulders square, hands over their hearts.

Rose touched her palm to her left breast. Would she go?

"I think I might," she said as the song ended.

Surprise flickered in Roxy's eyes, but she made no further comment. That was why Roxy was Rose's only friend—she might be blunt and even a little tactless, but she knew when to let things go.

AFTER THE GAME, Evan came out of the locker room feeling tired but satisfied. He'd seen his victorious players off and had wrapped up his various coaching duties. In the gym, the stands had emptied. Only a few loiterers remained. A lone janitor pushed a wide broom around the wood floor, sweeping up shredded candy wrappers and popcorn bags.

Lucy was waiting, holding hands with Rose Robbin. Evan suddenly found his second wind.

"Hi," he said. He tousled Lucy's head, aware that she no longer immediately ran to him after even a short absence. "What happened to Tess and Connor?"

"They remembered they had dinner reservations, so they left Lucy with me." Rose's lashes flicked at him. "Is that okay?"

"Of course. I hope that was no bother for you."

"I volunteered."

"We're not keeping you?"

"I managed to make an opening in my busy social schedule."

Her tone was so dry he almost missed the joke. "Thanks for pushing back dinner with the Queen." He looked at his daughter, who was still clinging to Rose's hand. "Ready to go, Luce?"

"Can Rose come along?"

"I have a car tonight," Rose quickly said.

Lucy tugged. "But it's a silly-bration."

Evan spread his hands. "We won."

"Yeah, I saw. Good game." Rose looked like she wanted to pull away, but Lucy wasn't letting go.

"I know it's late for Lucy to be up, but I promised her a treat since this is the first win of the season. We're having make-your-own hot fudge sundaes—"

Rose began shaking her head.

"—at home," he finished.

She stopped.

"In pajamas," Lucy added.

Rose's eyes widened.

Evan chuckled. "Guests are exempt from the dress code."

"That sounds like…fun." Evan was sure Rose only said that for Lucy's benefit. "But—"

"Please, Rose?" Lucy was using her big blue marble eyes, the ones that got to Evan every time. If Rose resisted, no doubt could remain that she had the hardest heart in all of Alouette.

"I want to show you my pictures that we did," Lucy

added. "Dad put frames on and hung them up in my room."

"I don't—" Rose frowned. "It's not—" She looked at Lucy and visibly caved, a smile softening her surly expression. Once more, Evan was reminded of the loveliness that was usually hidden behind the grim mouth and ruffle of black hair. "Maybe I can stop by for a few minutes."

Lucy hugged her.

Rose looked at Evan with a helplessness he well recognized.

Way to go, Luce.

LUCY WORE light blue flannel pajamas printed with fluffy clouds and even fluffier sheep. She was overexcited, chattering like a squirrel and constantly rising up to her knees on her chair, reaching for another spoonful of the assorted sundae toppings Evan had put out. Feeling a little queasy, Rose watched as the girl layered chocolate sprinkles over rainbow sprinkles over jelly beans over hot fudge *and* caramel sauce.

She hadn't needed to fret about feeding Lucy sugar. Evan obviously had no problem with that.

"All right, that's enough, Miss Lucy," he said in a firm father-knows-best voice. "Sit down and eat or you're going to bed right now."

Lucy stirred her melting concoction and took a heaping spoonful. She rolled it in her mouth before swallowing. "We have comp'ny," she said, showing fudge-rimmed teeth. "I want to stay up."

Evan rolled his eyes. "Oh, you're up, all right. Probably all night long after this treat."

Lucy popped back onto her knees. She leaned over

the table, making it wiggle. "Yahoo! Rose, do you want to sleep over?"

Startled, Rose stole a quick look at Evan. He watched her with a potentially wicked little grin picking up one corner of his mouth. "Um," she said, feeling every bite of cold ice cream solidifying in the pit of her stomach. "Maybe another time."

Lucy sighed with gusto. "Okay."

In a voice that was a shade too low to be innocent, Evan said, "We'll hold you to that."

Rose stared into her sundae dish, the spoon frozen in her hand. He didn't mean that. He was teasing her. Wasn't he?

She tossed her hair. Met his eyes. "Yeah, I'll be sure to bring a sleeping bag and toothbrush."

"And jammies," Lucy said, burbling with delight over the prospect. She poked a finger into her ice cream to rescue a drowned jelly bean.

Evan didn't hesitate. "Or a nightgown, if you'd prefer."

Rose blinked. This wasn't only teasing. It was *flirting.* She might be out of practice by a decade or so, but she still recognized it. Participating…that was more difficult.

"My best one is silk," she said, feeling slightly ridiculous. Such a lie. She slept in T-shirts or a tank top and panties.

Evan's eyes darkened, but he didn't take it further.

"Pretty," Lucy said. "I betcha you look like a princess." She was wiping sprinkles off a sticky finger onto the side of her dish. "I have a princess nightgown. It's pink with lace ruffles."

"Lucy, your manners are atrocious." Evan handed

her a napkin. "Here you go. Clean up and then go brush your teeth. It's bedtime."

Lucy wailed. "But you said—"

"I was joking. You know you can't stay up all night. You have school tomorrow." He stood and removed her dish, grabbing the back of her chair with the other hand and pulling it away from the table. "Go on."

"All…right…" Lucy dragged herself to the doorway of the small kitchen. "But I want Rose to come say good-night."

"She will," Evan said. "Shoo."

Lucy made heavy foot-stomps through the living room and into the short hallway that linked the bedrooms.

Rose took a deep breath and looked around. Even with one less body in the room, the kitchen had just grown smaller. Lucy had been her buffer. Now…her eyes were drawn like a magnet to Evan.

He'd scraped the dishes and was rinsing them at the sink, his back to her. The suit coat was off, the tie loosened and his sleeves rolled up. Her gaze dipped when he bent to open the dishwasher. His tailored pants pulled taut, displaying a firm, nicely rounded butt. She hadn't noticed a man's butt in…

Evan straightened. She looked up, horrified when her gaze met his in the black, reflective surface of the window over the sink. He'd caught her admiring his goods!

"Are you finished?" he asked.

No way could she talk. Her throat had closed. She managed an unintelligible sound.

"I'll take your dish."

Oh, she thought, flooding with relief. Until Evan

turned back to the sink, giving his rear end a funny wiggle that left no doubt he *had* noticed.

"Nice house," she blurted through the flame of embarrassment.

He slapped a wet hand on his butt, sending spray flying. "The glutes are in shape. I run twenty miles a week." He glanced over his shoulder and laughed at the expression on her face. "What? You didn't say, 'Nice ass'?"

"You know I didn't."

"Must have been wishful thinking."

"Quit teasing me. I know I'm not—" She bit her lip.

He closed the dishwasher, turned and leaned against the sink, wiping his hands on a dish towel. There was something so attractive about a man in a dress shirt with his tie askew and his sleeves rolled up, working in a kitchen with ruffled curtains and baskets hung on the lilac walls. She wouldn't have thought it would make him seem more masculine, but it did. Particularly in contrast to her memory of him pacing the sidelines during the basketball game, progressively more disheveled as his intensity level rose.

"Not what?" he said.

Oh, damn. No way to get out of this one. Maybe it was best to lay her cards on the table. "I'm not the kind of woman men like you are…looking for. I'm not cute, or cheerful, or funny, or feminine."

"No, you're not," he said, agreeing so quickly her heart sank.

"Not marriage material," she added in an almost angry tone. *That* should do it. *Finito.*

"Hmm."

Her jaw jutted. What did *hmm* mean?

"Feminine," he said. "You're a woman. How can you *not* be feminine?"

"Conventionally feminine," she said tightly. "Don't get philosophical about it."

"I think you underestimate yourself."

"Yes. But only because—" She closed her mouth.

"Because…" Evan drew out the word. "Because others do?"

She shrugged.

"My first coaching job downstate, I had this player." He tossed the towel aside, but thankfully stayed where he was. She couldn't have borne it if he'd sat across from her with a sympathetic look in his eyes while he gave her the "there-there, atta girl," motivational speech. "Bright kid. Fantastic talent. Sloppy skills."

"And yadda, yadda, you helped him to believe in himself and he went on to get a college basketball scholarship," she said. "Spare me the lecture. I've heard it before."

"Actually, no. He's in jail now."

Rose cocked her head.

"I tried. Set myself up as his mentor, whipped out every cheesy cliché in the book, and when that didn't work I simply became his friend. His family life was pure hell. No one expected anything out of him but the worst. He wanted to do better, and he tried, but…" Evan shrugged, turning over his empty hands in a gesture that said it all.

She saw in his expression that he still felt defeated. But that wasn't her concern. She wasn't his support. They were barely friends.

"Y'know—" She stopped and cleared her clogged

throat. "You need better stories, ones with a genuine moral."

"Life's not like that, is it?"

"Not for some of us."

A deep silence swelled, broken by Lucy's footsteps. She called for them, asking to be tucked in, wanting bedtime stories.

Evan held up a hand, as if she could see him and be silenced. He was looking at Rose. His eyes glowed with conviction. "You're more than you think."

Although she'd thought that she'd accepted her inadequacies, she felt herself nodding.

CHAPTER SIX

At Lucy's insistence, Rose followed Evan into the bedroom to say good-night. She seemed ill at ease—no surprise there—and wandered around the room while he did the ritual tucking-in procedures. When he went to the window to pull the curtain tight, he brushed against her and she nearly hopped out of her skin, even though she tried to make it look as if she'd merely gotten a sudden urge to bolt across the room to examine the drawings that Lucy had already shown her when they first got home.

A woman who was that sensitive to touch was either very shy or very stimulated.

Both, perhaps.

He wasn't sure how he felt about that. He *was* fascinated by Rose. But was that his Dudley Do-Right rescue fantasy talking or was it a sexual attraction?

Hell, yes, he wanted to help her. Help her with his hands on her waist and her breasts against his chest. Help her as her mouth lifted and her pink lips softened for his kiss.

The desire was so strong and sudden it stunned him. There was no doubt she'd be woman enough for him.

"Dad," Lucy said. "You're not listening."

He dragged his gaze away from Rose's cameo profile. "Sure I am."

"The ogre's coming to bite Princess Kristina's head off."

"Oh, no. Then we'd better think up a twist to the story real fast." Evan noticed Rose looking alarmed by the conversation. "Lucy has been making up her own bedtime story."

Lucy sat up in bed. "Rose can help."

"If she wants…"

Rose hovered nearby. Her expression was uncertain. "I don't know if I'm any good at telling stories."

Evan offered her a wry grin. "Neither am I. Lucy has enough imagination for all three of us."

Lucy patted the bed. "You sit on this side, Rose."

She perched. "What do I have to do?"

Relax, he wanted to say. She looked as nervous as he'd been the first time he'd held a pink, squawling, six-pound bundle named Lucy Victoria.

He nodded toward Rose's watercolor, now framed and set in pride of place beside a studio portrait of Krissa and Lucy on the bedside table. "Your picture of the roses started this story."

Rose stared in silence. He couldn't tell if she was looking at her painting or the photo of his late wife.

"Princess Kristina lives in Rose Cottage," he began.

Lucy picked up the familiar story. "She's cursed by an evil witch."

Most nights, they added a bit more to the growing saga. Though details changed from telling to telling, Lucy relished the dramatic points with a zeal that was either encouraging or disturbing. Evan hadn't figured that out yet.

"If she leaves her house," Lucy continued, "a big, mean ogre will chop her up and eat her for supper."

Rose shivered. "How scary."

Lucy nodded. "He's ninety-nine feet tall and his teeth are sharp as—"

"Razor blades," Evan supplied. "Like the ones I keep for shaving in the locked cabinet that you're not allowed to touch."

"Uh-huh."

"Don't forget that the princess is allowed to go into the woods around her house. The last time she was there, she found a magic stone."

Lucy screwed up her face. "She dropped it when the ogre started chasing her, Dad."

"Maybe a bird swooped down and picked up the stone," Rose said.

Lucy seemed to weigh the value of the contribution. "Then what?"

"Just when the ogre was about to snatch the princess, the bird flew overhead and dropped the magic stone into her hand."

Lucy nodded.

"Umm…" Rose pushed both hands through her hair, tucking it behind her ears.

"The stone began to glow," Evan said.

Rose smiled gratefully. "And the princess made a wish."

"To stop the ogre."

"Or to turn the ogre into a prince?"

"To turn *herself* into an ogre!" Lucy said with an excited jounce.

"Well, let's think on that one, shall we?" Evan got Lucy to slide down in bed. He kissed her. "We'll decide tomorrow night what Princess Kristina wishes for. Try to get some sleep, okay, kid?"

"'Kay." Lucy looked at Rose, who'd risen to stand beside the bed, and turned up her cheek.

Rose pecked her, darting in and out like a bird. Lucy sighed and settled down with surprisingly little complaint.

Evan moved to the door. Rose was frozen, her fingertips touching her lips. "Want to snap off that light?"

"Night, Lucy." She flicked the switch and quickly followed Evan out of the room. "I'll go now," she said, trying to slide by him in the narrow hallway.

He wanted to catch her, but this wasn't the place, with Lucy listening to every sound. She slipped by with a swish of black hair and a faintly woodsy scent of pine tar and smoke. "What's the rush?"

"I meant to stay only for ten minutes. I've been here an hour."

"Does that matter?"

She sent him a frown. "People will talk."

"Who cares?" But of course he knew—*she* did.

"I don't," she said. Her fingers pleated the ribbed hem of her sweater. "Not for me. But for you…"

"I can handle myself—and any talk."

They'd reached the living room of the modestly sized house. Krissa had decorated it long ago with pale-green walls, a scrolled wrought-iron shelving unit and a plump sofa patterned in stripes and big, blowsy roses. After she'd left him, he'd shoved the dozen pillows into a closet and taken down the watering cans, the pastel prints and the dried herb wreath that shed bits and pieces on the rug every time he walked by. He hadn't noticed before how empty and ugly the leftover picture hooks looked. Or how massive his new big-screen TV and leather recliner were.

Rose had inched toward the door. "I have a request," he said. "Another job."

"Oh, no. You've been generous enough—"

"This isn't about generosity." He motioned to the couch. "Please sit. Just for a few minutes longer."

She sat.

He was edgy. He paced back and forth like a zoo animal before realizing that wasn't making Rose any more comfortable. "You noticed how much Lucy likes the painting you gave her, right?" He sat on the ottoman that Krissa used to dress up with a tray and a tipsy vase of flowers. Now it was piled with newspapers that crunched beneath him. He wasn't right next to Rose, but near enough. "She looks at it every night."

Rose nodded.

He lowered his voice. "Well, see, Lucy's birthday is at the end of January. The depths of winter. It'll be two years since her mother died and I'd like to give her something special. She saw this decorating show on TV and ever since, I've been promising her we'd paint her room. But she has this imagination, and I—well, I don't. The whole deal baffles me. So I wondered if I could hire you to paint a mural. The kind of thing little girls like—" He waggled his hands, feeling out of his depth. "Castles and clouds and unicorns, you know?"

"Sure, I know what you mean."

"Yeah. Good." He exhaled. "Lucy would love that."

He'd engaged Rose's interest. She leaned forward, her fingers knotted and her shoulders hunched. Her eyes had lit up. "Do you want this to be a surprise?"

"I don't know. I hadn't thought about logistics, except I figured I'd better ask you far in advance since I'm not sure how long these things take."

"I can do preliminary sketches. The actual painting, if I'm prepped, might take a weekend. Maybe more, depending on how detailed the mural is."

"Have you ever done something like this?"

"Uh, not really." Her restless fingers rethreaded. "Did you want someone experienced?"

"Experience doesn't matter. You're the right wom—artist."

Her lashes lowered. "You have to understand. I'm not a pro."

He swallowed. "You'll do fine."

"But what if it turns out badly?"

He scooted forward on the ottoman, careful not to crowd her. He wanted to take her hand and still the nervous fingers. Stroke her. Instead he brushed his knuckles across her knee where her jeans were worn white and thin, as if to get her attention when he already knew he had it. "Are we still talking about the mural?"

She nodded and laid her loose fists on her legs.

He covered her right hand. "Sometimes I wonder."

Rose said nothing as he slowly worked his thumb into her fist, opening her curled fingers to his touch. Amazing. She hadn't pulled away. She was letting him hold her hand.

"About what?" she whispered.

"About us. If there's any chance of…that we could, you know, go out sometime." He hadn't been this bad at asking a girl for a date since he was fifteen and hoping to take Lori Carson to the movies.

For a moment, he had hope. Rose's fingers brushed experimentally over the side of his hand, causing warm tingles to skitter along his arm. Their wrists were pressed together, pulse to pulse in a way that had never seemed so intimate. With Rose, even the smallest liberty was sweet.

Her lips puckered, just a bit. He felt his own respond, which was a funny thing since normally he didn't give his lips a thought. But now they were sticking out on his face as if they'd swelled from an allergic reaction. They burned to kiss her.

When he leaned closer, the spell was broken and she slid her hand away, jumping up with a trembly laugh. "No. I'm sorry. I can't do that."

"Can't do what?"

"Go—" She took a breath. "Go out with you."

"I'm sorry to hear that."

She was only one person, but she managed to create a flurry out of leaving, turning one way, then another, making the air crackle with friction. He followed her outside as she mumbled excuses and apologies that didn't matter to him at all.

Her car door slammed. She roared away, a bad muffler making her departure even more noticeable. Across the street, he saw Mrs. Culhane's squat silhouette in her window. Rose had been right—people would talk.

So what.

So close.

He scrubbed his fist across his mouth and returned inside.

THE NEXT DAY, Rose sought out Roxy at the Whitaker's B&B. The sandstone mansion had been built by a lumber baron at the turn of the century and was one of the grand houses along Bayside Road, the nice neighborhood that perched on a hill above the town, blessed with lush forests and steep cliffs that offered a magnificent view of Lake Superior. With the trees stripped bare, it was possible to see the lake even from the parking area where Rose left her car. The water was steel-gray and rolling with waves. They crashed on the rocks with a force that had nothing on the discordant, clashing thoughts in Rose's own head. Particularly when she glanced next door at the Lindstroms' large white house, as well-maintained and forbidding as its owners. She considered herself lucky that their social circles were miles apart under most circumstances.

Hoping to avoid encountering the inhabitants of both of the homes, Rose hurried to the old-fashioned carriage house that was tucked away at the side of the garden behind a mass of denuded lilacs and ivy vines. Roxy had a roomy studio apartment on the second floor. Knocking roused no response. "Damn."

Rose was considering skulking back to her car when the kitchen door opened. "Who's there? I know I heard a car, so hurry up inside before all the heat gets out. The temperature has dropped twenty degrees since last week. We're sure to have snow—*oh*. Well, land's sakes. Wild Rose Robbin! There must be a blue moon tonight."

Rose shivered inside her roomy navy-blue peacoat.

"Don't just stand there, young lady. Get yourself in here." Emmie Whitaker, the grand dame of Bay House whose only airs were over the tenderness of her pot roast, grabbed Rose by the shoulder and urged her inside. "Don't be shy. I suppose you're looking for Roxy."

"Yes, ma'am."

"She's around and about," Emmie said vaguely. She eyed Rose up and down. "We never see you. How is your poor mother, dear? I hear from Alice that you've been taking good care of her."

Rose nodded, even though grandmotherly Emmie might think Rose's efforts were less than ideal. "She's holding her own, thank you."

"Well enough to venture out? I'd love to have both of you over for Thanksgiving dinner. There should be quite a crew here, what with Claire's family arriving to meet Noah, and Connor moving back in now that the weather's turned at Gull Rock, and all the usual suspects…" Emmie glanced past Rose's shoulder.

An older man sat at a small table, drinking coffee. Silent Bill Maki, a mine worker. Rose knew him from the Buck Stop, where he bought gas and the occasional bottle of beer or lunch-box apple pie. She'd never exchanged more than a "Snow again," or "Hot today, huh?" with him.

True to form, he nodded over the rim of his mug.

She returned the nod, wondering if he was a boarder or a suitor.

To Emmie, she made a regretful face even though there was no way in hell she'd be dragged into attending a Bay House dinner. Roxy had told her about them—where nobody's business became everybody's business.

"Sorry," she said, "but Maxine doesn't go out much. The cold weather's not good for her lungs. We'll be having a quiet dinner at home." With her mother complaining about the way the turkey was cooked and moaning over how much she missed her boys on the holidays.

"Isn't that a shame." Emmie had gone to the stove to mix a pot of stewing prunes. "I know. I'll send over a pie. Pumpkin? Apple? Rhubarb?"

Rose hesitated. Black Jack had been a stickler about accepting handouts of any kind, even when he'd drunk up the household funds and they had three cans of beans in the cupboard. Rose had her own pride, but the thought of one of Emmie's famous home-baked pies made her mouth water. And Black Jack wasn't here to tell her no.

"We'd really appreciate that, Emmie. Any flavor at all. Thank you." Rose lifted her shoulders as she slid her hands into the pockets of her coat. "I'm not much of a baker."

Emmie huffed. "Girls, nowadays." She tilted her head at Rose, making a sly Mona Lisa smile. "Any time you want a lesson…" She paused significantly. "Now that you've caught the coach's eye, you need to start thinking about keeping his interest. It's true about the way to a man's heart."

"Yah," said Bill.

Rose's face heated. For a second, her voice gurgled in her throat before she managed to spit out Roxy's name. Comment on Evan would only encourage the innkeeper's speculation.

Emmie chuckled. "You'll find Rox in Cassia's room. Through the dining room and it's the second door down the hall."

Rose fled.

The front hall of Bay House had a simple but rich elegance that made Rose slow down to admire it in awe. The walls were a soft golden hue, set off by a ruby Persian rug, large, healthy plants and a gleaming check-in desk with hotel register. There was a crystal chandelier, carved woodwork and a grand staircase. It wasn't at all what she'd expected from Roxy's descriptions of bursting pipes and muzzy wiring. At one point, the inn had even been in dire financial straits.

A glimpse into an adjoining living room full of formal antiques was equally intimidating. Rose couldn't imagine living in such a place. Or even taking a room for the night. She wondered how Roxy fit in, with her tool belt and practicality, but then Roxy had often said she escaped to her apartment when her aunt and uncle crowded her. And Roxy's bravado was real, while Rose's only hid her inner timidity.

Clanking sounds came from an open door down the hall, accompanied by female laughter. Rose followed the noise, cautiously peeping inside.

A slender young woman in a wheelchair spotted her. "Hiya," she said with a friendly wave.

"I'm looking for Roxy."

A *bang* and a ripe curse came from the connecting bathroom.

"Yeowch. You've found her," the redhead said with a laugh. "Roxy's installing grab bars in my bathroom." With a soft whir of the motorized chair, the girl wheeled closer to Rose and offered her hand. "I'm Cassia, by the way. You may enter the sanctum sanctorum."

Rose edged inside the lovely room, which was outfitted with all the luxuries like a full entertainment system, color-coordinated bedding, packed bookcases and a plump reading chair. An image of her cottage sprang to mind, seeming even more sparse than before. Maybe she ought to think about giving herself a few of the luxuries she sometimes longed for.

She looked at Cassia's white wool sweater. And a few new clothes wouldn't hurt. Something warm. Even…pretty.

Pretty, she silently scoffed. What's the point?

"Cassia Keegan, that is," the young woman said, with an expectant look.

"Uh, yeah. I'm Rose Robbin."

Cassia's eyes got round. "Oh my gosh! *You're* Wild Rose?"

"I suppose so."

"Oops. Pardon me. Does the nickname bother you?"

"Nope. I'm used to it."

"I'd love to be known for being wild." Cassia made a face. "But, oh, no—never! People take one look at me and assume I'm sweet and kind. Blech. What a bore."

Rose smiled tentatively. She wasn't sure how to take this woman. She was young, in her twenties, fragile in appearance but rather bold and lively otherwise.

Cassia cocked her head. Her green eyes danced. "What's it like, being wild?"

Rose opened her mouth. "I—"

"She wouldn't know," Roxy said, coming out of the bathroom with an electric drill and a wrench. She slung the wrench into a loop on her tool belt. "Rose hasn't been wild since—" Roxy frowned. "Man. Since when, Rose? The wildest thing you've done in the time I've known you was when you stood up to your mother about the sponge baths." She looked at Cassia. "And that's giving them, not getting them. To her *mother.*"

Cassia grinned. "And I thought my life was dull."

Rose decided now would be a good time to stare at

her boots. She knew she could trust Roxy with one or two of her confidences, but Cassia seemed like the chatterbox type.

"Hmm," Roxy said. "Rose?" No response. "What have you got to say for yourself?"

She looked up, narrowing her eyes. "Maybe you don't know me as well as you think you do."

Roxy pressed a button and made the drill blade spin. "Woohoo. *That* sounds interesting. Something happen last night? Toivo came home from the diner this morning, full of talk about how you've been seen visiting at Coach Grant's house."

"You know I've been giving Lucy art lessons."

"Not at home."

"Well…"

"And not at night." Roxy laughed. "Give it up, sister. The town grapevine was working overtime last night about you and Evan, so there must be something to tell."

"Evan Grant?" Cassia sighed. "He's dreamy. All that athletic energy."

"I can imagine him in the bedroom with his whistle," Roxy said. "Waving his arms. Giving directions."

Rose almost choked. "He's not a crossing guard."

Roxy went on, oblivious. "A' course, he would be good in a huddle. And he'd know how to make a hole in one."

"That's golf!"

"Okay, then, what do they call a basket?" Roxy rocked her hips and pumped one fist, the drill in her other hand whining in short bursts. "Slam dunk me, baby. Give me nothin' but net."

Cassia was roaring with laughter. Even Rose hid her smile behind her hand.

"Let's hear it for the old double dribble—"

"Stop it," Rose interrupted. "Just stop it. I'll never be able to look him in the eye again."

"Most people do it with their eyes closed," Cassia said. She grinned. "Kissing, I mean."

Thankfully, Roxy's attention swerved. "Yeah? I saw *you* talking with Pete in the parking lot yesterday when you were getting home from class."

"Oh, him." Cassia wrinkled her nose. "He doesn't even think of me as a woman. I'm just the kid he likes to tease. He's super annoying. I'd run him down if he came at me, and, anyway, all we talked about was school. He thinks I'll be impressed by the Ivy League education he's really put to use. *Not.*"

Pete Lindstrom, Rose thought. The youngest of the three Lindstrom brothers. Too young to have been involved in the drama between their families, but even thinking of the surname was too close for her comfort. Although she'd put her teenage crush on Rick aside many years ago and had briefly mourned his tragic death, she'd never be ready to forgive and forget his parents. If they—and her own father—hadn't forced her to make the rash decision to leave town, her future might not have seemed so hopeless. She might not have given away her baby.

Water under the bridge. Quit your belly-aching. Robbins don't cry.

"Sure sign that he likes you," Roxy said.

"Does not."

"What do you think, Rose?"

Rose kept her fists thrust in her coat pockets. "I have no earthly idea what goes on in men's brains." She winced, not believing she was doing this, but…

"I thought *you* could tell me," she blurted.

Roxy laughed. "Me?"

"Not me, either." Cassia shook her head. "What a sorry bunch we are."

"At least you know how to flirt," Roxy said. "Rose just runs in the other direction." She took in Rose's embarrassment. "Or at least she used to."

"Nothing happened. Not really."

"Aha. But it might?"

Rose winced. "Would that be wrong?"

"Wrong?" Cassia asked. "How could it be wrong?"

"I dunno. I'm his daughter's teacher...."

Roxy waved that off. "Pah. A few art lessons."

"Well, Lucy might get too attached. She lost her mother and she's vulnerable."

"You could be good for her," Cassia said.

Roxy went and closed the door, reminding them to keep their voices low. "I don't think Toivo's home but, still, the walls have ears."

"I shouldn't have come," Rose said.

Roxy patted her back, urging her toward the armchair. "Sure you should have."

Rose sat with a sigh. "Lucy will end up getting hurt because there's no way Evan and I—" She squeezed her eyes shut, scrunching up her face. "He's probably only attracted to my wild reputation."

"Not Evan," said Roxy.

Rose threw her a cynical glance. "Don't be too sure. The clean-living all-American jock types are the ones you have to watch out for. It's all cheerleaders and prom queens in public, but in private they want to find out what the girls are like on the other side of the tracks. That's happened to me before."

Roxy frowned, as if considering the possibility, while Cassia looked on with great interest.

Guilt crept over Rose. Out of her own insecurity, she was smearing Evan, who didn't deserve such treatment. "I shouldn't be here," she said, blushing hotly. "Please ignore me. Forget what I said. I'm completely wrong." She stood. "Evan's probably not even interested in me."

"Hey, now. I know for sure *that's* wrong."

"Has he tried to kiss you?" Cassia asked.

Rose closed her eyes. She remembered the previous evening, when holding hands with Evan had seemed a more intimate act than all of her backseat fumblings added together.

She blinked. "He hasn't really tried. Not all-out. But…"

If she'd dared to meet him halfway, they *would* have kissed.

"Um, I have to go." She looked at Cassia. "Please don't—"

Cassia nodded immediately, making a lock-turning motion at her lips. Rose hoped she could believe her.

Roxy caught Rose's arm at the door. "What really happened?" she said in hushed voice as they walked into the hallway.

"He asked me out."

"And?"

"I said no."

"Rose."

"Was that a mistake?" Her stomach clenched. *It was a mistake.*

"You tell me," Roxy said. "But since you asked, I think you should give Evan a chance. He's a nice guy.

A real *man*. Got to be a thousand-percent improvement over the walking-hormone schoolboys who were only interested in one thing out of you, last time you were free and single in Alouette."

"Yeah, I know." She shrugged. "I guess I'm scared."

"Why?" Roxy was obviously baffled—and curious. "There's no reason to be scared that I can see."

A heaviness sat on Rose's chest, weighing her down. She leaned against the wall, bone tired. Roxy was her only friend, and though she'd come here needing to unburden herself, the ugly words that would explain her fear just didn't want to come out of her mouth. She'd held them inside for so long, buried them so deep, that it seemed as if only a cataclysmic eruption could tear them loose.

Not here, in the hallway of Bay House.

Roxy frowned. "What is it, Rose?"

She soundlessly shook her head. A tear trickled down the side of her nose and she wiped it away. She didn't cry.

"I'm not good enough," she muttered, when Roxy continued to stare, her concern evident.

"Bunk. What makes you say that?"

Rose closed her eyes. "I was never good enough, even before the—" She clamped her lip between her teeth.

"Before what? I can see there's something you want to say." Roxy took Rose's arm and led her away from Cassia's door to the staircase, where she urged Rose to sit. "Go ahead. Tell me. I'm about as safe a confidante as there is in Alouette. I know how to keep my mouth shut."

Rose gripped one of the polished wood balusters.

A shocking memory ripped through her—the weight of wood in her hand, the wrench in her shoulders as she'd swung the broken tree limb at her assailant—

Oh God. She opened her hand, then fisted it in her lap when she saw it was shaking. *I don't want to remember. Don't make me remember.* She tried to push the horror back down inside her, but it wouldn't go.

Then make *it go. Get rid of it.*

She looked at Roxy, then shifted her gaze to the empty foyer. From the distant kitchen, the murmurs of Emmie's chatter rose and fell, seeming so normal, so…comforting.

Rose opened her mouth. A sharp pang tightened her throat, but she pushed the words out. "I was raped."

She wasn't quite sure she'd spoken aloud until the sound of Roxy's gasp reached her, in time-delayed action as if the world had slowed almost to a stop.

Ha. No chance of that. The world didn't stop for nobodies like Rose.

Not ever.

"I'm sorry," Roxy said. She laid a hand on Rose's shoulder and kept it there, warm and steadying, even when Rose flinched and pulled herself into a knot. "That explains a lot."

Rose licked her lips, putting her head down so her chin almost touched her knees. "Well, maybe, but it happened years ago, several months before I left town."

"Do you want to talk about it?"

"No. Not—not now."

A moment of silence passed. "Evan…" Roxy said eventually. "He would never hurt you—"

"I know, I know. He's a good man." Rose wound her

arms around her legs, squeezing even tighter, trying to control the emotions thrashing around inside her. "But I'm scared anyway. Plus, there are other complications. Lucy, for one." *Danny.*

"Listen," Roxy said in a low voice. "I know you won't want to hear this, but you have to quit hiding from your past, even though it's going to be painful to remember. We can call the women's crisis center for help."

"Thanks, but no. It happened so long ago. I'm over it."

Therapy. Rose had undergone a few torturous sessions when she'd been in the home for teenage runaways that Pastor Mike had sent her to downstate. At the time, she'd have sworn she'd detested every moment. In retrospect she knew the therapist had helped her cope. But she'd been coping on her own for a lot of years now. She was fine.

The recent turmoil was the only reason she'd started thinking of the rape again, after all these years.

But Roxy was insistent. "You're not over it if the thought of going out with Evan gets you this scared."

Rose tried to put on a brave front. "Maybe I will then."

Roxy patted Rose's back, looking skeptical, but she had the smarts to hold her tongue.

I can do it, Rose silently vowed. *I can be normal.* Just telling Roxy the bare minimum about the rape had helped, at least a little. Maybe that small relief would give her the strength to banish the memories again, even though she knew that denial wasn't healthy.

Especially now. Because as much as she tried to keep the incident out of her mind, it was no longer out of sight. Not with Danny living in the same town.

CHAPTER SEVEN

"LOOK AT OUR HAIR," Lucy said. She hung over Rose's shoulder, holding out strands for comparison. "Mine is white and yours is black."

Rose tilted her head, too aware of the glances they were getting from some of the crowd. "Yeah, like the good witch and the bad witch." *And guess which one I am,* she thought, narrowing her eyes and pasting on a mirthless smile for Teri Sjoholm and Gloria Kevanen, who put their heads together to whisper of the scandalous news: Coach Grant's daughter treated Wild Rose like a friend.

"I'm not a witch. We're Princess Kristina and her sister Princess Jade." Last week, Rose had gone for a quick coffee with the Grants after another home game. She'd ended up helping put Lucy to bed and adding on to the story at the girl's direction.

Apparently, she needed direction. She had no idea of how to push her relationship with Evan forward outside of the growing comfort zone with his daughter, even if she wanted to.

If? She was being less than honest. She did want more with Evan. Ever since her talk with Roxy, she'd bolstered herself with encouragement to accept his next invitation, to prove that she could overcome her past. But Evan had taken her previous reluctance as his cue and made no further personal overtures. They were a couple of days away from Thanksgiving and at this pace she'd be kissing no one but her mother at New Year's.

The thought of kissing Evan made Rose flush with a shy anticipation instead of the more familiar dread. She hadn't expected to be impatient to move their relationship along. Maybe that was Evan's plan, to go so slow *she* was forced to spur him on?

Lucy straightened and began gathering Rose's hair into a bunch. She was bored with the basketball game, and who could blame her? The Storm were losing by twenty points to the Negaunee Miners, a Class C school double their size. With eight minutes left to go in the game and a weather report that said the first big snow of the winter was arriving that night, the crowd had visibly thinned.

Lucy's busy hands tugged at Rose's hair. She wouldn't have gone home anyway when Danny was playing, but over the course of the past few home games, she'd become Lucy's unofficial game-time baby-sitter. Not by design. The girl had gravitated to her. And Rose had found that she enjoyed having a companion to share cheers and chatter. Almost like a normal person, except that her "girlfriend" was a five-year-old.

"I'm braiding your hair," Lucy said. "Alyssa in my class showed me how because Daddy can't make a braid. Dads aren't very good at hair."

"Well, me, either, I'm afraid."

Lucy breathed in Rose's ear. "Is that why you don't make your hair pretty?"

Involuntarily, Rose put a hand up. Several loose strands had sprung free from the scraped-together braid. It felt strange to have her hair pulled back, showing her face to everyone. Nothing left to hide behind.

She glanced back. "Do you think my hair is ugly?"

Lucy had pulled one of the purple glitter barrettes from her own hair and was opening it using her teeth. She clipped it onto the end of the messy braid. "That's okay. I fixed it."

"Thanks." Rose skimmed her hands over her head. Not exactly a neat job, but for a five-year-old....

She turned back to the game, catching another of Gloria's looks.

Lucy left the braid alone for ten seconds before she yanked the barrette off, pulling out a few strands of hair. "Ouch." Rose pressed her hands to her scalp. "What are you doing, Luce?"

"Playing hairdresser." She finger-combed until the braid was loosened, then dug into the pocket of her jeans. "I have a ribbon that will make you look beautiful."

Have at it, thought Rose. *Miracles may happen, even in a small-town gym at the frozen edge of the country.* She'd gone through her scanty wardrobe before the game, trying to find a garment attractive enough to entice Evan while not looking as if she'd tried too hard. She'd ended up in her same old boots and peacoat with a pair of gray wool pants and her best sweater—pale blue with only a minimal amount of pilling. Alluring she was not, but it was a step up from plaid flannel.

Lucy threaded the ribbon behind Rose's ears and tied a floppy bow on top of her head three times before she was satisfied. "There," she said with a smile, "you look like Snow White. That's what my dad says. 'Cause you have pale skin and black hair and you live in the woods. But you don't have any dwarves."

"I don't want any dwarves." Rose helped Lucy settle beside her on the bleacher seat.

The girl was running out of steam. She leaned her head against Rose. "How come?"

"Too many to pick up after. Seven pairs of boots. Seven pairs of socks. Seven hats, seven jackets, seven pickaxes…."

Lucy slumped lower, sliding until her head was resting on Rose's thigh. Rose put her arm around the girl as she scanned the basketball game. Less than a minute to go, eighteen points behind, and still Danny was playing his heart out, pushing the basketball up the floor as if another basket really mattered. A mere second before the buzzer went off, he sent an arcing shot swishing through the net.

Rose kept to a silent cheer. Lucy appeared to be sleeping.

For several minutes the shuffle of fans exiting the stands obscured the floor and she missed seeing Evan and the team enter the locker room. He always shot a thumbs-up or a wave into the stands for Lucy. Rose liked to imagine that he meant it for her as well.

"You're getting cozy with the coach's daughter," said a voice to the right.

As a couple of fans passed between them, footsteps ringing, Rose leaned back to look at Gloria in her team sweatshirt, white jeans and studded black boots with three-inch heels. Drawn-on eyebrows arched into a frill of fake blond curls. The woman's expression hovered between make-nice and make-trouble.

Rose chose her words carefully. She didn't want to send the woman in either direction. "It's a job." The art lessons must be common knowledge by now.

"Oh?" Gloria looked pointedly at Lucy, secure beside Rose, sheltered by her protective arm. "Is that all?"

Rose made her eyes wide. "What else would there be?"

Gloria laughed, not pleasantly. "You'd know better than me." Her lips pursed. "The boys didn't call you *Wild* Rose for nothing."

Rose fought down the shameful heat that wanted to climb up her throat and into her face. Gloria's nickname in high school had been Hally, from the "Glory Hallelujah!" her boyfriend Billy had shouted when he'd entered the boy's locker room the morning after he'd finally been welcomed into her "promised land."

"Why don't you ask Billy?" Rose snapped, completely aware that she was making a mistake. High-school escapades that would have been forgotten elsewhere lingered on in a town the size of Alouette. "He knows."

Billy Kevanen had come begging after Rose one night by the river. He'd sworn to her that he'd broken up with Gloria. She'd kissed him, that was all, but the talk had multiplied and before Rose had said one word in her defense, Gloria was wearing Billy's class ring again and had sworn hatred of the tramp who'd tried to steal her man.

Rose shook her head as soon as the words had slipped out. "I'm sorry. I shouldn't have said that."

Gloria let out a huff, but she followed up with a small smile and shrug. "Me, either. We're grown women, we don't have time for old high-school rivalries."

What a relief. If Rose had known that they would move past the ancient animosity that easily, she might have made an overture a year ago instead of going on believing that Gloria would only sneer at her.

"I mean…" Gloria flipped her bouncy curls. "I have a husband and four kids, a big house, a new SUV and a nail salon. My life is *so* full. And you—" She smiled at Rose. "I'm sure you're keeping busy. At the Buck Stop, eh?"

"That's right."

"Must be awful…" Gloria paused to shudder. "Awful scary. Working there at night, I mean. With the type of, uh, clientele you get."

"I can take care of myself."

"Of course you can." Gloria smiled, real big. "The way you grew up, poor thing. How are your brothers, by the way? Didn't I hear that Gary's in prison?"

"Yeah, I bet you did."

"And Jack, Jr.?"

"Jake. He was an Army ranger."

"Better than jail!" Gloria laughed gaily.

She stopped when Rose's face remained stony. "So. I'd better go warm up the car. I'm waiting for my son, Jeremy. He's the star center of the team. Coach has been a good role model. I've never had to question his judgment before." Her eyes went to Lucy, who had begun to stir. In her sleepy state, the girl automatically reached for Rose, snuggling even closer with her arms around Rose's waist.

"You're so close to her," Gloria observed with a small twist to her pinched smile. "How smart of you."

"I like Lucy for herself. That has nothing to do with—with whatever you're insinuating."

"Jeez. Don't get all defensive. I didn't mean anything."

Rose remembered. Gloria had been one of those girls who'd make snide remarks and then brush off the insult with a cheery "No offense!"

"All I'm saying is that you should think of the coach's reputation," Gloria went on. "You know. People in this town can be so quick to assume the worst."

Rose widened her eyes. "Have I done something horrible without realizing it? Run over a dog? Stolen candy from a baby?"

"That's so funny."

"Give me a break, Gloria." Rose kept her shoulders stiff and her jaw clenched as she swept her gaze across the gym. Two people caught her attention as they moved closer, following the sidelines.

"Just trying to be friendly," Gloria said with a bit of a whine. Rose didn't respond. "Hmph. See ya."

Not if I see you first.

Danny's parents were coming closer. Rose ducked her head under the guise of speaking to Lucy. "Time to wake up, honey."

Lucy straightened up and rubbed her eyes. "Are we going home yet?"

"Soon as your dad comes out." Rose began bundling the limp and compliant girl into her coat and mittens.

"Are you coming with?"

"Not this time."

The Swansons were hesitating, speaking quietly to each other before glancing at Rose, midway up in the stands. Still scorched by Gloria's remarks, Rose gave them her patented hard, blank stare and they moved on. Her stomach sank. Another opportunity gone because she couldn't let herself be vulnerable and actually *ask* about Danny's well-being.

Lucy and Rose waited without speaking. By now, the scene was familiar—the emptied gym, the glaring lights, the janitor and his push broom. Danny emerged from the locker room and ran across the floor to where his parents waited by the door. Not even a glance at Rose. His shoulders were slumped and he dragged a winter jacket. Ken Swanson put his arm around the boy in a comforting, fatherly way that sliced into Rose's heart. It hurt to see the gesture, but the moment also underscored her decision. She'd done that right—she'd given her son a real father.

She hadn't noticed Evan's approach, and looked up in surprise when he said, "Looks like we've got a sleepy girl on our hands."

Lucy blinked heavy eyes. She opened her arms. "Daddy."

He lifted her. "I'd better get her straight home." But he paused, looking down at Rose. "Thanks again for keeping your eye on Luce. Will you be okay on your own? It's snowing."

She nodded. "I'm heading home, too." With the winter storm warning in effect, she'd told Cross he could close up the store early.

"Drive safely." Evan carried Lucy out of the stands.

Rose realized she held the girl's muffler and hat. "Wait," she called, scrambling after them. She pulled the knit cap over Lucy's head and wound the matching scarf around her neck until she was swaddled like a mummy. Lucy's head tilted forward against her father's shoulder and she snuggled in closer.

Lucky girl, Rose thought.

"Thanks, Rose." Evan studied her. "Your hair looks nice."

She touched the forgotten bow. "Lucy did it."

"Like Snow White," the girl murmured, her lashes lifting briefly before drooping again.

Pure as the driven snow. Rose cringed inside, certain that Evan would be thinking of the reputation that was to the contrary. She tried to smile to show she wasn't mortified and managed only a weak flicker. "Who, me? Not exactly, huh?"

His eyes traced her face. "Close enough."

"You've been reading too many fairy tales."

He laughed. "There is that."

The agreement came too easily and again Rose was disappointed. She was fed up with feeling that way. Her old sense of defiance, of simply not giving a damn, grew stronger. The Gloria Kevanens of the town weren't going to make her feel bad about herself ever again.

She lifted her chin and looked straight at Evan. "Do you have plans for Thanksgiving?"

"We had a few invitations, but I turned them down. Had this idea I could cook dinner myself—" He broke off with a laugh. "Can we say overly optimistic? I'm having a hard time just making out the shopping list."

Rose wanted to speak, but there seemed to be a barbell weighing down her tongue.

"Do you know how to cook? Maybe if we put our heads together…" He looked at her hopefully.

"I'm passable," she croaked. She knew how to read a recipe, anyway.

"Should we team up?"

"I can't. There's my mother. She expects me to spend the day with her, so—" Rose swallowed, trying not to think of what her mother might say or do. "I don't guess you and Lucy would want to come to our house for dinner?"

The invitation had startled Evan. And pleased him, too. She could see that in the gleam of his warm brown eyes. "I do guess we'd be most appreciative," he said, lightly teasing her for the fashion of her offer.

She held her ground, even though she was backpedaling in her head. "I have to warn you, my mother's liable to make assumptions. It could be very—" Rose waved her hands.

"Embarrassing?" Evan didn't seem bothered. He hefted Lucy higher in his arms. "What's the holidays without an embarrassing moment with relatives?"

Rose smiled, grateful for his easy acceptance. She touched the curve of Lucy's cheek that showed between her hat and scarf. "You'd better get this one home. She's zonked."

"Thanksgiving, then," he said, turning to go.

"Thanksgiving," she agreed.

"Our first official date."

Rose's turn to be startled. She popped a hand over her mouth, searching for qualifications even as Evan walked away, chuckling to himself.

There were none. She'd asked him over and he'd accepted. They could say it was a family dinner, but the fact remained. In public, in private, in company or alone—he liked her. The notorious Wild Rose.

"ROSE?" Tess Bucek said. Her voice squeaked. "Is that really you?"

Rose reluctantly came out from behind the circular rack of dresses in Shumanski's Clothier, the only clothing store in Alouette aside from the used garments available at Goodwill. "Yeah, it's me. Hi."

Tess blinked in surprise, but was quick to recover. "Looking for a new dress?" She lifted out a bright print dress with a polyester lace collar and cuffs. With a quick grimace, she shoved it back on the rack. "Very 1980s bible-school teacher."

Rose was glad to have her faulty fashion radar confirmed. "I'll never find anything here."

"Just a warning—Betty Shumanski doesn't get rid of old stock," Tess whispered. "Have you tried the mall in Marquette?"

That would have been too much like a shopping trip. Shumanski's was Rose's speed. "I'm only browsing."

"Lucy's wearing a pumpkin orange corduroy jumper," Tess volunteered with a smile. "If you're thinking of coordinating."

Rose looked up sharply. "How'd you know?" She gulped. "Not the coordinating, the—" She shook her head. "Forget I asked. Of course you know."

Tess laughed. "Lucy and Evan stopped in the library this morning and she told me all about it. You're going to get a construction-paper turkey centerpiece as a hostess gift. She made it in school."

"Good. One less thing for me to fuss over."

Tess frowned at another print dress. "I'm glad the Grants have a place to go. I was with them last year, but I'll be at Bay House tomorrow. Lucy misses her mom even more around this time, and I think Evan's at a loss about how to stage a holiday. You know men."

Rose hesitated. She heard very little about Krissa

Grant except the tidbits that Lucy dropped, and that Evan had said they were getting a divorce. In the photo on Lucy's night table, her mother was a slender blonde with a tight smile and an air of delicacy. Lucy looked a lot like her.

"What about Evan?" Rose asked.

Tess was quizzical.

"Doesn't *he* miss…Krissa?"

"I'm sure," Tess said. "But it was a different kind of situation."

"Yeah, he told me how they'd split up before she got sick. Did you know her?"

"Briefly. Krissa wasn't that happy about moving here from downstate when Evan got the new job. She felt so isolated. You could tell by looking at her that she wouldn't last the winter."

Rose clasped the hook of a metal hanger as she leaned into the rack. "What happened? She just up and left him?"

Tess gave a dry chuckle. "What am I, the talk clearing-house?" She glanced around the store, empty except for Betty Shumanski at the cash register, idly watching them as she cut coupons out of the newspaper's Day-after-Thanksgiving advertising circulars. "Shouldn't you ask Evan about this?"

Rose lowered her eyes and pushed an entire section of dresses aside with a screech of the hangers. "We're not that close."

"Hmm. Then I wonder why he was asking me the same kind of questions about you."

Oh! Rose didn't dare ask what Tess had said, even though she knew that the librarian was probably the kindest person Evan could have asked.

"Never mind," she muttered. It was hard for her to imagine a woman who would choose to leave Evan and Lucy. Unless the wife had taken Lucy with her. Evan must have been—

"This one's not bad." Tess held up a knit dress with bell sleeves. "Very pink, but that's a good color for you." She evaluated Rose's coloring. "You'd be a knockout in red."

Vigorous head shake. "I don't wear dresses."

Tess's brows went up, but she didn't ask why Rose had been hovering at the dress rack. "Just try it on," she urged, pushing the dress into Rose's hands.

Betty swooped in, and soon Rose found herself alone in a cubicle staring at the pink dress the saleslady had hung from a hook beside the narrow vertical mirror. She looked at her reflection—haphazard hair, pinched face, an outfit that would suit a lumberjack—and thought of the bright, smiling women in the ladies' magazines she'd snatched up at the supermarket checkout when she went to buy the turkey and other fixings. The least she could do was *try*.

She peeled off her jacket and sweatshirt, kicked off the boots and dropped her jeans. The soft knit of the dress was strange against her skin, so light and airy it was like wearing a nightgown. She'd feel half-nude if she wore this, especially around Evan.

"What's the verdict?" called Tess.

"Um." Rose fiddled with the satin tie at the keyhole neckline. *"No way."*

Betty pushed back the curtain. "But it's lovely!"

Tess stared. "Wow, Rose. Who knew? You've got a very nice shape."

"It doesn't feel right." Rose plucked at the dress,

sneaking peeks at her reflection. The woolen socks scrunched around her ankles didn't go and her legs were deathly white, but otherwise she didn't look half bad. Not that she was even *thinking* of buying the dress...

The saleslady grabbed a handful of fabric, tugging the dress tighter around the hips. "Panty line. You'll need a girdle and a slip."

Tess grinned at the mirror Rose with a certain kinship, making Rose smile back, wondering why she was suddenly so elated. It took her a few seconds to figure out that it was the female camaraderie—after thirty-three years, she was finally "one of the girls."

"No one wears girdles anymore," Tess said. "I don't suppose you sell thongs, Betty?"

The elderly woman peered through her half-moon glasses, her lips wrinkling with disapproval. "That's all the girls want these days. I've got some on order."

"You're not serious." Tess's laughter was infectious. "Whoa. Shumanski's enters the twenty-first century."

Betty *tsk-tsked* at their frivolity and announced that she would find Rose a proper slip.

Rose quit laughing and said, "Good time for my getaway." She whipped the curtain closed, tore off the dress and was yanking up her jeans by the time the saleslady returned with a handful of pastel nylon. "Thanks, but I think I'll just take the jeans and the sweater."

Tess looked like she wanted to speak, but Rose didn't give her the chance. She paid cash for the clothing she'd picked out earlier and was heading toward the door with Betty calling after her. "We've got a wonderful selection of holiday sweaters, girls!

Turkeys, pilgrims, candy corn, Santa, snowmen, jingle bells…"

"Next time!" Tess let the door swing shut. She buttoned up her shearling coat. "Next time I'm on an Osmond Family holiday special."

Rose stuck the shopping bag under her arm and dug her hat and gloves out of the peacoat's deep pockets. The wind was swirly, blowing a few light, downy snowflakes in wide spirals.

"The dress," Tess said tentatively.

Rose shook her head. "It wasn't for me."

"Pfft. It was *made* for you."

Yeah, sure. Me in an alternate reality.

Surprisingly, it wasn't that difficult for Rose to imagine the other her. Perhaps she'd always done so, at the back of her mind. Starting with a Rose Robbin who'd seen that Rick Lindstrom was only temporarily indulging in a walk on the wild side. A Rose who'd understood that she didn't need male approval, especially the wrong kind. A Rose who'd fought just a little bit harder—

No, that way of thinking was self-defeating. She wanted more than the cold comfort of regret.

"Silence? Okay, I get the message. I'll stop pushing." Tess gave a funny grimace. "Connor says that sometimes my enthusiasm makes him want to crawl under the covers and not get out of bed at all. But he's contrary, that way." She cocked her chin at Rose. "Like you."

"What do you mean?"

"Aw, you know. Doing the opposite of what a buttinsky like me tells you to do." Tess set her hands on her hips, giving in with a laugh. "Even if that dress did suit you to a T and you're crazy not to buy it."

"I'd look—" Rose winced at herself, but she didn't want to admit to *desperate.* "Obvious. It would be so obvious that I was trying to attract a man. People would see me and smile."

"And that's a bad thing?"

Rose shrugged. Tess was right. She needed to get over her shyness and the debilitating worry about what others thought of her. But it wasn't easy to take the first step.

Unless she figured that she'd already done it. She'd stepped out of her comfort zone on the day she'd agreed to give Lucy the lessons. And when she'd gone to their house. And the Thanksgiving dinner invitation had been the biggest step of all.

Rose looked at the scraped sidewalk, scuffing the side of her boot along a ridge of ice. *Wait and see. Tomorrow you may fall.*

"Have you ever considered," Tess said, her expression so thoughtful it was clear she was treading carefully herself, "that it's possible the smiles come because some of us truly care and want you to find happiness?" She gave Rose's arm a pat. "I've never known exactly what went on back then, but I know about living down the past. I had my own to get over."

"Yeah." Rose sniffed, the cold air prickling in her nostrils. She'd been long gone by then, but she'd heard from her mother about the car accident that had killed Tess's fiancé. She'd been driving and some had blamed her for the tragedy.

"You don't have to say another word. Just know that I know. If you ever want to talk…" Tess grabbed Rose in a quick hug, not letting her protest.

Rose wiped her nose with the back of a gloved hand. "Thanks."

"Anytime. I'm always good for advice—solicited or not." Tess walked off with a wave. "Happy Thanksgiving!"

"Happy Thanksgiving." Rose watched Tess go, feeling less alone, even when she noticed the lunchtime crew at the corner café watching her through the picture window, their heads nodding with what she imagined were the typical comments about her family's sorry state of affairs. "Happy Thanksgiving," she repeated for their benefit even though they couldn't hear. And then she summoned up her courage to add a smile and cheery wave, inordinately pleased with herself.

Wild Rose being friendly. They wouldn't know what to make of *that*.

CHAPTER EIGHT

LUCY TUGGED on Evan's jacket. He bent so she could whisper in his ear. "Dad, what is *that?*"

"Why don't you ask? Mrs. Robbin won't mind."

Rose took their outerwear and hung it on a coat rack that was already hump-shouldered with thick winter gear. They'd had six inches of snow on the night of the basketball game and it was sticking, two days later.

Lucy shook her head, burying her face against Evan's back as he kneeled to help her off with her winter boots. She slipped her feet into the dress shoes they'd carried in from the car, along with a bottle of wine, the slightly crushed centerpiece and a casserole dish of yams he'd slapped together after the first batch had been overcooked into hard, cracked hillocks when he forgot to set the oven timer.

Lucy had been clingy all morning, even though he'd reassured her that she'd have a nice time today. Spending Thanksgiving with Rose wasn't a problem, but the holiday hoopla combined with the unfamiliar house and the presence of Maxine Robbin added up to too much. She'd regressed into shyness again.

"So, we really do have company. This is novel." Maxine wheeled her oxygen tank toward the crowded entryway. Metal clanked and oxygen hissed as she sucked in a lungful through a mask held over her mouth. Lucy took another look and darted behind Evan, holding on to his belt loops so he couldn't pry her free.

Maxine hooked the mask on the tank. "Can't say I believed it when Rose told me. Far as I knew, she didn't have a friend in the world aside from that tomboy up at Bay House. But isn't it always the mother who's the last to be told?" Maxine narrowed her eyes at Evan. "You're a tall one."

"This is Evan Grant, Mom. Evan, Maxine, my mother."

He offered his hand. "Good to see you again, Mrs. Robbin."

She waved him off. "Germs."

Looking miserable, Rose hurried to the kitchen with Evan's offerings. She was back in a few seconds, in time to stop Maxine from circling him to get a look at Lucy. "Let her be, Mom," she mouthed.

"What?" Maxine spoke loudly. "What's she so shy of? Can't be me. I'm not scary. Never have been, never will be. Now, my late husband—he rousted out the quiet ones and made 'em stand up for themselves and speak clearly."

"Mother." Rose took her arm. "Let's go into the living room and sit down."

Maxine turned away. Evan tugged Lucy by the hand, urging her forward. She stared, her irises rimmed in white. The frightened gaze followed the older woman as she went to sit in a dumpy easy chair, the tank keeping pace at her side like a poodle.

Rose's face was pale and nervous. Wordlessly, she motioned them to the couch.

Lucy let out a little scream and hop when Maxine leaped out as they passed, snatching at the air with spindly fingers and saying, "Gobble, gobble, gobble" in a cackling voice.

"For God's sake, Mom! Sit down." Rose pressed the woman into the chair. "Give Lucy a chance to adjust."

"I was just having a little fun." Maxine's head snaked forward, looming at Lucy. "Don't you like to have fun, little girl?"

Lucy shrank toward Evan on the couch.

"What's the matter with her?" Maxine asked without a shred of compassion.

Behind her mother's back, Rose made a gesture of frustration that spoke volumes. She looked helplessly at Evan.

He spoke. "She's wondering about the oxygen tank."

"This old thing." Maxine gave it a kick with a slippered toe. She waggled a finger at Lucy, who'd peeked out from Evan's side. "Don't smoke, girlie, that's all I have to say. It's very bad for you. None of us knew what we were doing, back in my day."

Rose explained. "My mother has emphysema, Lucy. That's a disease of the lungs, sometimes caused by smoking. When she's feeling short of breath, she breathes oxygen from the tank through the mask. That might seem a bit scary to you at first, but you'll get used to it."

Evan held a hand over his mouth and made a *shush*-ing sound. "Luke," he intoned, "I am your father."

Maxine dangled the mask. "Want to try?"

Though Lucy had followed the explanation with interest and even smiled at her father's joke, she quickly shook her head at the offer. Evan couldn't really blame his daughter for being dumbstruck. With Maxine's disarranged hair, sunken cheeks and lined face, the woman looked like a crone. An odd outfit of worn house slippers, a black skirt so large it dragged on the floor and a top printed with cartoon jack o' lanterns didn't help.

Maxine gave a throaty chuckle and set aside the mask. "She seems smart enough, even if she's shy."

"Want to come with me to the kitchen, Lucy? We can put the marshmallows on your dad's yams and toast them in the oven." Rose sent Evan an apologetic look. "If you're okay here for a few minutes…"

"Go on," he said.

Maxine picked up a remote control. "We'll watch football."

Rose held out her hand to Lucy. She hesitated for a few seconds, then darted across the room, giving Maxine's chair a wide berth.

Maxine cocked her head at Evan. "You a Packer fan?"

"Lions."

She hooted. "Didja hear that, Rose? Enemy in the camp! If Black Jack was here, you'd be booted out on your tailbone, for sure. But I've got an open mind. So long as we win, you can stay."

Evan settled in. This wasn't exactly what he'd imagined, but at least the turkey smelled good. And Rose…his eyes went to her as she and Lucy began laying the dining table with stack of plates and bundled silverware. She saw him looking and smiled shyly. She was different, he decided. Lucy's blue ribbon had made a second appearance, tied around her glossy black hair. If he wasn't mistaken she'd put on makeup. Just a little. Her lips had a shine and there was something about the shading around her eyes that made them stand out.

He heard Lucy say what he'd been thinking. "You look pretty, Rose."

"Thank you, sweetheart. But I'm not as dressed up as you." Rose leaned down, putting her hands on her knees as she admired Lucy's jumper, lace tights and handmade popcorn kernel pin.

Evan was relieved. Getting Lucy dressed had been a trial. First she'd wanted the blouse that was in the laundry hamper, then she'd asked for French braids. He could barely manage ordinary braids, but she'd started to cry when he'd refused, so he'd looked at the illustrations in her hairdo book and faked it, flattening out the alarming number of stray strands and general fuzziness with hair gel. Lucy had been dubious about the results. Her lower lip had wobbled, but then the yams had started smoking in the kitchen, the alarm had gone off with a shriek, and he'd dodged *that* bullet.

"You're wearing my ribbon," Lucy said.

"Yes, I am." Rose smoothed her hair. "Is that okay?"

Lucy nodded with obvious pleasure, and Evan found himself nodding as well. For weeks, he'd held himself back from pushing for more while waiting for a signal from Rose. Today was it.

A blue-ribbon day.

Lucy and Rose came into the living area with offerings of simple crudités. When Evan jumped up to rescue Lucy's plate, she shrilly insisted that she could do it. The platter tilted dangerously, but she managed to set it on the coffee table without spilling any of the vegetables.

"Dinner will be ready in a few minutes," Rose said, speaking each word as carefully as Lucy had balanced the platter. She looked up from watching her mother grab a handful of cheese cubes and party mix from her tray. "Would you care for a glass of wine, Evan?"

He wondered if she'd written out a script beforehand. Her concern for proper etiquette was touching, particularly in contrast to the gruffness she had exhibited only a couple of months ago. Still, he didn't want her to be formal with him. He declined the drink and took her hand instead, making her sit beside him on the couch despite her protests that she had gravy to make and a salad to toss.

"The food will keep," he said as Lucy squirmed in between them. "Take a breather."

Rose gave him a small smile, unconsciously fingering a silver necklace, the first jewelry he'd ever seen her wear. Peacock-blue collar and cuffs showed beneath a white sweater that was clingy rather than thickly knitted. He tried not to be too aware of the curves the sweater revealed. Staring at any breasts other than the turkey's would definitely qualify as a holiday faux pas.

Maxine let out a cheer as the Packers kicked a field goal. Pretzel crumbs flew from her mouth. She looked at Evan while dusting off the front of her pumpkin top. "Take that, Lions fan."

"Ouch," he said. "Four minutes to go and we're losing by ten."

"Never gonna catch up." Maxine cackled and rubbed her hands as the Packers kicked off.

"It's not impossible."

Rose teased him for his optimism. "You might as well give up. Your team doesn't have a chance."

"I never admit defeat," he vowed, even as a pass bounced to the turf, incomplete. He groaned. "Have to set an example for my own team."

"Never? Want to make a bet?"

Evan kept one eye on the TV, where unfortunately the Lions' quarterback had been sacked. Third and eighteen. It didn't look good. "What kind of bet?"

"Loser washes the dishes."

He looked down at Lucy. "What do you say, kid? Are you on my side?"

"Dad, it's third and eighteen," she said very seriously, making Rose laugh. Lucy looked like she wanted to defect, but he'd taught her better than that— no jumping on and off the bandwagon. Her skinny shoulders hitched higher. "Okay."

"Then we have a bet."

"Sucker!" Maxine yelled. The Lions' pass had gone incomplete and they were forced to punt.

"We're only four people," he said. "How many dishes can there be?"

Rose's eyes glittered. "Obviously you've never cooked a Thanksgiving dinner."

"IT'S THE TWO-MINUTE DRILL," Evan said a couple of hours later. "Team Grant is down to their last suds and they still have the pots and pans to wash. Do you think they can make it in time?"

Lucy waved a damp linen towel. "We can do it, Dad!"

He had to hand it to her—she'd stuck by his side the entire time, drying dishes as they came out of the rinse water. She'd fallen behind now and then, but Rose would swoop in and rescue a few items under the guise of putting the dishes away.

"Don't forget—one drop means the challenge is over." Rose patted Lucy's back. "But rah-rah, go, team, go!"

"Ew. Mashed potato pot." Evan scraped it, pulling a disgusted face for Lucy's benefit.

"Come on, Dad. Quit fooling around."

He looked at Rose. "She's as tough a coach as Lombardi."

"Doing dishes isn't everything, it's the *only* thing."

Evan washed and rinsed the heavy pot and gave it to Lucy, who balanced it on the edge of the countertop while she dried the cavernous bottom. "All we have left is the roasting pan. It's worse than the mashed potato pot."

"Disgusting!" Lucy agreed.

"Clock's ticking." Rose was arranging stainless steel flatware in a drawer.

Evan scraped glop into the trash can while Lucy urged him on. "Here we go, sports fans." He plunged the pan into the gray wash water. "Sponge, Lucy." She leaned over the sink from her step stool by the drying rack. He worked on the pan, then wiped his forehead and asked for another squirt of detergent. "Lucy?"

"Yes, Dad?"

"We're going to need the scrubber."

Rose was giggling in the background.

He scrubbed every speck out of the pan and together they polished it dry. Lucy presented the clean roasting pan to Rose as if it had been a bouquet of flowers. She seemed just as pleased.

"Mere seconds before the buzzer," she announced. "Team Grant wins the Thanksgiving dishwashing challenge. Pie for everyone!"

Lucy cheered.

"Oh, no." Evan groaned. "More dishes…"

"I HAVE SKETCHES FOR YOU," Rose said, sipping coffee in the kitchen. They'd played several rousing games of cards before stopping for dessert. She and Evan had just cleared the plates. He'd started to do the washing up, but she'd said to leave them.

"They're at my cottage," she added, giving him a shy glance.

"Can we sneak out?" Evan looked at the dining table, where Maxine was teaching Lucy how to play several versions of solitaire. They hadn't become the greatest of friends by any means, but at least Lucy wasn't shaking in her shoes. In fact, she seemed warily fascinated with the older woman.

Rose set aside her coffee cup. "It'll only take five minutes."

"Hey, Luce," Evan called. "Rose and I have something to do. We'll be back in ten minutes. Okay? Do you mind staying with Mrs. Robbin for a bit?"

Lucy looked up from the table. After a moment of hesitation when he thought she was going to crumple, she nodded. Brave girl.

"I said five minutes," Rose pointed out while they hurried into their coats.

He grinned. "Well, you know how everything takes twice as long as you think it will."

"Oh, yeah," she said with a flippancy he wished she'd show more often. "And sometimes it's over before it's begun."

"Not with me."

"We'll see about that."

"You should know by now. I love a challenge." He leaned in to lift her hair from the collar of her jacket and managed a quick nuzzle before she pulled away and opened the front door. "Right back," he called again to Lucy.

Maxine flapped her hand at him. "Get outta here. You're interrupting my concentration."

Outdoors, the pearly sky had darkened to slate. Spiky shadows from the bare deciduous trees cross-hatched the frosting of snow. Rose was already making her way along a mossy path that led past several of the small stone cottages before disappearing into a small forest of evergreens. Evan hurried to catch up. From his first visit, he knew that Rose's house was the last one, hidden from view around a bend in the path as it curved deeper into the trees, closer to the river. The trees grew so thickly that only narrow, sugary drifts of snow had made it past the overhanging boughs.

"Here we are," Rose said brightly when they reached her storybook cottage. She withdrew a key from her pocket and unlocked the door.

"You keep your door locked? No one in Alouette locks doors."

"I do."

They entered. Evan looked around while Rose flipped on the lights and went to a table beneath a window that was stacked with many books, drawing tablets and artist's utensils. There was no other clutter in the space. It was utterly clean and spare, one half of the room set up as sitting area, the other as the bedroom.

He looked there first. The white iron bedstead was narrow, high and spindly. A rustic end table with chipping paint held an old-fashioned bell alarm clock and a milk-glass lamp. For comfort, there was only one pillow and a pastel blue down comforter folded at the end of the bed. A cotton cloth had been strung across a corner, apparently to form a makeshift closet. Two pairs of shoes peeped out from the hem—sandals and sneakers.

If Evan hadn't already been aware of how different Rose was, he'd know it now. When Krissa had moved out, she'd packed her entire car with her wardrobe. There wouldn't have been room for Lucy even if she'd been invited.

"You like the simple life," he said to Rose, stating the obvious. The sitting area boasted a small woodstove and was furnished with the table, the two mismatched wooden chairs that were pulled up to it, and a faded flower-print armchair with a birch-bark, rawhide-laced reading lamp. That was it.

Rose sounded apologetic. "I'm not into accumulating stuff." She asked for his coat and when he gave it she hung it on the back of a wooden chair.

Evan was still looking around, not sure what he'd expected, but not this. Maybe he'd thought the invitation into Rose's cottage would make him privy to the inside of her mysterious mind.

Instead, her living space gave away next to nothing. Sliding glass doors overlooked the river. A basic kitchen was set up along one wall, partitioned by folding doors that had been left open to reveal no more than a tiny sink, a microwave and a sputtering miniature refrigerator. Another open door allowed a glimpse of a claw-foot tub and shaggy pale-green bath mat.

The windows were small and deep. The walls and

floors were cold, hard stone. The few woven rags that were scattered about were no way to keep feet warm in the winter.

The rustic simplicity suited a temporary summertime vacation. Evan couldn't imagine why Rose would want to live here when the weather turned. "Do you stay at your mother's house during the winter?"

"Only on the coldest days, or when she's not doing well." Rose hugged a sketch pad to her chest, looking defensive. "I have electric heat when the woodstove's not enough. It's not so bad."

"Isolated," he said. "You must do a lot of shoveling when there's a snowstorm."

"The trees have grown tight enough to act as a windbreak. I don't get the really deep drifts until later in the season. And I have snowshoes. Besides, I like the seclusion."

"To each her own." He noticed the drawings tacked to the stone walls and even the slanted ceilings where they dipped low. "Are these yours?"

"Yes." She shuffled self-consciously to the center of room as he circled, examining the artwork.

"You're really good."

"I'm just an amateur scribbler."

"These are amazing. I mean, I'm no art critic, but…" She'd made detailed drawings of birds and other small creatures, insects, flowers, ferns, even blades of grass. He examined a colored ink drawing of a frog, every splotch and bump detailed. "These are just as good as the illustrations in our school textbooks."

"No," she said, blushing.

"Honestly. I teach Biology and Earth Science at junior high level. You could be a—what do they call it? A botanical artist?" He spied a book among the stacks on her table. Many of them wore the Alouette Public Library label. "Like Audubon."

Rose shook her head, although she seemed pleased.

"You should send samples to a publisher." He realized he was talking out of his hat and shrugged. "But what do I know?"

"More than me," she ventured.

"Let's see the sketches for Lucy's room."

She opened the spiral-bound book.

"Can we sit?"

"On the bed." She blinked. "The light's better there."

It wasn't as if they'd entered a private bedroom, Evan told himself, so why should it matter? There shouldn't have been a hollow in his stomach, either. He'd eaten more than his share of the Thanksgiving dinner, wanting to impress Rose with how good her cooking had been.

The springs creaked as they sat on the bed. There was no box spring, only a mattress with a hollow in the center that would have sucked them both in it if they hadn't perched on the edge, feet planted on the floor. Rose flipped pages. "Seeing as the Princess Kristina story is close to Lucy's heart, I decided that we should go with a storybook fairy-tale theme."

She'd painted several pages of pastel watercolors to give the overall view of the mural—a scene of golden fields and green hills, gamboling deer, a dark forest, with a castle and village in the distance.

"And here…" She showed him pencil sketches of the mural's details—the princess's stone cottage, the magic, glowing stone, an ogre peering from a cave. "I'm not sure about the ogre. I don't want Lucy to be frightened of the mural when the lights go off."

"We can ask her about it." They'd already decided that they would show Lucy the sketches for approval and even let her help with some of the preliminary painting. The detail work would be done by Rose alone so the final unveiling could be Lucy's birthday surprise.

He heard Rose swallow. "What do you think?" she asked.

"I'm astonished. This is more than I imagined."

"You approve?"

He nodded. "Lucy will love it."

"I think so. I *hope* so."

He turned the pages, looking over each painting again. "I was picturing—I don't know, maybe a few cartoons. This is real artwork."

Rose peered at him, her head tilted to one side. "Too much?"

"Not if you're willing."

"Willing?" Her cheeks pinkened.

"To take on the job."

"You don't have to pay me. I'd like to do it as my present to Lucy."

"Thanks for the thought, but that's nonsense. You're an artist. You deserve to be treated professionally."

A smile twitched at her lips. "What if I charged plumber's rates per hour?"

He acted staggered. "How about a professional who gives friends a price break?"

"We'll compromise on a flat fee. That way I won't worry that I'm taking advantage of you if I go slow."

"You have slow hands? Mmm. Then go right ahead and take advantage of me."

She sent him a scolding look and ignored his lame come-on. "This project will take some time. I'll have to be at your house quite a bit. For hours at a time." She shifted on the bed. "Is that okay?"

"You're thinking of the gossip again."

"I've decided—" She sucked in a deep breath. "I don't care about that anymore. Let them think whatever they like."

He became aware of his heartbeat. "Maybe we should give them something real to talk about?"

"How do you mean?"

"On second thought, forget that." He slid his hands beneath hers, using them to close the sketchbook. For a moment, they stayed like that, hands clasped, and then he took the book and tossed it aside on the bed. He found her hands again and raised them to his shoulders. Set them there, waiting for a moment to see if she'd pull away. When she didn't, he inched forward, reaching for her waist. He wanted to pull her into a deep, consuming embrace, but instinct stopped him. *Go slow.*

Rose's eyes had darkened. Her voice was velvety. "What are you doing?"

"I've been wanting to kiss you for some time," he said. His own voice was gritty with a harsh longing. "Except I don't want it to be about anyone but us."

"I d-don't know what you mean."

"Not about the gossips." Raising one hand, he stroked her hair away from her face. "Or Lucy. Not your mother, my wife, not the team, not your rep—" He stopped, his fingers buried in her hair. There'd been a reaction in the depths of her eyes. Apprehension?

But she hadn't pulled away.

"Did I say the wrong thing?" he asked.

Her lips rounded. "No." She stroked her fingers across his shoulders, the first time she'd made a conscious decision to touch him for pleasure's sake. "You said everything just right."

"Then…" He brought his face next to hers, nudging her with his nose. A slight bump so she angled her head up, her eyes closing. "May I kiss you?"

She breathed, in and out and in and out, before finally whispering, "Yes."

He brushed his mouth across her lips. The sweetest touch. She shivered from deep inside, her body filled with such tension her teeth came close to jittering. He couldn't tell if she was afraid of him…or her own desire.

"Again?" he said.

Her tongue darted across her teeth. She nodded, eyes shut tight.

He kissed her. Gently, opening his mouth only a fraction over her full lower lip, giving it a sensuous, too-brief suckle and release, then once more, making a small, wet sound in the silent room. She sighed, shifting toward him with her shoulders beginning to relax. A few more kisses and she'd be melting.

He was winding his arms around her when the sound of a deep, clanging bell shattered their quiet intimacy.

Rose leaped off the bed, her face draining to chalk-white as she listened to the ongoing clamor. "My mother's ringing the bell—or Lucy—" She looked at Evan with a horrified alarm. "Something's gone wrong."

CHAPTER NINE

"LUCY."

"I'm sure she's—" Rose started to race after Evan, then returned for their winter coats. "My mother rings for all kinds of reasons," she called, grasping for a weak explanation. Too late. He was already gone.

She ran along the incline, slipping a little on the stone path. Evan was shouting Lucy's name in the distance.

Maxine stood in the open doorway of her house, shrilly explaining her summons when Rose arrived. "I don't know what happened. She was skipping around my tank, so I tried to get her to sit down and be quiet. Then she turned scaredy-cat again and before I knew it she'd grabbed her jacket from the closet and run straight out the door. Didn't say a word."

Rose thrust Evan's coat at him. "Which way did she go?" he asked as he shrugged into it, already dancing away. He searched the path for footprints, but the snow was hard-packed near the house and trampled around the cars from their comings and goings. His gaze swept the bleak landscape. "Are the other cottages locked?"

"Yes," Rose said. "But the keys are in the office, right by the front door." She pushed past her mother. "I'll check if any are missing."

Maxine wrung her hands. "I didn't see where she went. Figured she would find you and Rose easy enough. But then I heard something, like a cry, or a shout…"

Rose rushed out of the office. "The keys are all there."

Evan threw back his head and bellowed. *"Lucy!"*

The call was met with silence, complete except for the rushing river. Rose's gut tightened at the familiar sound. The rapids wouldn't freeze over for at least another month.

Her horror was doubled—tripled—in Evan's expression.

"We have to check the river first," she said, but he was already moving, running behind the house, dodging through the jack pines.

"Go back inside, Mom." Rose stopped to look for signs of Lucy's footprints in the snow of the backyard before she took off after Evan, losing her footing on the slick pine needles halfway down the slope and scrambling back up again.

Evan slid down the steep bank to the river, calling his daughter's name. The black water rushed by, ice-cold and turbulent. There was no sign of Lucy, but a child as light as she would be swept away in an instant.

Rose grabbed Evan's arm. "Would she come this way?"

His harsh breath made great clouds of vapor in the air. "Normally, no. The river would scare her. But if she lost her way…"

Rose checked again for tracks in the snow and found only their own zigzagging trail. "Go downstream. The current slows farther along. I'll go back up the hill to search the cottages on the other side."

Evan was off, clambering over rocks where they impeded his path. "Get on the phone and call for help if you don't find her right away."

"I will. Don't worry. She's okay."

Rose's breath caught short in her chest, but she loped back up the hill in ground-eating strides, grabbing onto branches where she could for support. Maybe Lucy had simply gone in the wrong direction, to the other cottages that were spread haphazardly over the property. She'd never been to Rose's house, and each one looked much like the others except for their different settings. Rose's was the most secluded, out of sight of the others. It was likely Lucy had tried to find her and Evan and hadn't known which way to go. There would *have* to be some sign of her in the soft snow if she'd wandered off the path.

The frigid water of the rushing river didn't bear thinking of.

Rose hurried from cottage to cottage, checking the doors and calling Lucy's name. She found a couple of small footprints in the snow outside the last cabin on that side of the house, where the path ended at a dense wood. It looked as though Lucy had stopped there and turned in a circle.

Betting that the girl would have turned back when she realized the cottages along this path were all unoccupied, Rose returned to the main house, watching more carefully for footprints. There were very few— the snow had been shoveled and scraped too well.

Maxine poked her head out the door, wrapped in a scarf. "Anything?"

"I found footprints."

"Should I call for Search and Rescue?"

"Wait a minute. I wonder…" Rose looked at the cars. If Lucy was frightened and couldn't find her dad, where would she go? Not to the river or the woods, especially in the dark. She would go to the *familiar.*

At first the car looked empty and Rose's hopes dropped. But then she peered closer into the shadowed back seat and saw Lucy, huddled in a ball, her head tucked as deep as a turtle's.

Rose waved to her mother. "Ring the bell for Evan. I've found her."

She opened the door. "*Lucy.* Didn't you hear us calling for you?"

The clanging was terrible and loud, even as a salvation. Rose crawled inside the car and closed the door, blocking out some of the clamor. She reached for the girl, draping her arms around the pitiful, huddled form. "Oh, Luce."

Lucy raised a tear-streaked face to let out a muffled sob, then grabbed blindly. Her cold bare hands clung to Rose's neck. "Nuh-unh-unh," she blubbered, trying to speak but unable to catch her breath.

Rose held her. "Shhh. It's okay. I've got you."

"Duh—Dah—Daddy…"

"Don't worry. He's coming." The ringing had stopped. She rocked Lucy, letting the girl catch her breath and quiet down.

The door on Lucy's side was flung open. Evan appeared, bending to reach into the backseat. "My God. Lucy."

She threw herself into his arms. "Daddy! Where were you?"

He staggered, half in and half out of the car, before slumping onto the seat. Lucy's face was buried in his neck. He cuddled her, patting her back for a while before pulling the door shut. She sniffled and clung, but the sobbing had stopped.

"What happened?" he asked, looking at Rose.

"I think she couldn't find us in any of the cottages—" Rose pointed toward the unoccupied structures to the right. "And then she must have gotten scared out here and climbed into your car for safety."

Evan stroked his daughter's hair. "Lucy? Why didn't you answer me? Did you hear us calling? I thought you were lost." He kept his voice even and steady but threw a starkly emotional glance at Rose, one that spoke volumes of the fear they'd shared by the river.

If this is parenthood, Rose thought, *how did anyone survive?*

Lucy was whispering. "I didn't know where you were…you left me! And Mrs. Robbin tried to grab me and she l-looks like a witch…."

"But you know she's not. And I told you I'd be back." He gave a sigh and set her back a little, making her sit up on his lap so he could look into her face. "You know that I'd never leave you, *really* leave you, right? Haven't I told you that, over and over?"

Lucy nodded miserably. Rose's heart went out to her, thinking of what Evan had recently explained about his daughter's mother—leaving once, coming back, then gone for good. Really gone. No reprieve.

No second chance.

"I know you were scared, Luce, but don't ever do that again. If I'm calling, you have to answer." Evan folded her into his arms. "I'm sorry for leav—" He stopped to take a steadying breath. "For taking so long.

But…there are going to be times I'm not with you, honey. You're going to have to learn not to panic. You always have to stay with an adult, not take off on your own without permission." He nudged her with his chin. "Okay?"

Lucy nodded.

Rose swallowed, hoping her voice wouldn't shake. "Hey, it's cold out here. Let's get you inside." She looked at Evan's pants—soaked to the knee. "Both of you."

Lucy's face was peaked, her eyes enormous behind dampened strings of hair. She looked at the Robbins' house and cringed. "Do I have to?"

Rose was dismayed. "Oh, no, of course—"

Evan interrupted. "Yes, in fact, you do, Miss Lucy. I want you to see there's nothing scary inside that house. We'll go and get warm and before we leave you'll thank Mrs. Robbin for her kind hospitality."

Rose got out of the car, struggling with her own emotions even though she knew that Evan was doing what he thought best. She'd run away from her parents' house so many times she could identify with Lucy's desperation. Perhaps if she'd had someone who'd forced her to stop and look her fears in the face…

Maxine opened the door, still draped in the scarf. It hung around her shoulders like a shawl. Her face was wrinkled and sallow. One scrawny, knobby hand clutched the doorknob. She really did look like a witch.

Rose glanced at Lucy, carried in Evan's arms.

She wished she felt so safe.

DECEMBER ARRIVED. And with it snow. Soon the ground was permanently blanketed and snowbanks began piling up, deposited by plows and shovelers. The branches of the evergreens grew heavy beneath mantles of white. Days passed without sunshine, a succession of skies layered with white cotton batting. Alouette social activity began to slow as the days grew shorter and townspeople opted to spend the frigid evenings at home.

With Rose's hours at the convenience store lessened, Maxine expected her daughter to keep her company more often. They watched TV every night, it seemed, though Rose would usually take out her block of watercolor paper and work on a painting from the sketches she'd done over the summer, adding strokes of soft color to blossoms and leaves and skies while her mother droned on about the machinations of *Survivor* or her expanding knowledge of dead bodies and criminal procedure learned from *CSI* and *Law and Order.* A couple of times Alice Sjoholm stopped by with a friend and they'd partner up for a few rounds of canasta. On her free days, Rose would snowshoe along the river to see the frozen waterfalls, enjoying the sharp chill of the air in her lungs. One clear evening Roxy showed up and they drove to Marquette to take in a movie and see the historic buildings of the downtown area outlined in white lights for the holidays.

More than ever, Rose looked forward to her evenings at the high-school gym. There was usually at least one home game each week, and though Evan's team was struggling to keep at the .500 level, the hometown support never wavered. No matter what the temperature, a vocal crowd turned out to cheer for the Storm.

Gradually, Rose realized that she was no longer an

anonymous fan in the stands. Lucy was her constant companion at the games, and that had drawn Rose out of her usual distant seat to a position in the middle of the action. Various people waved hello and stopped to chat for a few minutes about the team's chances, discussing Jeremy's rebound record or Evan's coaching tactics. Rose was mostly silent at first, but by mid-December she had even initiated a couple of brief conversations.

She felt accepted. She felt good.

Particularly on the evening that Danny, coming to the sidelines after warm-ups, had looked up into the stands and said, "Hi, Lucy. Hi, Rose. We're gonna kick butt tonight." She hadn't come down from her cloud to actually watch the game until midway through the second period.

Soon it was a week before Christmas. It finally occurred to Rose that she should start thinking about gifts. For all of her adult life, Christmas had been a quiet affair. During the years when she'd drifted from job to job and avoided coming home, there'd been no need to participate in the festivities of the season. The past few Christmases had been most humble, with her father's death, her mother's ill health and her brothers far from home. This year was feeling quite unique.

Having a child in her life made all the difference. Lucy wasn't Danny, but she did bring Rose much joy. They'd devoted their most recent art lesson to cookie decorating, prompting Rose and Maxine to reminisce of the years when holiday baking had been a rare opportunity for mother-daughter bonding. Soon Maxine had been making a shopping list, and with the appearance of bricks of butter, spices, colored and powdered sugar had come a revived holiday spirit.

It wasn't only Rose who was different.

Life was good.

SCRAPING NOISES WOKE Rose on the Saturday before Christmas. For a couple of minutes, she burrowed deeper beneath her covers, smiling to herself. She knew that sound—Evan was shoveling her path again. He'd done it several times lately and was even threatening to buy her a snowblower for Christmas to make the job easier.

When the shoveling sounds got a little closer, Rose slipped out of bed and turned up the electric heat. She showered in three minutes flat, threw on jeans, heavy socks and a cable-knit sweater, then went to the kitchen to make coffee and see if she had any cinnamon bread left for toast.

This was becoming a routine on snowy weekday mornings—Evan would either bring Lucy along or drop her off at her baby-sitter's house if it was one of her free mornings, then drive out to Blackbear Road to shovel from Maxine's door to Rose's. He'd usually come inside for a quick cup of coffee before he went on to school.

Rose had tried to insist that she was perfectly capable of doing the shoveling herself, but Evan had only nodded and continued to show up anyway. After years of solitary independence, she found it strange to be taken care of, but not as hard to become accustomed to as she'd expected. It was nice, feeling this way. Not permanent, she tried to remind herself every now and then, because she didn't quite dare to believe that such goodness would last forever, but still very nice.

When she heard him stomping his boots on the front

steps, ridding them of snow, she went over to open the door. "It's Saturday," she said, peeping at the wintry view behind him as he batted snow off his gloves. The fresh snowfall had capped the pine trees and turned bare branches into lacework that stood out against a clear blue sky. "Where's Lucy? Up at my mom's?"

"Nope." With a huge smile, Evan stepped inside. He took off his heavy jacket and hung it on the doorknob, then turned to look at Rose with his hands resting on his narrow hips, long fingers splayed. In jeans and a gray wool pullover with a black turtleneck showing underneath, he exuded such a healthy, masculine vigor that he took her breath away.

"Good news," he said, looping one arm around her waist and pulling her to his chest for a quick, friendly kiss.

Rose gave a breathless laugh as she pulled away. Her hand rose to touch her cheek where Evan's stubble had grazed it. He hadn't shaved that morning. "What's going on?"

"Lucy is spending the *entire* day at her classmate's birthday party. Apparently it's a big production—sledding, ice skating, lunch at Pizza Hut, birthday cake and presents back home…"

Rose nodded. "So she decided to go after all."

After the Thanksgiving debacle, Rose had worried that Lucy would retreat into her shell, but the girl had bounced back quicker than expected, recovering much of her composure even before they'd left the Robbins' house. A few days later, Rose and Maxine had each received handmade cards thanking them for their hospitality. Rose had been touched, while Maxine had acted all abrupt and dismissive. Somehow, though, her card had wound up stuck to the refrigerator with magnets.

At the last basketball game, Rose had heard all about the birthday invitation from Lucy. The girl had veered between chatterbox excitement and an obvious case of nerves. Evan had explained privately that he'd had to rescue Lucy from the last outing she'd attempted—a class field trip—and that she'd been so miserable about getting teased for being a baby that, except for school, she'd refused to leave him for any length of time.

"Made up her mind late last night," Evan said. "Thanks to you. The idea about the cell phones worked."

Rose was pleased. "No, really?" She'd suggested that Lucy would feel more secure about leaving Evan if she could call him any time she wanted throughout the day.

"I took her out yesterday and she chose a little pink phone for herself. We programmed in my number—" Evan patted the pocket where he kept his phone "—and she tested it out only about a dozen times. When I dropped her off this morning, she was so keen on getting inside to show the girls her new phone that she hardly cared when I drove away."

Rose beamed, feeling like a mother bird watching her baby fly for the first time. "How many times has she called since?"

"Only once. And sent me a couple of text messages." Evan shook his head. "Toys have changed since I was a kid."

"Yeah, you're such an old man." She patted his cheek, keeping it playful even though her underlying motive was getting to touch his whiskers again. They gave him an edgier look she found most attractive.

"Not so old that I've forgotten about the date you promised me. If Lucy had made up her mind sooner I wouldn't be asking at the last minute, but what do you say? Want to make it an all-day thing? I hope you're not scheduled to work."

"No." Cross had been crabbier than usual because with winter hours he was getting only ten or fifteen hours a week. She'd offered him today, thinking that she could use the time off to get her shopping done. "The thing is—I was planning to go Christmas shopping."

"With Roxy?"

"Well, no. Roxy hates to shop."

"But you don't mind it?"

"It's not my habit. But I haven't had much reason to shop, before. I actually have a list this year." Rose grabbed the scribbled-over notepaper off the table before Evan could see that his name topped it. "I want to get something special for Lucy, except I'm kind of at a loss."

"I come armed." Evan pulled a much-folded sheet of notebook paper out of his wallet. "Lucy's list. She started it the day after Thanksgiving. I've ordered some of the stuff online, but there's plenty more to choose from." He examined the list, which was done in colored markers with illustrations, making a puzzled face. "Do you know what a Hollywood Hairdo Glitter Pack is?"

"Hell, no."

"We can hunt and gather as a pair. Maybe check out a few of the local shops, then drive over to Marquette for lunch at a good restaurant before braving the mall. Not the ideal date, but…"

"That sounds very nice," Rose said, wincing inside over her formal tone. By now, she'd spent enough time with Evan that she should have been comfortable with him. But as soon as she started thinking in physical, intimate terms, the old nervousness came back.

"We could even go to a movie," he said. "If Lucy cooperates, that is. I arranged for MaryAnn to pick her up from the party in case I got held up." The baby-sitter. He tugged at his turtleneck, getting ruddy in the face. "Not for, um, the entire night, you understand. Just the evening."

"Ohhh." Rose exhaled. The scent of the freshly brewed coffee reached her and she gratefully turned away to pour it into mugs. She handed one to Evan. "Do you want cinnamon toast? I was making a piece for myself."

"I'll take an answer first."

"Right." She shook a packet of NutraSweet into her coffee, made a clatter stirring it. "I'd love to spend the day with you. But I should warn you—I'm not good in crowds. Can we keep the shopping trip as short as possible?"

Evan laughed. "Hey, I'm a guy. You even need to ask?"

She smiled sideways at him and took a sip of coffee. Even though he'd treated her as a friend more often than not these past several months, never once had she forgotten that he was a guy.

THEY'D FOUND SEVERAL ITEMS from their lists in the quaint shops of Alouette, but for the real power shopping they headed to the mall, twenty miles away. The sun was out, the roads were clear, and the trip went by in a flash. Rose gave the Buck Stop a laughing salute as they drove by. "For once, this buck does not stop!"

Evan was struck by the change in her. She still tended to be quiet and watchful around others, but with him and Lucy she was almost vivacious. She laughed easily. Her eyes sparkled with clarity, a deep pansy-blue rimmed with black lashes. Even her posture had changed. She was no longer the dour lurker who'd made him so suspicious. Although he hadn't learned her secrets—aside from what he'd put together on his own—he sensed that they were not as heavy a burden as before.

His motive to help her remained. But when he looked at her as he did now, knowing the woman behind the reputation, there was no doubt that his interest went beyond charity.

You thought that with Krissa, too.

"New slippers and a robe for my mother," Rose said, consulting her list. "Check." She crossed off an item, frowned, then drew a line through whatever had been listed below it. "Fuchsia velour zip-up. Shumanski's is just my mom's style."

"Not yours?" Evan asked. She'd searched the dress rack twice.

"I have no style. Or if I do, it's straight off the shelf at the sporting goods outfitter."

"Not so much." Evan touched one of the sparkly butterflies she wore in her hair, letting his hand slide down to momentarily cradle her head. "Are those Lucy's?"

Rose nodded. "She loaned them to me at the last basketball game. Too young for me?"

"No. They suit you. I can see you, standing in a field

of wildflowers, with butterflies lighting in your hair…."

"How poetic."

"That's all I can manage for now. Wait till spring. A young man's fancy—"

Rose interrupted with a loud, obvious clearing of her throat and a studious contemplation of her list. "I need to figure out something for Alice, my mother's friend. She's been a big help to me. Maybe a gift for Tess…the library's another lifeline."

"A wedding gift?" Tess and Connor had set their wedding date for New Year's Eve, as a playful nod to the Bay House legend that said inhabitants of the Valentina Whitaker bridal suite would marry before the year was up. When he'd first come to Alouette, Connor had been given the anointed room. He swore that the inn's mavens, Emmie Whitaker and Claire Levander, had conspired against him. Tess only smiled and reminded him that he'd been damn lucky to get her.

"I'll buy the wedding gift later," Rose said. "And have it delivered."

"You're not going?" Evan clenched his teeth, a moment too late. The wedding was supposedly small in size, with the reception at Bay House. Maybe Rose hadn't been invited.

She moved her lips. "Um, probably not."

"Come with me," he said on impulse.

"My mother…"

"Don't use her for an excuse. She's not *that* ill."

"I'll think about it. Right now, the Christmas revelry is about all I can handle."

"Have you made all of your holiday plans?"

They'd left the countryside behind and arrived at a

stoplight. Evan took one hand off the wheel and dropped it over Rose's clenched fist, wishing she'd relax again, go back to the saucy woman who'd been telling him how her scattered relatives used to re-gift each other with the same hard fruitcake every year, until her father had taken the tin out back, put it on a chopping block and hacked it to pieces with an ax.

"I was going to ask what you and Lucy were doing." Casually, Rose turned her hand, taking hold.

He squeezed. "Will you come over on Christmas Eve? We have a tradition of putting up the tree that afternoon, then a light dinner and church, and when we get back Lucy is allowed to open one of her gifts. Your mother's invited, too, of course."

"Mom probably won't want to go out. I can't leave her for too long, but maybe I could help with the tree trimming? That would mean a lot to me."

"And the dinner," he prompted. "You know what happens when I try to cook." Just last week, he'd managed to create an explosion in the microwave. "You have to come. Hey, it's Christmas Eve. The firefighters deserve an evening off."

Rose's eyes glinted. "Oh, so I'm to be the scullery maid?"

A car honked behind them. Green light.

Rose pushed his hand away. "Drive."

"You'll be the guest of honor," he said, making his turn. They were going for lunch at a luxury hotel near the downtown shopping district. He knew she would balk, so he hadn't told her. The place wasn't *that* fancy.

"What's this?" she said when they pulled into the parking lot. "A hotel?"

"For lunch." He lifted a wicked eyebrow. "Not afternoon delight."

"Well," she said with a blink, "of course not."

He wondered if she was *too* comfortable with him. That had happened to him before—be the good guy long enough and females stopped thinking of you in romantic terms. They wanted you as a friend, the one who'd pick them up at the airport, help them move, change the oil in the car. Take care of them when they were sick.

He'd do all of that for Rose, but he had no intention of stopping there.

The entrance was decorated with swags of evergreens wound with red berries. Inside, tiny white lights sparkled among urns of ruby-red poinsettias. A black-and-white marble floor gleamed. Through a doorway they could see the formal dining room, richly carpeted, decked out in elegant holiday decor and white linen tablecloths.

Rose looked down at her peacoat and jeans, her eyes big in her face. Many of the diners were dressed casually, but Evan saw that wasn't the point. He wanted her to feel special, not uncomfortable.

He noticed another option and touched her arm. "Should we try the pub?"

She followed his nod. "Oh, yes, please."

They were greeted by a hostess at the open door to the wood-paneled pub and brought to a recently vacated booth. Rose was visibly relieved as he helped her out of her coat. The place was packed with patrons and noisy seasonal cheer. The menu ran the gamut from fancy salads and London broil to cheeseburgers and fries.

"I don't get the chance to eat out a lot," she said.

"There aren't many options in Alouette." They had no fast-food franchises, only the café, one family-style restaurant and the ice cream stand in summer. "Next time," he said, giving her a reassuring but meaningful glance, "I'll plan ahead. You can wear a dress. I'll put on a suit and tie. We'll be grown-ups."

Rose mumbled into her menu.

"I've never seen you in a dress," he said.

"Don't be too sure you'd want to."

He shook his head. "Why do you say things like that?"

She looked straight at him and said, "Low self-esteem," surprising and intriguing him with the direct answer, as she did every now and then.

"I don't get it. You're talented, attractive, independent…"

"Uneducated, uncouth, unwanted."

"That's so wrong I can't begin—" He stopped abruptly as the waitress arrived to deliver water glasses and take their order.

After she left, Rose said, "You don't understand."

"Then tell me."

"So you can fix me?"

He felt himself flushing and took a long drink of ice water. "Yeah, you got me there. I do have a habit of acting like Mr. Fix-It. That's why I got into teaching and coaching."

She fiddled with her napkin. "There's nothing *wrong* with that."

Might as well confess. "When we first met—I mean, that first time I really talked to you, at basketball practice, I was thinking that I could help you."

Her head reared back. "Help me with what?"

"I didn't know. But I could tell there was something."

"It's too complicated." She let out a soft moan and ducked forward, covering her face with her hand. "It's not fixable."

There was such anguish in her voice, his own throat became tight. "What is it, Rose?"

She refused to look at him.

"One of the boys on my team," he prompted, making the leap he'd been looking at for months now. He hoped Rose would meet him on the other side so they could finally get past this and become...what? Normal and happy? A couple? Was that what he wanted?

Her hand dropped. She stared at him across the table, her eyes liquid and wary. "What do you know?"

"Nothing. Only supposition."

"I've been very careful not to be obvious."

"Aw, Rose." He wanted to reassure her, but she was pressed against the high wooden bench, out of his reach. "Don't you realize? You give it away every time you look at him."

She didn't respond. Even her expression was stark and frozen.

"It's okay," he said.

Her pale lips barely moved. "You're mistaken."

Evan had tried so hard not to push her, but it was time. "Oh?" he said. "Then Danny's *not* your son?"

CHAPTER TEN

AFTERWARD, Rose would remember that her heart had stopped. She truly believed it did, before taking up again with a horrid thump that felt like a hammer against her breast. "How— There's no way you could know that."

"I don't have proof," Evan said. "Just you."

"Me?"

"He looks like you."

"You're imagining that."

"It's true. The dark hair, the shape of the face, even some of his gestures…"

She couldn't speak. There had been times she'd noticed a resemblance, but always she'd convinced herself she was seeing what she wanted to see, and that no one else would notice. Elation laced her fear—the usual mix of emotions whenever she thought of Danny.

"And there's also the way you watch Danny. At first I wasn't sure which player had your interest, but when I got to know you better, and I saw how you reacted to them individually…" He shrugged. "Two and two made four."

This was huge. Too huge to deny. She scanned the pub for familiar faces. Licked her parchment lips. "Does anyone else know?"

"Not as far as I'm concerned."

She was trying to add up Evan's equation, but it didn't compute. Even if she'd given away her interest in Danny, for him to reach his conclusion…there had to be more.

Let him see her suspicion. "Where did you get the two and two?"

He answered easily enough. "Danny's parents had me over for dinner not long after I came to Alouette. His dad joked about having no athletic ability, so it was just as well that they'd adopted Danny. They were very open about that. But it didn't mean much to me at the time. Danny's a bright, well-adjusted kid. I've never had a problem with him."

At another time, she'd have relished that praise as proof she'd made a good choice. "That's fine, but it doesn't prove a thing. What else do you have?"

"I'd been told about your past. How you left town when you were a teenager."

"So?" The old sense of shame burned in her. Even worse, her front of bravado had been worn away. She was vulnerable, but tried to hide that. "Didn't they tell you? I was in trouble with the cops. I was *sent* away."

"I believe that you were in trouble, but not that kind."

"Think you're smart, huh?"

Evan made a small, soothing smile. "Ah, Rose."

She dashed at her eyes. "What?"

"I won't tell anyone if you don't want me to."

"Doesn't matter. Danny's parents know about me."

That had surprised him. "They do?"

"It was a private adoption. I chose the Swansons from several couples who applied, all of them living somewhere in Upper Michigan. I knew it might be complicated, them being from Alouette, but I wasn't intending to return."

In her lap, she pressed her knuckles together. "They know I'm Danny's birth mother. Over the years, they've sent photos of him, wrote me letters…"

"They seem very accepting. Why don't you approach them about—"

"*No.*"

"But, Rose. You're not happy this way."

"My happiness doesn't matter. Think of Danny. Word would get out about me being his mother—you know it would. And then he'd have to live with the stigma." She shuddered.

"Stigma? Aren't you exaggerating? I don't think the situation's that bad."

"You've only been here a few years. You didn't know my father or my brothers. You don't know the reaction I got when they found out I was pregnant. It was horrible, especially when the cops came to threaten my dad."

Evan frowned. "You lost me. Why would there be police intervention? Unless—" His eyes became flinty. "He didn't hurt you, did he?"

"No. It wasn't like that, exactly." Her father had bellowed about throwing her out of the house—until he'd started getting ideas about making her baby his meal ticket. "There were other complications." She shrugged. "Doesn't matter now."

"No? I think it matters a hell of a lot to you."

She realized that she wanted to tell Evan the story. She really did. Early on, trusting him was a reach. But now she knew beyond doubt that he was fair and kind. He wouldn't judge her harshly.

Not caring about etiquette, she put her elbows on the table and leaned closer. He followed suit. She fixed her gaze on a loose thread in his sweater and started. "I was sixteen when I got pregnant. Seventeen when the baby was born. In between, a lot of jumping to conclusions happened. They all thought the baby's father was a guy I'd gone out with, sort of. Do you know the Lindstroms?"

"Sure. But not well."

"He was their son. Rick. We were the total cliché—rich boy, poor girl, Romeo and Juliet. Except that what happened between us wasn't so noble or poetic. I did have a crush on him, but he—he just, y'know, wanted a piece of ass."

Being crude hadn't worked to keep her tears at bay. She squeezed her eyes shut. *Oh, damn.* No crying allowed.

Evan was apparently at a loss for words. He knew boys—he couldn't say it wasn't true that frequently hormones ruled their actions.

Rick had first approached her on the night of a school dance. Rose—she'd been only Rose then, sometimes even Rosie—usually avoided that type of extracurricular activity, but it was a casual come-as-you-are event, and she'd begun to yearn for more of a life than she had, always being alone and forgotten even at home. So she'd put on her nicest jeans and top and gone to hang out for a while at the dance. She must have looked okay; several boys had asked her to dance. They'd even wanted her to come partying with them, but she'd been too shy and cautious for that. She'd escaped to the bathroom, where a couple of the "popular" girls, led by Gloria, had made no pains to hide their disdain. Rose's jeans had no designer label. She had short nails and no makeup and didn't even smoke. She was from the wrong side of the tracks. The girls had told her to keep away from their boyfriends.

Rose had fled. But on the walk home, a familiar sporty convertible had driven up. Rick Lindstrom. He'd smiled, chatted to put her at ease, then offered her a ride.

"I was naive. Actually, dumb. I was flattered by his attention," Rose told Evan. "I started meeting him after school, then in the evenings after I'd sneaked out of the house. We didn't do much—rode around the countryside and talked. He said he loved me…" She shrugged. "I *wanted* to believe that. He was the first guy who'd showed genuine interest in me. And so we—well, you know what happens with teenagers in the back seat of cars."

Rose could feel a dull embarrassment heating her cheeks. She was grateful when the waitress arrived with their food and she could busy herself with dumping condiments on her burger. Too much. The sandwich was already stuffed with a thick patty, cheese, lettuce, tomato, pickles and onion. She squashed the bun down and took a large bite, squirting excess ketchup and mustard out the other side. No class.

She juggled the burger, her fingers dripping as she tried to slide a napkin out from under the utensils.

"Let me." Evan liberated the napkin and daubed her fingers.

"Thanks." She pulled away. "Not much different than having lunch with a five year old, is it?"

"Only if you spill your drink, too."

"I'll try not to."

"Don't worry about it." He lifted his fish sandwich and a tomato slice slid out the back end of the kaiser roll. He laughed and stuck it back in, licking the tartar sauce off his fingers when he was done.

Rose went back to her burger, taking smaller bites as regular as a metronome. If she kept chewing, she wouldn't have to talk.

They shared a plate of onion rings. "Have some," Evan said. "They're good."

She swallowed and reached for a golden ring.

"Are you going to tell me the rest of the story?"

She dropped the onion ring on her plate. "It's predictable."

"These things usually are. We humans keep making the same mistakes."

We, Rose thought. Who was he kidding? He'd probably never broken a law or struggled with a moral ambiguity in his entire life. Look at how he'd cared for a sick wife even though she'd left him. The man was a paragon.

"Rick Lindstrom was Danny's father?"

She put down the burger and took up the napkin, carefully wiping her greasy fingers and mouth, her mind racing with possibilities. It would be easy to point the finger at Rick. He was gone now. He couldn't be hurt. And part of her still wanted to blame him. He'd been good to her when their liaison was a secret, but when the rumors grew and his parents put the heat on him to stop seeing her or else, he'd dumped her. After she'd realized that he hadn't really, truly cared for her, she'd given up hope and started hanging with the rough crowd, smoking and drinking, staying out all night and getting into trouble just like her brothers. Exactly as the townspeople predicted.

But Danny deserved better than a lie. And so did Evan.

"No," she said, surprising him again.

"No?"

"Someone along the way saw me and Rick together and word got back to his parents. They considered my family scum. He was told he couldn't keep seeing me. For a while, we met in secret, but then they threatened to take his car away." She tried to smile, but her mouth felt twisted. "By then I'd realized that he never had taken me out in public. He was just as ashamed of being seen with me as his parents. So we broke up. And then there were other boys who…" She gulped. She could let Evan believe her bad behavior had included multiple partners, or she could tell him the most painful truth of all.

The rape.

She looked around at the other customers, a merry bunch, fit for the season. Now wasn't the time to dredge up her nightmare.

Finish it, she said brutally to herself. *Any way at all.*

"When my family learned I was pregnant, they assumed Rick was to blame. So my dad got the idea that the Lindstroms should pay. He called it expenses and damages. They called it blackmail and got the police involved. That was when I decided to end it by getting the hell out of town."

Evan was nodding. "And because the police had been seen at your house right before you left, the rumor spread that you'd been taken away to jail, or whatever."

"I guess so."

"Where did you go?"

"Not far. I hopped a bus with about three hundred dollars to my name."

Even now, Evan was disheartened by that prospect. "God, Rose."

"There was one person who helped—Pastor Mike Greenlee from the Lutheran church where I'd gone to Sunday school. He was new here then. When all the trouble started, he'd tried to counsel me and my parents, but my dad had pretty much tossed him out on his ear. Pastor Mike had told me to get in touch with him if I needed help, and when I got desperate enough, I did. He sent me to a home for unwed teenage girls downstate." She made a face, even though she'd been grateful for any kindness at all at the time. "*That* was a fun four months, let me tell you."

Finally, she looked at Evan again, dreading what she'd see in his face even though she knew his soul was as generous as they came. She'd called him a paragon, but the truth was that not even Evan was flawless. How could his feelings *not* change toward her, for the worse, given that she'd led him to believe she'd earned her nickname by being wild in every way?

"I know how hard that must have been," he said, putting his hand over hers on the table top. He squeezed, but she kept her hand lying flat and unresponsive. "You're some kind of woman, Rose."

Her eyes narrowed. "*Feh.* I was a knocked-up teenager who gave her baby away. Happens to thousands of girls. Common—" Tramps. That was what Black Jack had called her—a common tramp. "Common as lice."

"You're not common to me."

She pursed her lips, shaking her head at his rose-colored glasses. "You have a savior complex."

"Yeah, maybe, but that doesn't mean I can't be experiencing real feelings."

Could he? Could they?

The emotional possibility—falling in love, even though she wouldn't let herself call it that—was scary to Rose, even scarier than the thought of letting a man touch her in a truly intimate way. She'd tried several times over the years, wanting to be normal again, but it had never worked out. She was as prickly as a porcupine around men, and the only ones who'd been willing to put up with her antisocial tendencies were not the kind she wanted in her life. Losers, mostly, looking for a cheap lay on a lonely night. Even the one or two nice guys she'd run across had eventually given up on her when she couldn't reciprocate with any real affection.

Only Evan had managed to get under her skin. That didn't mean she was entirely comfortable with him. Hell, she wasn't always comfortable with herself. But…he was there. Offering himself. If she could only accept the gift.

"Are we finished?" he asked, startling her until she realized he referred to the lunch.

"Yeah, I'm done."

He signaled for the check. "Ready for more shopping? Or would you prefer to head back? We can do this another time."

Thoughtful of him. Her knees *were* a little shaky as she rose from the booth, but she was glad he was acting normally, as if their conversation had been no big deal. "That's okay. Might as well keep on, since we're here and all. I'm a tough girl."

"That you are." He left the waitress a hefty tip, the way she'd known he would, then paid the check at the till and took her hand as they collected their coats and walked out of the pub into the fancy lobby.

Rose smiled to herself, amazed she was still at ease with him. *Tough girls need love, too.*

THREE DAYS LATER, when Ken Swanson walked into the Buck Stop while Rose was on duty at the cash register, the first thought that entered her head was that Evan had sent him. She might have blurted out an accusation if she'd been able to talk past the enormous lump in her throat. Her book dropped to the counter, unnoticed.

"Merry Christmas," Mr. Swanson said. He was in his middle-fifties and somewhat pear-shaped, especially in a quilted down coat. His face looked like a potato.

"Merry Christmas," she muttered, turning to check if he'd pulled up to the gas pump. Nope.

He took off his glasses and puffed warm air on the fogged lenses, squinting at the humdrum shop. Aside from a scrubby old wreath on the door and one string of bulbs that hung in uneven loops around the front window, Christmas cheer had skipped the convenience store. "You're probably wondering why I'm here."

Rose said nothing.

"The wife and I got your card."

"Oh." One of Rose's stops during the shopping trip with Evan had been the card store in the mall. Her mother had sent cards to a short list earlier in the month, but Rose had never gone in for that kind of thing. There were very few people she'd wanted to keep in touch with. But suddenly, standing in front of the racks of holiday blessings and cheer, she'd thought of the Swansons. And then of Pastor Mike and his wife. Roxy, Tess. Lia Pogue, a divorced mother of three who'd lived next door to Rose when she'd been a checker at a grocery store in Cadillac. When Rose had moved, Lia had said how much she'd be missed. Rose had thought that was only because she'd been a convenient baby-sitter, but now she realized they'd been *friends*.

"Was it…did it…" Mr. Swanson seemed as unsure as she.

"It was only a card," Rose said. She frowned. "To let you know that I, um, appreciate everything you've done."

"We've been wanting to talk with you." They'd made a couple of strained attempts to speak to her when she'd first moved back to Alouette, but she'd been dealing with her mother's bereavement and ill health and had kept the conversations to a minimum, certain that they were only being polite.

"That's not a good idea," she said.

"Why?"

She shrugged.

"Danny has asked, you know. About who his birth parents are."

Rose's heart leaped back up into her throat.

"We'd like to tell him, but not without your permission, of course. We'll continue to respect your wishes." Mr. Swanson smiled tentatively. "Except we're hoping you'll change your mind. It doesn't have to be a secret."

Yes, it does.

Reluctantly, she shook her head. "Trust me, it's better this way." *Don't make me explain.*

Mr. Swanson didn't go, he just stood there, waiting and watching her, with his hands tucked in the pockets of his coat. She gripped the worn counter, biting her tongue as a hundred questions about Danny's life ran through her mind. This was her chance—she could talk with another person who loved him as a parent. All that stopped her was the painful knowledge that she was *not* a parent.

Even so, she was on the verge of caving when Danny's father sighed. "Well, if you ever change your mind, let us know. We think it would be good for Danny to meet you and see where he came from."

"No." Her voice was flat and dry. *That would only bring up more questions—he'd want to know about his father next.*

She cleared her throat. "But thank you for…offering."

Mr. Swanson shrugged. "At least I can tell the wife I tried." He walked to the door. "Have a good Christmas."

"You, too," Rose whispered. She closed her eyes as the door banged shut. *A family Christmas.* Her longing was fierce, until she remembered that she would finally have a family Christmas of her own. Incomplete without Danny, but it was a start.

"DOES LUCY STILL BELIEVE IN SANTA?" Rose whispered to Evan as they retrieved a stack of presents from his bedroom closet. It was their first moment alone together since she'd arrived to trim the tree. As much as it pleased him to see Lucy so animated, he was wishing for a little quiet time with Rose.

"Last week, she came home from school in a funk. Some of the older kids had been saying there was no Santa. I talked about the true meaning of Christmas and how she should keep the magic of Santa in her heart—"

"In other words, you fudged."

"I fudged." He nodded. "Why not? She has her suspicions, but so far she wants to believe."

"That's nice." Rose added a small gift to the lopsided stack in Evan's arms, then turned back to check the closet shelf. Her gaze moved slowly across the rack of his dress shirts and business suits.

There was extra space in his closet since Krissa had removed her things. Before she'd died, she'd set aside a few garments and mementos for Lucy when she was older, along with a journal, video and photos. Krissa and Evan had both wanted Lucy to *know* her mother, even years from now, but he hadn't counted on how it would be for another woman coming into their life.

Rose had seen the box in the largely empty side of the closet. Krissa's name was on it. "I think that's everything," she said.

"Ha," he said. "I have more presents in the trunk of my car, but those are the ones from Santa. I think Lucy's been sneaking peeks in here."

"But of course." Rose backed out of the closet with the final gift. "This one has my name on it! From Tess."

"She dropped it by early this morning. Said she knew you'd be here later on."

"I mentioned that when I was at the library. But I don't know why she gave me a present, or why she brought it *here*...." Pink-cheeked, Rose shook the rectangular present, wrapped in shiny foil with a huge red bow.

"None of that," Evan said. "You'll shake something loose. All I know is that Tess said the gift was something she wanted you to have for today or tomorrow."

"But…" Rose's eyes darted toward the bed. "It's not like we're a couple."

"Not officially."

She raised her eyebrows. "Not even unofficially!"

"I need to remedy that." He looked around the room, pretending to search. "Where's that mistletoe again?"

"Dad?" Lucy called from the living room. She was rattling one of her favorite holiday decorations—a string of bells that hung from the doorknob to catch Santa's entrance. They had no fireplace. "*Rose?* Are you coming?"

"Saved by the jingle bell," Rose said with an anxious laugh, and hurried out of the room.

Evan followed, smiling to himself. They hadn't seen each other since the shopping trip, when he'd believed they'd made a big leap forward in their relationship. Though one leap forward might be followed with another step back, at last he was sure that Rose trusted him. He only had to get her alone and prove that she could be comfortable with him as well.

And solve her other problems, too. There'd been half a thought in his head to invite the Swansons over today, in the spirit of the season, but he'd known that much interference would be pushing his luck with Rose. But soon…

And then what? he wondered. They became an official couple? Was he ready for that? Was *Lucy?*

Judging by the way she danced between him and Rose as they arranged the presents beneath the Christmas tree, Lucy would have no problem accepting Rose. But she'd been ready for Tess to become part of their lives, too, and disentangling had been a delicate operation. After that, he'd vowed to be more careful about letting Lucy see him with a woman unless it was serious, but here he'd gone and let her become attached to Rose, who was far less stable than Tess.

Sure, *his* feelings were strong. That didn't mean they were strong enough for both of them. Or all three. He'd learned that lesson with Krissa, and even then he hadn't taken his wedding ring off until the past summer.

"Dad, can I open a present now?" Lucy knelt in front of the tree, checking tags. "This one's for me, and this one's for me, and this one."

"Not yet, not until after dinner. You know the rules."

"I forgot Rose's present!" Lucy charged off to her room, where a small number of gift boxes were guarded by her favorite stuffed animal.

She came back waving a medium-sized box flecked with ragged tape squares and arranged it at the front of the pile. "There. We have a present for everybody. And lots for me."

"Rose is special, too," Evan said. "She has three to open."

"Three?" Rose said, caught by surprise. She'd been gazing at the tree, which they'd decorated with flashing lights, tinsel, paper chains, popcorn strings and a mishmash of gaudy and handmade ornaments, all of it to Lucy's precise specifications. In the fading afternoon light, it was a tree that could only be called a thing of beauty by a child…or a woman who was more sentimental than she wanted to admit.

"One from me, one from my dad, and one from Tess." Lucy pawed through the presents, knocking several over. "Tess said Rose should open it right away."

Lucy handed the box to Rose, who demurred. "Oh, no, I'll wait."

"Go ahead," Evan said. "Lucy's been dying to see something opened, so you might as well stave her off."

Rose gave in, sitting on the couch and asking Lucy to help her peel back the wrappings. She lifted off the lid of a Shumanski Clothier box and parted the tissue. "Ohhh…"

Rose started to lifted something pink and soft from the box, then stopped abruptly, letting it fall. She looked stunned.

"It's a dress," Lucy said, clapping gleefully.

Rose smoothed a hand over the garment. "I can't believe Tess bought me the dress."

"Put it on!" Holding out the sparkly blue velvet skirt, Lucy twirled in her own brand-new Christmas dress. "Then you'll be pretty and fancy just like me."

"I can't. I'm not wearing the right shoes, and I don't have nylons—"

Lucy got in Rose's face with steepled prayer hands and an angelic pout. "*Please.* Tess said she wanted you to wear it."

"That's true," Evan said.

Rose shot him a "thanks a lot" look as Lucy led her off to the bathroom.

The changing and primping seemed to take an exceptionally long time, so he headed toward the kitchen, which was emitting the savory scent of baking ham. He'd teased Rose about having to cook their dinner, but had surprised her with a selection of prepared deli food and a smoked, spiral-cut ham that only needed warming. She'd put potatoes on to boil while they decorated the tree, so he switched them off and got out the potato masher. Lots of extra trouble, he thought, when it was easy to make baked potatoes in the microwave, as long as he remembered to poke holes with a fork.

He was trying to think of what else needed doing when Lucy and Rose walked into the room. "Look, Dad."

He looked. Rose stood in the doorway, wearing the dress, her arms folded and her cheeks burning bright. Fashion he couldn't care less about, but he knew he loved that dress. It was smooth and clingy, and the Rose who wore it was a new Rose, a soft, pink blossom emerging from the thorns.

"Quit staring at me," she said, looking at the floor. She'd taken off her boots and left her feet bare.

"All right," he answered, not quitting because he wasn't able to.

Lucy took Rose's hand. "Isn't she pretty, Dad?"

"Pretty as a rose in winter." He forced himself to turn his eyes toward Lucy. "And you're my little Christmas berry, aren't you?"

"But holly berries are red." Lucy swished her skirt. "I'm a blueberry."

Rose brushed by. "Let me take over in here," she said, intent on being efficient as she clapped a lid on the pot of potatoes and began to drain the water into the sink. "You two can go and straighten up the ornament boxes in the living room. I thought we could be casual and eat in there, so we can admire the tree—" She stopped, catching herself. Steam curled against her blushing cheeks. "I mean, if that's all right with you, Evan."

"Sounds like a good plan. You think so, Luce?"

"Whatever Mom says," Lucy said as she ran through the dining room back to the tree.

Evan saw Rose catch her breath. His own gut gave a hitch at the casual reference. "Hey," he said, going for a cavalier brush-off. "That's okay. I don't think she even realized what she said."

Rose set the steaming pan on a hot pad. "Yes. Just a mistake. It didn't mean anything."

"Well, maybe it meant *something*." He was like Lucy—he wanted to believe. "But there's no need to worry about it."

"No, I won't." Rose threw him a forced smile. "Go ahead, clean up in there. I'll have dinner ready in ten minutes." And then she turned even pinker, hearing herself. It *was* a very Mom kind of thing to say.

Probably, given his doubts about her, Evan should have been concerned. But the truth was…he didn't mind in the least.

CHAPTER ELEVEN

THEY LOADED UP THEIR PLATES with ham, potatoes, a variety of deli salads and hot rolls and ate in the living room as Rose had suggested. Darkness fell around five-thirty, but Evan kept the lights off, except for the blinking rainbow of bulbs on the festive Christmas tree. After a while, Rose forgot about being uncomfortable in the dress, and she sat with her legs drawn up beneath her, smiling over Lucy's antics as she poked and prodded, trying to guess the contents of her gifts.

Evan returned their plates to the kitchen. When he came back, he pulled a chenille throw off the back of the sofa and wrapped it around Rose. He sat beside her. "You looked cold."

She leaned against him, loving the weight of his arm around her shoulders. "Mmm, this is wonderful."

"It's okay that we pulled you away from your mother?"

"She's fine." Maxine had complained some, but that was standard form. "I called her earlier and Alice had been by. I shouldn't stay too much longer though."

"You won't go to church with us?"

"Oh, no." Luckily she'd promised to take her mother on Christmas morning, because merely the prospect of going with Evan gave her the willies.

"Too public?"

"It's not that I *care,* exactly…" Who was she kidding? "It's just that, you know, people will assume—"

Evan put his mouth near her ear. "That we're a couple?"

She nodded.

"What if I'm assuming the same?" he asked.

She gave him a long look out of the corners of her eyes. He was smiling. Teasing…perhaps. Or not. Desire slipped through her, liquid and warm. And thrilling. Her skin prickled with the urge to lean even closer and kiss him.

His hand lifted off her shoulder and stroked her hair. She tilted back, letting him cup her nape and turn her face toward his, an inviting smile springing to her lips. *Yes,* she thought. Inviting. All she really wanted for Christmas was *this*.

"Is it time for presents *yet?*" came Lucy's plaintive voice.

Evan stifled a groan. "I guess it is. But let our guest go first."

"No, I already opened one." Rose gave Evan's leg a pat and went to kneel by the tree. She sorted through the piles of gifts to find the ones she'd brought with her. "For you, Lucy. From me."

The girl took the gift into her lap. "It's big!" She looked at her dad for the go-ahead. He nodded, and she tore into the present, pulling paper away in long strips. Rose laughed to see her.

A fine wooden box was revealed. Lucy fumbled with the latches. "What is it?"

"Art supplies."

The lid opened. "Oooh." Lucy stared in awe at the rows of colored pencils and markers.

"If you lift the tray, there's more." Rose helped her. "Pastels and paints and brushes. And your name is engraved here, on the little plaque."

"It's awesome." Lucy snapped the lid shut and hugged the case. "Dad, did you see? I'm gonna be like a real artist. I can go sketching in the woods just like Rose."

"It's a great gift." Evan squeezed Rose's hand as she returned to his side. "And what do you say?"

"Thank you." Lucy came over to kiss Rose's cheek. Her arms went around the girl and they hugged, a rush of affection making Rose's eyes sting. She squeezed them shut and buried her face in the girl's corn-silk hair, astonished at how right she felt about all of this.

With a sweet smile, Lucy passed out other gifts, dancing between the tree and Rose and Evan on the couch. Evan laughed over the cookbook Rose had found for him, comically illustrated with simple, foolproof recipes aimed for the mistake-prone bachelor.

Rose received a matted and framed painting from Lucy, her own work. "Princess Jade," Rose guessed, examining the black-haired figure painted in bright purples with orange-hued skin and splotches of pink and green in the background. A sun beamed from the corner of the picture. She tapped the blob of blue above the head. "Wearing her tiara."

"No, it's you!" Lucy chortled. "That's a hair ribbon. And those are the roses by your house, 'cause it's summertime in the picture and that's when they bloom. And here's the river." Lucy indicated a thin line of blue in the background. "It's small because it's in the distance, like you taught me."

"Ah, of course." Rose smiled at Evan over Lucy's head. "Thank you so much. I will treasure this. It's my very best Christmas present."

"You have one from my dad, too." Lucy brought over another gift.

"Wow," Rose said, overwhelmed. "This is too much. Maybe I should save one for tomorrow."

"Uh-uh. Tomorrow you open Santa's presents."

"Go on," Evan said, reassuring her that the gift wasn't too personal by adding, "Lucy helped pick it out."

"All right then." Rose peeled back the candy-cane paper to find a vanity set—a brush, comb and hand mirror made of polished wood with pearl and gold insets. "Oh, gosh. This is beautiful. Thank you, Evan."

He cleared his throat. "It's pretty much a girl gift," he said with a crooked grin. "Anyway, it's teak. We almost picked the fancy silver set, but this one seemed more like you." Lucy, who was leaning over the open gift box with her elbows resting on Rose's leg, nodded very sagely.

Happiness took hold in Rose. "I'm…I'm…" She lifted her hands, having to gesture helplessly. Four months ago, she'd have never imagined a Christmas like this one. "I'm at a loss for words." One arm went around Lucy and the other reached for Evan, pulling them both in closer with a crinkle of discarded wrapping paper as she kissed their cheeks. "Merry Christmas, Luce." *Smack.* "Merry Christmas, Evan." *Smack.*

Golly gee, it's like a Christmas miracle, she thought, aiming for sarcasm and missing by a mile. She was practically a new woman. And not because of the dress, although the outer trappings had made a difference. The real miracle was the way she felt inside.

THE REMAINDER OF Rose's holiday season was quiet. They got a telephone call from her brother, Jake, on Christmas Day and that put her mother in a mellow mood, even though he resisted the pleas to come home for a visit. He'd been honorably discharged from the Army and was making good money working on an oil platform off Louisiana, in the Gulf of Mexico. When Rose came on the line, he asked how she was holding up and she could honestly say, "Good," for once. Apparently Maxine had given away secrets, because Jake teased her about her new boyfriend, making Rose remember the old, innocent days of their youth. Or not-so-innocent, she supposed, given that they'd always been a dysfunctional family.

With no basketball games or art lessons on the schedule, Rose had no excuse to see Evan. Maybe that was why, when he phoned, she let him talk her into going to Tess and Connor's wedding reception on New Year's Eve at Bay House. Or maybe it was the new her—no longer quite as timid about going out and mingling. She knew that most of the wedding guests were friendly types, even to her.

It turned out that the event had unexpectedly become a double wedding at the last moment. Several explanations swirled around Bay House. One variation had it that Noah Saari had lost a bet at the bachelor party. Others said that his fiancée, Claire Levander, was—ahem—expecting. Toivo Whitaker, Emmie's brother, went around the reception boasting that it had been his doing. According to Valentina's wedding prophecy, bad luck would befall them all if Noah and Claire hadn't been married before the end of the year.

"What is *that* about?" Rose asked Roxy, midway

through the reception. The first floor of the inn was filled with guests, and they had grabbed seats on the stairs, out of the way. Rose wore her pink dress, but Roxy had on pants—the silky fabric being her only concession to formality. That, and leaving the tool belt at home.

"Valentina's wedding prophecy?" Roxy asked. "You don't know about that?"

"Of course I know." Everyone in Alouette knew. Legend said that any single person who slept the night in Valentina Whitaker's bedroom would be married by the end of the year. "I'm just surprised that anyone actually believes it enough to schedule their wedding that way."

"Tess and Connor went along for the fun of it. As for Claire and Noah…" Roxy shrugged.

"Maybe it was wedding fever," Cassia said, emerging from the crowd that had spilled over into the foyer. She drove her chair up to the foot of the stairs, looking flushed in a heather knit sweater and long suede skirt.

Roxy nodded. "Or honeymoon anticipation."

"No, I am *not* pregnant," said a voice above and behind them. Rose looked back in time to see one of the evening's brides, Claire Levander Saari, sit down on the steps. "Let's squelch that rumor here and now. I'm not that irresponsible."

Rose winced.

"Maybe Noah's that virile," Cassia teased.

Claire laughed. "No comment."

"Was it the wedding legend, then?" Roxy asked.

"I'm still not sure what happened." Claire fingered the ivy, holly and white rose bouquet in her lap. "Two days ago I was at the bridal shop with Emma and Beth, doing the final try-on of our bridesmaid's dresses—" she smoothed the red gown over her knees "—and the next thing I knew, Noah had busted in and was begging me to set the date already. Then Tess suggested making it a double wedding, and right on the spot we picked out a veil and, well, here I am." She held up her left hand, showing off the gold band that had been added to her engagement ring. "Married."

"It was Toivo," Cassia said. "Noah's been over every day this winter working on the attic renovation and Toivo kept after him. He didn't want the legend to die."

"Especially since he was the one who put me in Valentina's suite in the first place," Claire agreed.

"Emmie's been bragging on that, too," Roxy said. "Two weddings in one year." She shook her head. "Shari will never give up now."

Shari Shirley was the inn's single, middle-aged housemaid, hell-bent on testing the prophecy's legitimacy. Emmie wouldn't let her into Valentina's room on the excuse that the legend wasn't meant to be a marriage free-for-all. According to Roxy, the real reason was that Emmie feared Shari would snag Bill Maki from under her nose.

The talk of weddings and romance made Rose uncomfortable. She shifted on the step, pulling her dress down farther over her calves as she wondered how soon she could get Evan to take her home. By the sounds of male laughter, he was having a good time hanging out in the sunroom with the male half of the wedding party.

Rose's movement had drawn Claire's attention.

"What about you, Rose? Aren't you going out with Evan? Should we sneak you into Valentina's room when Emmie's not watching?"

Rose blurted out a loud, "Hell, no!" then slapped a hand over her mouth. A couple of the guests turned toward the stairs to see about the commotion and she wanted to bite her tongue for being so gauche.

No one else seemed to think she'd been out of line. They all laughed. Claire was soon looking at the other women. "Roxy? Cassia?"

Roxy snorted. Cassia tried to look innocent. "I don't know. Do I get to pick my groom, or is it random luck?"

"Got your eye on someone?"

"I spoke to your brother, Jesse, on the phone again when he called before the wedding." Cassia fanned her face. "That man gives me heart palpitations and prickly heat rash."

"No, no," Claire said, laughing. "I told you, my other brother is more your type. He's the solid and sincere one. Jesse's currently living aboard a sailboat without a penny to his name."

"Then we'd never work out." Cassia gave her wheelchair a slap. "I'm a landlubber all the way. Oh, well. It was just a fantasy. Of course I'm not *really* interested in getting married."

"Valentina's prophecy is too risky," Roxy said. "You could end up with Pete Lindstrom by mistake. He's right next door and up for grabs."

Cassia opened her mouth and stuck a finger toward her throat, and everyone laughed except Rose. She didn't know what animosity there was between Cassia and Pete, but the oldest brother, Terry, remained a thorn in her side. Up until this past summer, he'd come into the Buck Stop every month or so, to check up on her and make sleazy insinuations. He'd even asked about the baby once, and she'd lied and said she had no idea who'd adopted the child. The Lindstroms had always maintained that their son couldn't possibly be at fault for Rose's pregnancy, but she sometimes wondered if Rick's death had made them regret that stand. The very last thing she needed was to have the Lindstroms decide that they wanted to find and accept Danny as one of their own. If she was backed into a corner, she'd have to admit the truth. As if her reputation could sink any lower....

"I don't think Valentina makes mistakes," Claire said with a loving, gooey smile as Noah entered the foyer from the direction of the sunroom. Evan and Connor followed, all three of them tall, manly and breathtakingly gorgeous, even though they'd discarded their suit jackets and loosened their ties.

Rose pressed herself closer to the wall, ostensibly to let Claire pass, but mostly wanting to blend into the woodwork. Granted, she'd been welcomed as Evan's date without excessive fanfare. But it would take more than one or two public outings to make her comfortable around so many people.

Tess was making her way toward them from the opposite direction. "It's time for the tossing of the bouquet!" The crowd stirred, pouring into the hallway to watch the tradition.

"Gather 'round, girls," Emmie was saying.

Roxy and Rose exchanged a horrified look. "Get me outta here," Roxy said, leaping off the steps. She bounded into the gathering throng with Rose following in her wake, but Emmie grabbed hold of both their wrists and hung on for dear life.

Tess had lifted the skirts of her flowing cream silk dress and climbed the curving staircase. Claire joined her, an unconventional bride in the red dress and lace veil. They carried identical bouquets.

"One for both of you," Emmie said with determined cheer, trying to nudge Roxy and Rose forward. They resisted, letting the other single women move to the base of the steps with their hands outstretched.

"Aim one of them boo-kays right here at me," brayed a woman at the center of the knot, to genial laughter. Rose recognized the distinctive, mannish voice of Shari Shirley, who came into the Buck Stop for scandal papers and cigarettes and the occasional bottle of peach schnapps.

Tess went first, turning on the wide step and tossing the bouquet over her shoulder in a high, wide arc. Rose's eyes widened. It was coming straight at her. She stepped behind Emmie. Roxy ducked. And Emmie, both hands manacled to their wrists, was left defenseless as the bouquet smacked her in the middle of the forehead and rebounded into the arms of one of the bridesmaids. A cheer went up.

"That was a pitiful effort," Emmie scolded Roxy and Rose as she gave their arms a shake and let go.

No time to regroup. Claire made a quick, purposeful toss, aimed low toward the front of the crowd, where the flowers landed directly in Cassia Keegan's lap.

"Bull's-eye," Claire said, applauding her own accuracy.

Cassia picked up the bouquet, blushing with pleasure, or possibly embarrassment. "I'm going to get you for this," she said with a flustered laugh.

Rose squirmed along the edge of the group, making her way out of the limelight as the photographer organized the women for group photos.

Evan's voice stopped her. "You didn't even try for it," he said into her ear.

"I'd sooner die," she mumbled.

"That's not very complimentary to me."

She narrowed her eyes. "Maybe you're meant to marry Emma Koski," she said, naming the first recipient of the bridal bouquet. Emma was a lovely woman, graceful and willowy, and she was even a teacher like Evan. They'd make a stunning pair, perfectly suited. Jealousy spurted through Rose. "She's just your type."

"I thought so," he said. "But…nope. No chemistry."

Rose blinked. "Is there a woman here you haven't dated?"

Evan scanned the crowd. "Shari Shirley."

"Seriously."

"I missed Claire—Noah found her first." He shrugged. "Can I help it if every woman in town got all softhearted and maternal toward me after I became a widower? They showered me with sympathy and baked goods and offers of comfort."

"That's unseemly." Rose couldn't believe how prissy she sounded.

Evan caressed her neck, beneath her hair, and the gesture felt secret and intimate for all that they were surrounded by people. Prickles rose all along her neck and arms. "I like it when you're jealous," he said. "At least that means you're thinking of me…that way."

"You know I am." She couldn't deny it.

"Then maybe we should get out of here and take advantage of our time together? I have the baby-sitter until one a.m."

The invitation pulled Rose in several directions. She wanted to get away from the party, she wanted to be alone with Evan, but she didn't know if she could follow through on his expectations. She might lie there like a cold fish. She could even freak before they got to the lying-down part.

He was leading her toward the door. She tugged on his sleeve. "Wouldn't it be rude, leaving early, before midnight?"

"Let me handle the goodbyes. I'm experienced with inventive excuses—my students come up with some wowzers."

But they ended up saying goodbye to the newly-weds together, Rose shyly hanging back until Tess grabbed her in a warm hug. "You look great in that dress," the bride whispered.

"I'm supposed to be telling *you* that." Rose looked into Tess's eyes. "Thank you."

"Wear it well. Or not." Tess laughed as she moved on to hug Evan. "Don't do anything I wouldn't do," she told them.

That was too much for Rose—she was out the door, carrying her coat in her arms. "Slow down," Evan said, grasping her elbow as the door closed behind them. "You'll slip on the ice."

Rose stopped on the front porch and pulled on her same old peacoat. The sounds of revelry carried even beyond the thick stone walls of Bay House, which was decorated with evergreen swags, a five-foot plastic candy cane and strings of red-and-green lights.

The relative quiet and darkness eased her flight mode. Evan linked their arms and they walked down the circular driveway, lined with vehicles. He'd had to park outside of the grounds, on the verge of Bayside Road.

Rose let out a large, relieved sigh once they were well away.

"It wasn't so bad, was it?"

"Very nice," she said, watching as her new boots crunched through the snow. She was glad she'd gone. But even better was walking with Evan like this, in the bracing air, with the sounds of the reception growing distant and the stars as bright and hard as diamonds in the night sky.

"We've got an hour until midnight," he said, escorting her into the car. The interior was frigid and she huddled inside her coat, understanding why she hadn't missed wearing dresses, even with a pair of tights on underneath. Thermal underwear would have worked better.

Evan kicked at the chunks of snow behind the wheels before he got in and started up the car, turning the heater way up. "What should we do?"

Rose's teeth chattered. "Get warm."

"Ah. I was hoping you'd say that."

Her eyes widened. "I didn't mean—"

"Let's pretend you did."

Maybe she had, subconsciously. She tucked her chin inside the collar of her coat, smiling a little to herself.

"Should we try one of the bars? Or I could find us a bottle of champagne?"

"Honestly, I've had enough." There had been champagne at the reception and the bars in town only made her think of her father. "I'm not a big drinker."

"We could drive into Marquette and watch the ball drop." The small city did their own version of the New York City New Year's tradition, with the downtown packed with rowdy celebrants.

"Too crowded."

"The restaurant is serving a midnight buffet and hot buttered rum."

"I've eaten enough." Emmie had laid out an immense spread. "But if you want to go…"

"No," Evan said. He fell silent. The engine purred, pumping heat into the interior of the car. "The baby-sitter's at my house, so we can't go there."

"And my mother's home, of course. There's my cottage. It's not the most comfortable place, and not really set up for visitors, but if you wanted to come over for a while, that would be—"

"Thought you'd never ask." Wasting no time, Evan put the car in gear and maneuvered out of the bumper-to-bumper spot. It didn't take long to drive through town and soon they were pulling up to the cabins. There was an awkward moment when Rose realized she'd have to go in to say good-night to her mother, but Evan told her to go on without him while he called home to check in with the baby-sitter.

A few minutes later, they were tromping along the treed path. Rose felt slightly foolish, like a teenager sneaking behind a parent's back; she'd told her mother that Evan was only walking her to her door. Maxine was already tucked in for the night, doped up with cold medicine, and she'd merely grunted in vague, sleepy disapproval.

I can do as I please, Rose told herself. *I don't have to feel guilty. Sex doesn't always lead to trouble.*

Except for her.

She unlocked the door and they went inside. At least the heater was working and the temperature in the cottage was comfortable. Because of the stone walls, it was never warm enough, it seemed, but they weren't going to freeze. Especially if they got under the covers.

She pivoted away from the bed, nerve ends flittering, and took Evan's coat. She hadn't thought this through. "You can have the chair," she said. "Should I make coffee or tea? Hot chocolate?"

He sat, dusting a few flakes of snow off his hair. "No, thanks, I'm good."

She perched on the edge of the bed and unzipped her boots. "Need help?" he asked, watching with bright eyes as she peeled away the leather.

Her fingers fumbled. Was boot removal a provocative act? The boots were knee-high, with a two-inch heel, but underneath she wore opaque white tights that had bagged around her ankle. She ran her fingers over her leg, smoothing out the wrinkles.

Evan was still watching, his short hair bristled by the melted snow. Hot excitement swirled inside her as the flame in his eyes ignited her own desire. Each breath seemed to catch short so she wasn't quite able to breathe right. She felt skittish, but also absolutely wonderful. At last, she was a normal woman, experiencing a natural, normal attraction.

"No TV?" he said, looking around. "What about music?"

She licked her lips. "There's a radio."

While he went to tune the radio to a music station,

she pushed higher up on the bed, pulling her legs beneath her.

"Can I get in?" he said, not waiting for her answer as he kicked off his shoes, tossed his suit jacket aside and stretched out on the bed beside her as if they'd done this a hundred times. He caught her around the waist. "C'mere."

She slid closer. He had to feel how tense she was as he put his arm around her shoulders. "We don't have to do anything," he whispered in a low, velvet voice that was muffled by her hair. "Just hold each other."

She giggled—actually *giggled.* "And get warm."

"But if I wanted to kiss you…"

"I would say yes." And hope like hell that she'd only think of Evan.

He patted her arm, settled back like a contented man. "Okay. Good to know."

She waited a beat. He didn't move.

Several seconds went by. "Um, Evan?"

"Yeah?"

Okay, he was teasing her. She sucked in as deep a breath as she could manage. "What if it was me—if I, you know, if I wanted to, um, kiss you?"

"I'd say, um, *yes, ma'am.*"

She didn't look at him, just closed her eyes and pressed higher against his chest to reach his mouth, finding it with a slightly erring instinct as her nose bumped on his chin before their lips met, sliding into place like a lock and key. The moment stretched, with him letting her lead the way as the kiss slowly deepened.

She pulled back, waiting for his reaction instead of fearing her own.

"Ummm." He smiled. "You taste like peppermint."
Oops. She'd sneaked a breath mint on the drive over.

"The air is chilly in here. Let's go under the covers."

"Is that a line?" she asked as they rummaged about, pulling the duvet and blankets out from beneath them.

"It's a necessity." He chattered his teeth against her throat. And then they were laughing softly, rolling back and forth in the bed in a tangled embrace as they kissed and cuddled and burrowed deeper among the pillows.

The bedsprings creaked. Evan started serenading her in a joking way, half singing the lyrics to "Lay, Lady, Lay," but all he could remember was the part about the big feather bed. She smiled as she kissed him, stroking her fingers through his clipped hair, exploring the shape of his skull and the long lines of his throat. She nuzzled inside his collar, exultant. The hesitancy was gone.

He undid the loops of the satin cording at her neckline and slowly spread the edges, his large hand pressing flat and warm against her breastbone. "Your heart is pounding."

She was lying on her right side, and her left breast made a deep curve against the edge of his hand. Wanting to know his touch there, she angled toward him. His fingers spread, cradling her breast, his thumb rubbing her nipple through the nylon lace of her new bra. She shivered into the delicious sensations of warmth and arousal.

Evan kissed her, squeezing her breast in his hand as he turned her onto her back, his weight coming down on top of her. "Ahh, Rose," he breathed, layering her in heat and hard muscle and the masculine energy that was usually so overwhelming to her. She tensed, then made herself relax. This was good, she liked it. He wasn't hurting her.

It's good. One word and he'll stop. I know it.

But she didn't want him to stop.

"You okay?" he asked, rising up a little and trying to look at her face even though she hid it against his shoulder, clutching his shirt in her fists.

"Uh-huh." She wanted him to kiss her again; that would take away the doubts. But he was hesitating. "Kiss me?" she prompted, lifting her face.

His knuckles grazed her cheek in a thoughtful caress before he lowered his mouth over hers. She gave a soft moan in her throat, surrendering to the feeling, relieved that it was still there. He eased partway off her and held her in his arms, only that, while kissing her for long, loving minutes—a comforting, deeply sensual experience. She was enveloped but not overpowered. She was lulled.

His arousal was evident, but he made no moves to satisfy himself. After a while, she stroked a hand along his side. "Should I touch you?"

"Just keep your arms around me. That's all I want."

"No, really..."

"Really." His voice rasped and she felt him swallow and knew he was fighting to maintain control.

She pressed her cheek to his. "Thank you. I'm really sorry that I—I'm not very good at this—"

He chuckled. "If you get any better, I won't be able to stop myself."

"It's just that..." She hesitated, wondering if she should tell him about what had happened when she was sixteen. *Later, tomorrow, next year,* she decided, not wanting to ruin the tender moment with ugly memories.

"I guess I need to take this slowly." Dumb. That's what they'd been doing.

He was too much of a gentleman to point that out. "It's okay. I like this fine." He snuggled her against his chest. "But, you know what? I think we missed midnight."

"We did? I'm sorry."

"What for? I can't think of a nicer way to greet the New Year."

She smiled, bathed in the safety of feeling truly cared for by a man who put her comfort above his pleasure. He was a beautiful liar.

And she was falling in love.

CHAPTER TWELVE

"HEY, MR. SWANSON, can you wait up?" Evan abandoned the rack of basketballs he'd been pushing toward the locker room and trotted across the gym floor. "Do you have a few minutes?"

"Sure thing. But you have to call me Ken." The two men shook hands.

"Of course. Ken. Am I keeping you from anything important?"

"Only a roast beef," Swanson said, zipping up his quilted jacket. "It'll wait." He turned to his son and tossed him a jangling key ring. "Danny, you want to go warm up the car?"

The boy snatched the keys out of the air. "What, so you two can talk about me?" he asked, sheepishly tousling his hair while he looked from his coach to his father.

"Have you gotten into trouble I should know about, son?"

A wide grin split the teen's face. "Jeez, not that I can remember."

Evan waited a beat—confessions were often blurted out to fill a silence—then relented. "Don't worry. You're not in my doghouse. Except for those free throws you missed against the Hawks."

"I'll put in some extra practice, coach." Danny pulled on the hood of the gray sweatshirt he wore under his letterman's jacket and hurried from the gym. He straight-armed both double doors, shoving them wide open.

"What can I help you with?" Swanson said after the doors had swung shut.

Evan cleared his throat. He wasn't sure how to open the subject of Rose Robbin with a man he knew only in a professional capacity. If Danny had seemed troubled, Evan could have justified his involvement. But as it was, he suspected that this could only be called meddling.

"Just touching base," he said.

"Then Danny's not giving you a problem?"

"No, not at all. At the beginning of the season I was concerned about how he'd handle a starting position as a sophomore, but he's come through with flying colors. His grade point average could be a little higher, but it's well above the minimum."

Swanson was nodding. "Alana and I keep after him about always making time for studying first. We appreciate that you back us up on that. Some coaches are happy to let their athletes slide through on the academics."

"Not on my team." Evan rested his hands on his hips. "Danny seems to have no real problems there, if he stays dedicated. He's a smart kid."

"We're proud of him." Swanson pushed up his glasses and cuffed Evan's shoulder, rather awkwardly. The gesture wasn't natural to him. "So, coach, you planning on making a late run and coming on strong in the tournament?"

"We can hope."

"Competition's tough for a small school." They nodded in agreement, then fell silent. The last of the players left the locker room, calling "See ya, coach," as they departed.

The doors clanged shut. Evan knew it was time to explain. "This isn't really my place, Ken, but I wondered if I could speak to you about Danny's adoption. Maybe make a private appointment, so we can include your wife?"

Lines corrugated Swanson's high forehead. "Danny's adoption? I'm not following."

"I'm aware of the situation with the birth mother."

"Aha, I see. Last I heard, Wild—ah, Ms. Robbin wanted that kept quiet."

"She still does. This is only between us."

"She's had a change of heart, then?"

Evan wasn't sure what Swanson meant by that. "About?"

"Meeting Danny. The wife and I, we offered. Several times, but we were always cut off. The last was several weeks ago, around Christmas. Rose had mailed us a greeting card, and Alana said maybe she was softening up, so she sent me to the Buck Stop…" Swanson trailed off. "You don't know about that, eh?"

"No," said Evan. "Rose didn't mention it."

"Nothing to tell, I guess. She turned me down cold."

"I'm surprised to hear that."

Swanson shrugged. "No interest whatsoever."

"You're wrong there. You must have noticed how she's in the stands for every basketball game, watching Danny play."

"Of course."

"She does want to meet him, I know she does." Evan's gut wrenched. "But something's holding her back."

Swanson shrugged. "Sorry, I can't help you on that. Like I said, Alana and I are willing. I won't say we haven't had our worries about the outcome, but we never wanted to exclude Rose from meeting the boy entirely."

"How does Danny feel about that? What does he know?"

"Only that he's adopted, and that we've sent his birth mother updates on him. He's asked us about both of his birth parents, many times, but we kept telling him the mother's name was private and the father unknown."

Unknown. Aw, Rose.

Swanson continued. "Danny hasn't brought up the subject in a while, but there's always the legal approach when he turns eighteen. We won't be able to stop him then. And I'm not sure that we'd want to. It seems wrong to us, keeping the secret from Danny when Rose is right here in town."

Evan wondered if the boy would become angry when he realized that, for a couple of years now, his birth mother had been living nearby without him knowing it. No doubt. They could be opening up the proverbial can of worms, and at the busiest time of the year, with the last month of the regular season coming on and then play-offs in early March. But that was hardly a concern. Rose and Danny's welfare had to take precedence.

Evan eyed Swanson, who'd always seemed like a levelheaded, sensible guy. "Then you and your wife would be open to an introduction, if Rose will agree? I don't want to get her hopes up if you have any qualms about Danny's reaction."

"Well." Swanson frowned. "I'm not guaranteeing there wouldn't be some upheaval. Teenagers are volatile. And Alana will probably worry herself into a tizzy about the outcome. But, yes, go ahead. Set it up. If you can get Rose to agree."

There was the sticking point.

They shook on it anyway.

ROSE BEGAN TO GET BUSY in earnest on the mural for Lucy's room. One weekend toward the end of January, they got together to clear the bedroom of smaller items, grouping the large furniture in the center and covering it with a tarp. For the next week, Lucy would bunk on the couch.

With Lucy "helping," Rose and Evan primed the room and began work on painting everything but the white baseboards a pale sky-blue. Partway through the job, they took a long lunch break. Over sandwiches, chips and fruit, Rose explained her plan to work every morning for the next week on the mural, while Lucy and Evan were at school. Saturday, she and Evan would rearrange the furniture, hang new curtains and unveil the room for Lucy, in time to show it off for her birthday party the following day.

"And no peeping till then," Rose said, giving Lucy's nose a tweak over the kitchen table.

Evan reached for another handful of red grapes. "Ha. I'll have to nail the door shut each day."

Rose smiled. "I'll seal it with tape when I leave for the day."

"I *promise* not to peep." Lucy flopped her arms on the table and gave Rose and her father an exasperated eye roll. She was no longer the timid child who'd approached Rose in the woods nearly five months ago. Evan reported that she still had her fears and occasional panics, but they were not debilitating. She'd begun to thrive at school. All eight of her female classmates had been invited to the birthday party on Sunday.

"You sneaked a few peeks at your Christmas presents," Evan said.

"Dad, I was only *five* then."

"Ah. And now you're grown up?"

"Six takes two hands." Lucy rested her chin on the table, squinting one eye at the six fingers she held up with her arms extended. "How old are you, Rose?"

Rose opened and closed her hands, flashing fingers until she held up the remaining two in a peace sign.

Lucy calculated. "Fifty-two?"

Rose laughed. "Ouch."

"You did it too fast," Lucy complained.

Rose repeated the motion while Lucy counted by fives.

"And two." Peace sign.

"Thirty-three," Lucy said. "Wow. You're old."

"Lucy," Evan said, half laughing, half scolding. "Don't be sassy."

"That's all right. I'm feeling my age today." Rose stretched her arms overhead. "Painting's strenuous work." She caught Evan looking at her with an interested gleam in his eyes and she realized the shrunken T-shirt she'd worn for the messy job had pulled taut over her breasts and ridden up to her rib cage. She brought her arms down, but not all that quickly. "Your dad seems to be raring to go," she said to Lucy. "Should we let him finish up?" They still had two walls to paint.

He grinned. "No problem."

"You can do the walls while I start on the clouds." She intended to paint clouds on the ceiling today while the paint was fresh and she could blend the edges more easily.

Lucy wasn't paying attention. Her head lolled on the table and she let out a deep moan, flopping the noodle arms and being quite the actress.

Evan reached over and gave her shoulders a rub. "Luce, you've put in your time. Why don't you go and watch TV while we work?"

Her head popped up. Her rosy cheeks were sprinkled with blue paint freckles. "Can I take cookies and a juice box?"

He looked at Rose. She'd told him that he fed Lucy too much junk food.

She flushed. "Don't look at me. I'm not the boss of this house."

"Go ahead," he said to Lucy.

She grabbed the juice from the fridge, got cookies from a drawer and ran off to the living room, then was back two seconds later to say, "Thank you, Daddy, thank you, Rose." She made a thoughtful face. "Rose…if you're so old, how come you don't have a little girl of your own?"

Rose tried not to react, but she knew that Evan had seen her flinch. She opened her mouth and started to stammer a say-nothing response.

Evan interrupted. *"Lucy,"* he warned. "Scoot."

Rose gave a shaky laugh. "Kids cut straight to the chase, don't they?"

He began clearing the table, a transparent excuse to give her time to collect herself. But he didn't let the subject drop. "Do you ever consider it?" He rinsed glasses and returned to wipe the table. "Having another child?"

She swallowed. "Not really. I didn't think of myself as the motherly type."

She never used to. Now…she wondered.

The prospect wasn't as far-fetched as she'd once believed. She'd even had a few daydreams about marrying Evan and being Lucy's stepmom—not that she'd admit it out loud. He might become alarmed that his temporary fix-it project had already gotten too attached.

Not to mention having fallen in love, goon that she was.

Evan's take on their situation remained bewildering. She knew for sure that he wanted to *make* love to her. Since New Year's, they'd gone out a couple of times and had managed to steal a few private minutes here and there for kissing and cuddling. Nothing heavy. But whenever she got close to him, she felt Evan's lust—and his control of it. At times, she was nearly as hungry as he, and had almost convinced herself that she was ready to say yes.

But the possibility of hurt feelings and bad endings was stronger than her tentative progress toward love, and so far that had always stopped her. She had no faith in happiness.

And then there was the last remaining secret that stood between them—the true circumstances of Danny's conception. A lie of omission on her part, but a lie nonetheless. Evan's feelings for her might change once he knew the whole story.

She was startled out of her glum thoughts when he laid his hand on her shoulder. "I've said it before. You underestimate yourself. You're a very capable person."

"Motherhood takes more than capability. I already failed once."

"You were young. You didn't get the chance to try."

She shrugged. "Can we just go back to the painting?"

He agreed, though he *still* didn't give up on the topic. Once they were in Lucy's bedroom, him busy with the roller and her mixing shades of off-white and blue-gray, he brought it up again. "Maybe you're not ready to think about having another child because you need to, you know, fix things with Danny."

The stir stick became suspended in midair. Rose watched paint droplets splat into the pan. Finally she cleared her throat. "Fix things, huh?"

Evan continued painting. "Yeah, I said it. Fix things."

"I'm guessing you're here to tell me how to do that?"

"Not to *command* you, but I'm ready to do what I can to help you."

"And that would be?"

The roller moved up and down the wall. His biceps flexed. He looked at Rose sidelong, gauging her reaction. Her tone had been dry and cool. His was casual, chatty. They were both putting up a good front.

"Coming clean," he said.

The stick clattered against the mixing pan when she dropped it. "Clean?" She laughed shortly. "You have no idea. That's not an option."

"Of course it is."

"No, it's not. You really don't know how—how—" Her voice constricted, then came out in a tight, hurting fury. "It was all so *dirty.*"

He'd finally stopped painting and was looking at her, baffled. "What? If you're talking about your wild reputation, I don't think that even matters anymore. It's been more than a decade, Rose. No one—"

"That's not it," she said between clenched teeth.

"Then what? Because I talked to Ken Swanson, and he mentioned he'd invited you to meet Danny, and—"

"Oh, God." Rose moaned. "You two were talking about me? Conniving behind my back?"

"It wasn't like that. Or maybe it was." He put the roller in the pan, looking confused. "I had good intentions."

Still crouched, she dropped her head, pretending great interest in the contents of her mini paint pans. "I know that."

"But I'm wandering around blindfolded," he said.

She almost laughed. He had that right. The explanation was right there in front of him, ready to trip him up. But he didn't see it.

She'd have to explain if she wanted to move forward, and that meant digging deep to carve out her heart.

Not necessarily. Maintain your distance. It's been more than fifteen years. That's long enough for the tears to dry up and the wounds to heal and even for the scars to fade.

Then why did she feel so raw?

Ignoring Evan's expectant look, she began arranging her paint pans on the tray of the ladder. She laid out assorted brushes and stuck clean rags in the pockets of her jeans before climbing the ladder.

He tossed a hand up, obviously frustrated with her stonewalling. "That's it? Subject closed?"

The noise of the TV carried through the house—frantic, zippy jingles and the accompanying sound effects of children's programming. So normal it comforted Rose. She took a brush and painted in a few blue-gray streaks, then boldly swished the off-white paint alongside, making a free-form blob, which she quickly blotted with a rag, softening and rounding the edges, blending the two shades to give the cloud depth. She was hyperaware of Evan, standing to one side, watching silently.

She knew she had to "come clean." No matter what the result. But it was so hard. She remembered how it had been with Roxy, telling her of the past she'd buried. Once the first words were said, the stone on her heart would lift and maybe she could go on this time. Evan deserved to know what he was getting into with her.

"I was raped," Rose said. Suddenly the floodgates opened. "Rick Lindstrom wasn't Danny's father. His father—his *biological* father—was a rapist. For me, that's always seemed to be reason enough to keep my mouth shut."

She closed her eyes for a few brief seconds, leaning heavily into the ladder because it felt like she might lose her balance. Evan had made a sound, a short, harsh grunt, as if he'd been sucker-punched, but that was all.

Shock, she thought, easing her grip on the ladder.

She straightened and stared up at the cloud without seeing it. "So, uh, can you hand me a clean brush? I need a big one."

Evan obeyed by rote, his face a mask. Except that she saw the concern and confusion clouding his eyes when she reached for the brush and made the mistake of glancing into his face. A glut of emotions threatened to rise up, but she battled them back, concentrating on the ceiling. *Swish, swish, swish.* With a deft touch, she dragged the dry brush back and forth over the edges of the cloud, blurring and blending. Dulling the pain, too.

Years and years ago. Decades. Ages. She was over it.

"Rose," Evan said. "Why didn't you tell me?"

"What's the use?" She shrugged. "You can't fix this one."

"No, but at least I'd have understood better."

The brush stilled. She studied the cloud for a long minute, not wanting to turn, but in the end she couldn't help it. She looked at him.

The unpleasant truth was hitting him now. His face was red, and his muscles were bunched up. Tension radiated off him like steam. A very male reaction. Which might have been disconcerting, if she'd believed even a shred of the anger was directed at her. With other men from her past, maybe, but with Evan, she knew it was not. He wanted to dispense justice. Punishment.

Too late. I blew the chance for that.

"Then you agree," she said. "It would be wrong to get involved in Danny's life when that would mean exposing him to a lot of ugliness."

"Wait. I didn't say that."

"I've already made the decision." She went back to painting, daubing in the bright white. "He's better off without me."

"You're wrong."

"What do you know?"

"I know that Danny wants to meet you. He needs to know—" Evan flexed his fists. "Maybe not the whole story, but…"

"I'm sure he's expecting something different. A sweet, beautiful mother, a dashing father. Lovers torn apart." Rose snorted. "Talk about your far-fetched fairy tales."

"Danny's fifteen, not five. No doubt he's figured out that a woman doesn't give up her baby unless she's troubled."

Troubled. Such a polite way of putting it. Wounded, terrified and half-crazy was more like it.

Rose climbed down the ladder. "It's one thing to suspect and another thing to know. It may have been a long time, but people here still call me Wild Rose. Can you imagine growing up in the same small town all your life, secure in a respected family, and then one day finding out that your mother is the town's outcast?"

"You have a point," Evan said. "But you're not an outcast now, if you were before."

She thought of the past several months and knew he was right. And even when she had been an outcast, it was of her own making. She'd always withdrawn or run away rather than stand her ground and fight for herself.

She'd tried to run, the night of the rape, when her instincts had warned her to get away. He'd caught her. She'd tried to fight. He'd been stronger. Of course he had—she'd been a skinny girl who talked tough to hide a broken heart and he'd been an older man, midthirties, one of a small hunting party who were staying at the cottages. Smelling of booze and cigars and sweat and stale blood…

Revulsion rolled through her. She swallowed hard, avoiding Evan's eyes while she mindlessly fiddled with her paint pans, preparing to move the ladder.

Suddenly he was there. His arms going around her, hugging her against his chest. "You're not an outcast. Don't even think that way. Danny will be lucky to know you. He'll grow to love you."

She could only shake her head; her throat was clotted.

"You've already made contact. The first meeting will be hard, I know. You'll both be nervous. But after that, it'll get easier. I promise."

Oh, God, she wanted to believe him! If only she could turn her life over to Evan and let him solve all her problems. So easy. So seductive.

So wrong.

Really? said another part of her head. *Seems like he's been doing a damn good job of fixing you up.*

"You promise, hmm?" She took a big sniff. Wimpy, but better than crying. "Your powers reach that far, do they?"

His chest gave a hitch. "Huh. Remember, I'm Mr. Fix-It." He kissed the top of her head. "And I'm only paying back the favor. Look what you've done for Lucy—she's a changed girl."

"That wasn't me."

"You had a hand in it. So let me take a turn and set something up with the Swansons." He squeezed her. "Okay?"

She leaned the side of her head on his crossed arms. "I'll think about it."

"Don't let the rape—that *man* stop you. He's caused enough hurt. Don't let him have power over your future."

That sounded good, but easier said than done. Evan couldn't possibly understand the layers of guilt and shame and fear that kept her muffled.

She sighed, savoring the feeling of being held by him for just another moment before pushing away to return to her painting project. "You haven't asked. Everyone asks." Roxy hadn't, but she wasn't nosy or judgmental—like Rose's parents. "If you can call the few people I've told a consensus, that is."

"Asked…about the rape?"

She climbed onto the ladder. "Who he is." Second rung. "How it happened." Third. "Why I didn't press charges." Fourth rung. High enough to reach the ceiling. She picked up the pan of blue-gray, mindful of Evan staring up at her. *No, don't look down. Keep busy.*

"I don't know if you should tell me. If it's someone local…" He didn't need to say more. His voice seethed.

"Don't worry. He's long gone."

"Free."

"I'm afraid so. He was never arrested, because I didn't tell anyone what happened."

"Not even your mother?"

"She may have suspected that something was wrong. But she didn't ask." No one had been allowed to make a fuss in their household except Black Jack. "Even if she had, I wouldn't have told. I was used to keeping secrets and hiding my pain. I'd been in a funk anyway, about getting dumped by Rick, so I guess she assumed my snarly, don't-come-near-me act was just another teenage mood."

Pretty amazing, she thought, swirling paint on the ceiling. She'd managed to say all that in a conversational tone. As if that injured girl had become more removed from her, now that she'd finally taken steps to change her attitude.

"He was a hunter from Illinois, that's all I know. Oh, and his last name, or maybe his nickname, was Pike."

"There would have been a registry, for the cottage."

"Probably. I could have looked him up. I never did." She slapped paint against the ceiling, blinking at the overspray. Too hard. "I didn't want to know."

"The statute of limitations—"

"Don't, Evan. After all this time, there's no chance of conviction. I made my decision. Yeah, I regretted it later, when I grew up a little, got some education on rape violence and became really angry over the injustice. But I'm over it now—as over it as I can be. If there really is a hell, or karma, he'll get what he deserves."

"But I want him to suffer."

She set the paintbrush aside. "Hmm."

"What?" Evan demanded. "He shouldn't suffer?"

"Oh, yes," she said. "Excruciatingly so." Over the years, she'd imagined a number of gory, tortured ends for the guy.

"Then what's the hesitation for?"

"It's complicated." Hot blood rushed into her face as she sent up a prayer. *Please let Evan understand.* "I, uh…I flirted with the guy when his party arrived at the cottages. Even though he wore a wedding ring. I wasn't entirely innocent."

She took a quick look at Evan's expression and hurried on. "I'm not saying the rape was my fault. For a while, I was fooled into thinking that maybe it was. The old 'she asked for it' excuse. Y'know." It always amazed her how many men were quick to latch on to that one. Even good guys.

"I was rebellious by then. Their first night, before the hunt, a couple of the group were hanging out around the cabins. They offered me a beer and I took it. I was putting on an act, flirting, drinking, thinking I could handle it. Nothing happened then, but I ran into the one called Pike the night before they were leaving. I was coming home around three in the morning, cutting through the woods near the cabins. He called me over. I went and talked to him. He kissed me. I'd smoked weed earlier with a couple of other outcasts and I was still a little high, so I let him, but he was awful—drunk and smelly. It got weird. I knew I should leave. He tried again and I hit him in the face with a broken tree branch. Broke his nose. Enraged him, too. I ran, but he was faster and stronger and that's when…it happened."

Silence. She stared at the clouds, wishing she could soar away.

She heard Evan exhale. "There's no question. It wasn't your fault."

"I know that now. But I wanted you to have the full story."

"Why didn't you—" He shook his head. "Dumb question. Sorry."

Call the police. Tell your parents or a friend. Go to the hospital. She'd tortured herself many nights with thoughts of how she might have done any of those things and turned the course of events onto a path that led to her keeping her baby.

"A couple of months later, I realized I was pregnant. My mom caught me throwing up one morning and she freaked out. Then my dad got into the act." Rose shuddered. "I told you about the rest of it—the fighting, the 'consultations' with the Lindstroms. You can imagine how thrilled they were with the prospect of my carrying their grandchild. Even so, for a couple of minutes, I thought I might be able to pretend that Rick was the father and that we would get married, but…"

She looked at Evan from the ladder. His face was as drained as she felt. "He said no way was he going to marry me, even if the baby was his. I was Wild Rose Robbin, a slut. If we tried to press for child support, he'd get a bunch of his friends to swear they'd been with me." She lifted her shoulders and screwed up her face in a grimace, then went limp again. "That was finally enough for me. I ran away."

Evan backed up until he could lean against the wall, forgetting about the fresh paint. "God, Rose. That's horrible." He slid down to the floor, his knees up. "I'm so sorry that happened to you."

"Yeah." She tried to smile. "Me, too. It sucked."

"Danny—"

"No, I'll *never* tell him. I don't care if he thinks I really was a slut who slept around with half the town. That's better than the truth."

"Not for you."

"It's all I have to give him," she said with the last of her reserves. A deep fatigue hit her and it took a moment to manufacture her old I-don't-give-a-damn attitude.

"Anyway, it's been fifteen years, right? Who cares anymore?"

"Nobody," he said. She'd never heard Evan be that sarcastic. "Except us. And the Swansons. And a few other people you haven't yet managed to chase out of your corner."

He was so dead-on she almost smiled. It was strange, not standing alone. She wasn't sure she liked it, but if Evan and Lucy came with the deal she might be able to adjust.

Enough of that. Rose went back to painting as if she hadn't spilled her guts. Evan seemed as if he wanted to keep talking, but she kept busy and didn't give him the chance, intent on creating a storybook heaven for a little girl who'd already known enough of the harsh reality of the world.

Rose wanted this for Lucy. For every child. Perhaps it was a gift to herself, as well.

CHAPTER THIRTEEN

ROSE PAINTED with a purpose for the next week, until her head swirled with stone walls and green fields and mountain caves where ogres dwelled. Their schedules rarely connected, so she didn't see much of Evan. They left notes for each other on his fridge—cozy, domestic stuff like "There's leftover stir-fry, if you want. I used the cookbook and didn't set off any alarms," and "Hi, I drank the last of the orange juice. See you at the basketball game."

Snow fell heavily throughout the week, but nothing could keep Rose from finishing the mural. Early every morning she made breakfast and an easy lunch for her mother, then performed the dozen other tasks that Maxine manufactured to set her up for the day. But as soon as the snowplows had been down Blackbear Road, Rose was in the car and on the way to the Grants' house in town. Afternoons and evenings she continued with her drudge work at the convenience store, needing to accumulate enough hours so she could afford to take the weekend of Lucy's birthday off.

By Saturday, they were all three ready for the project to be done. Evan and Rose moved the furniture in, making up the bed with new white eyelet lace bedding.

They hung a matchstick blind from Target and simple, blue cotton curtains sewn by Maxine as her contribution to the makeover.

By then, Lucy was outside the door, rattling the knob. "Is it ready yet?"

Evan glanced over the room. "Ready?"

Rose wadded up the packaging from the comforter and blinds and stuck it under her arm instead of in the empty wastebasket. With a stomach full of butterflies, she tucked a strand of hair behind her ear and said, "Okay. Ready."

He went to the door, making a megaphone with hands. "Lucy, back away from the door. I'm coming out to get you."

Rose followed closely, slipping sideways out into the hallway in case Lucy tried to peek.

"What should we do, make her put on a blindfold and say, 'Surprise'?"

"Oh, Dad." Lucy took charge, flinging the door open and bursting into the bedroom before either of them could protest.

They looked at each other, laughed and chorused, "Happy Birthday!"

Lucy had stopped short when she saw the room. The fairy-tale mural was all-encompassing, the ceiling and every wall painted, and even the wood floor, which was an emerald green with patches of wildflowers, dressed with a lily pond rug. The princess's rose-covered cottage was the most prominent feature, but there was also a thick, dark forest, two castles on the hills, a village, sheep and snow-capped mountains in the distance. A hundred small details awaited Lucy's discovery.

Rose couldn't help herself. "Do you like it?"

"Of course she likes it," Evan said. "Look at her."

Lucy was speechless.

"Here's Princess Kristina," Rose pointed out. She'd painted the blond princess near the cottage, tending a rose garden.

Lucy gasped. "And the ogre!" She laughed, rushing over to examine the scene. The ogre was hidden among the trees near his cave, watching the princess.

"Princess Jade is here, standing on the ramparts of the family castle." Rose traced her fingertips over a small figure featured in the hilltop castle. "And here are the king and queen at the front door, waiting for Kristina's return."

"What about the prince?" Evan asked. The prince was a recent addition to the story, but Lucy hadn't decided yet if he was to rescue the princess or be eaten by the ogre.

"There he is, Dad." Lucy ran over to another wall, where Rose had painted a river, an arched stone bridge and a prince on horseback, riding the trail that led to the princess's cottage. "Swans," she said, discovering details. "And a jumping fish. And a frog on a lily pad." She followed the meandering river into the corner of the room, sliding behind the armchair and out the other side. "Look—a little boy fishing!"

"You're amazing, Rose." Evan put his arm around her.

"It was fun."

"This could lead to a part-time job for you. After Lucy's birthday party, every six-year-old in town will want one of your murals."

"Oh, no, I doubt it."

"No need to be modest. You're talented. It won't hurt to let people know."

"I have been thinking of—" She stopped. Then made herself start again. "Now that the mural is finished, I'm going to work on my watercolor paintings. Maybe in the spring…well, we'll see."

Evan nodded, his eyes warm and encouraging.

She stood a little taller. His hand rested on her upper arm and her shoulder nudged his side and it all felt so fitting she wanted to stay like that forever.

"Where's the green bird that brings the magic stone?" Lucy said without looking at them.

"Hm. I don't remember. You'll have to find the bird yourself." Rose had glued an actual polished stone to the wall so it looked like the bird carried it in its beak.

Lucy sighed happily. "Oh, boy."

Evan leaned his forehead against hers. "Thanks."

"You're welcome."

"I'll write you a check."

She blinked. "This wasn't about money."

"I know. Even so…"

He brushed his lips over her cheek and whispered in her ear, so quickly she wasn't sure she'd heard right, but her heart was suddenly pounding like a drum because he might have said, "Love you." He cleared his throat, raising his voice for Lucy, who couldn't have cared less about the adults—she'd discovered the small band of wild ponies Rose had painted in one of the golden fields. "Be right back."

Bobble-kneed, Rose went and sat on the bed.

"I like the little black-and-white one," Lucy said, standing on the mattress for a better look. "Rose…do you think the ponies would be faster than an ogre?"

"I'm pretty sure."

"Then Princess Kristina could ride one home."

"That's a great idea."

"Maybe. But it's a long way to go." With a contented sigh, Lucy plopped onto the bed beside Rose. "This is my best ever birthday."

"I'm glad." Rose put an arm around the girl, sliding her palm along the narrow shoulder blades, thinking of how familiar and precious Lucy had become to her in the past months. Rose knew the girl's moods and dreams, she knew that Lucy liked to watch *Dexter* on Saturday mornings, got hives if the wrong detergent was used to wash her clothes, and had memorized all the words to "Superstar" and sang them to herself in the bathtub.

She was presumptuous, Rose knew, but she felt as if she finally had some idea what it was like to be a mother. Accepting the invitation to meet Danny seemed almost possible.

You're normal now, you can fit in, she thought, as Lucy hugged her around the waist. *Lucy grew to love you. Danny might, too.*

Rose stroked the girl's hair. "Yes, the best birthday ever. And just think, it's barely begun."

A WEEK PASSED and February arrived with a blustery fury. At school, Evan was extremely busy with his classes and his team. At home, he was barely maintaining order in his household. Now that Lucy was more active and social, he was expected to keep up with a growing schedule of skating and sledding dates, after-school activities and even sleepovers. Giving her the cell phone had turned into a mistake. She called her little friends more than she called him, which pleased him, but also made him wonder when she'd grown up into this female-type creature who giggled and squealed and had suddenly developed a fashion sense that was diametrically opposed to his method of pulling two garments from the closet and handing them to her.

It was all so perplexing. At six, *he'd* been into mud puddles and rock piles.

On a Friday morning after a short and lousy night's sleep, Evan woke to a thick, fresh snowfall that was still coming down. His bleary eyes widened as he stared out the frosted window at the winter wonderland. A swirling wind had sculpted the snow into waist-deep drifts, including a deep curve with a knife-sharp edge that curled back from his windowsill like a wave crashing on a rock. The snowboarders and skiers would be out full force, and once he'd have been among them.

Now he had responsibilities.

Maybe not today. Before starting the morning routine, he went to the kitchen and turned on the radio, finding one of the local stations that gave reliable school closing updates. He went to the bathroom and returned in time for the weather report, dry swallowing a couple of aspirin tablets as he listened. The prediction was for snow. Thirteen inches had already fallen and there was no end in sight.

Lucy stumbled into the kitchen holding a stuffed animal. Her pajamas were askew and her ponytail had migrated across her head so it stuck out on one side like a misplaced antenna. "Mmph. Daddy?"

"Shhh, baby."

The announcer had started in on the list of school closings. "Come on, come on," Evan coaxed, feeling like a kid again. Last night, the basketball team had had a miserable road game. They'd traveled nearly two hundred miles for the privilege of losing by a free throw at the buzzer. The players' bus had pulled back into Alouette at two o'clock in the morning and it had been even later when Evan got home, meaning he'd had about four hours of sleep. He needed this day off.

The announcer reeled off a list of schools before finally closing with "…and Alouette public schools are closed today due to snow."

Evan let out a whoop and swung Lucy off her feet. "No school today!"

She giggled. "But I wanted to go to school."

He set her down. "I can see I haven't been teaching you right. Snow days are Mother Nature's special treat to schoolkids—and teachers. We have to use this day as the gift it is."

Lucy hugged her puppy-dog. "What do we do?"

"First thing we do is go back to bed."

She wrinkled her nose.

"My room," he said. "Just this once." After her mother's death, when he'd been cut down with his own grief, Lucy had gotten into the habit of sleeping in his bed. Even when he forced himself to be strict and make her sleep in her own room no matter how much she cried, she'd sneak into his bed during the night. It had been many months before she'd sleep the entire night through on her own.

This time, he was thinking of his own needs. "Give me another hour to sleep and then I'll make you whatever you want for breakfast," he bargained.

"Pancakes?" she said, taking his hand.

"Pancakes," he agreed.

"Shaped like animals."

He fixed her antenna. "As long as they can be alien animals that no one on earth has ever seen before."

"I'LL BE LEFT ALONE all afternoon," Maxine said from her chair in front of the TV. She flipped back to the weather channel. "Might as well shove me into an old folks' home and forget all about me so you can go gallivanting all you want."

Gallivanting? Rose hadn't gallivanted since she was sixteen. "You're only fifty-six, Mom." But the attitude added thirty years. "There are still things you can do."

"I should sell this place and move away. The doctor says Arizona would be good for my lungs."

If only. "Go ahead. Anytime. Let me know and I'll call the real estate agent."

Maxine noisily sucked air through her mask. "Oh, you're a hardhearted girl! I get no sympathy."

"You get more than enough," Rose muttered under her breath. She was sitting at the table, paging through well-thumbed ladies' magazines while she waited for Evan to pick her up. The skies had cleared and the plows had been through. He'd called right after lunchtime to ask if she wanted to go sledding with him and Lucy. Maxine wasn't happy about the prospect of being left alone, even through Rose had been boxed in the house with her for the past twenty-four hours.

"Where's Jake? Why doesn't my Jakey come home to take care of me and put this business back on its feet?" Maxine fumbled for the cordless phone. "Give me Jake's number. I want to call him and tell him how you're neglecting me."

Maxine's voice had drilled into Rose's skull. She

gritted her teeth and pressed her fingers to her temples to keep her brain from exploding out the holes. "Jake doesn't have a number, remember? He's out at sea on an oil platform, making good money." Smart guy, getting away. The farther the better.

Maxine's head and shoulders slumped. "I wish Jake was here. Or your father."

Absence makes the heart grow fonder. Rose exhaled and tried again. "Mom, I am not neglecting you. I'm getting out of the house for a couple of hours to have some fun. You don't begrudge me that, do you? Is it so wrong of me to want a normal life?"

"But then you'll leave me alone….."

Finally Rose understood. This wasn't about today. "Mom, I promise. I'm not going anywhere anytime soon."

Maxine's head bobbed. "That's right. Don't get your hopes up. Most men can't be trusted to do the right thing, especially with a girl like—"

Rose cut her mother off. "That's enough." She shot up and went to the front closet to get her jacket, hat and gloves. "I'll be outside, shoveling the walk, until Evan and Lucy get here. See you in a few hours."

"But, Rosie…"

She let the door slam shut behind her.

"YOU HAVE NO IDEA how much I needed this," Rose said an hour later from the top of Bayside hill. The sky was a soft blue that looked like more snow, but for now the downfall had stopped. A steep expanse of white stretched before them, dotted with the color and activity of at least a dozen snowsuited kids and a few teenagers and adults as well. Every few seconds another sled shot down the hill, accompanied by gleeful shouts. The freedom of getting a day off from school enhanced the enjoyment.

Rose and Evan panted companionably, having just trudged up the hill for what must have been the tenth time. "Being cooped up with my mother was driving me crazy."

He kissed her forehead. "You're a saint."

She laughed sheepishly. "Hardly. I take care of her out of guilt, not goodness." The kiss was stinging cold, but very heartwarming.

"I left her alone with my dad for a lot of years. No matter how she talks about him now, I know that was no picnic."

"You're not to blame for saving yourself. You had to get out."

She punched his arm. "How come you always say the right thing?"

"Practice?"

He said that like it was a joke, but Rose became thoughtful as they waited for Lucy to rejoin them. Which was taking a while, since she'd found a school-mate and the two girls were making snow angels in a patch of untrampled snow midway up the hill, giggling as they fell over backward and swooped their out-stretched arms through the snow.

Evan stabbed Lucy's bright pink plastic sled into the softer snow piled at the edges of the sled run. He put his arm around Rose. She leaned into him, perfectly content.

Except for the reminder that she was Evan's latest project. That didn't mean his feelings for her weren't real, but she wondered—what happened when the project was complete?

They hadn't talked much about Krissa except how her death had affected Lucy. But there had been little hints along the way, and Rose had collected them to draw her own picture.

"Practice?" she echoed. Her tone was arch.

"Placating females," he said easily.

"Is that so?" Darting like a rabbit, she scooped up a handful of the sugary snow and shoved it down the neck of his jacket.

He howled, shaking the snow out as he came after her. She was ready, packing another scoop into a snowball that she tossed at him point-blank, splattering his chest. Suddenly another snowball flew through the air from the opposite side, almost knocking Evan's knit hat off. "Lucy!" he said, acting shocked. She stood beside her friend, laughing behind her snowy mittens.

Within seconds, the white missiles were flying in all directions as others joined in. Evan was getting pelted the worst, stuck in the middle of the melee. He grabbed his daughter's sled, threw it down and jumped onto it on his stomach. "I'm making my getaway," he yelled, shoving off.

"Not without me!" Rose ran behind him as he picked up speed, making a last-second belly flop right on top of him.

They careened down the hill, skidding sideways as they hit a ridge near the bottom. The sled tilted and they toppled over in a tangle of limbs and laughter and a dusting of snow.

"You're a bad driver," she said, trying to catch her breath, but she couldn't stop laughing.

He rolled over on top of her. "We were top-heavy. Like this."

She pushed at him, and he flopped onto his back. "No, like this." She slung her right arm and leg over him.

"Not exactly." He took her by the collar and pulled her close enough to kiss. "But it'll do."

His lips were cold but his tongue was warm. Rose broke off the kiss after only a few seconds, lifting her head. "Where's Lucy?"

"It won't hurt her to see us kiss."

Rose sat up and dusted off her front and sleeves. "How do you know? She might be traumatized. Her mother..."

"I know. But months ago, she asked me if I kissed you. She wanted to have mistletoe at Christmas, but I couldn't find any."

Rose laughed, startled. "The little matchmaker."

"She likes you."

"But that's different than...you know."

"Seeing you take her mother's place?" Evan rose to his elbows. "We've talked about that, and she understands as well as a six-year-old can that she never has to replace her mother. But she was so young when Krissa died. It's inevitable that she's going to forget."

"That's sad."

"Yeah. But I'm doing my best to keep Krissa's memory alive for her. We tell stories about her mother all the time."

"That's important." Rose plucked at the fingertips of her gloves. Her face was beginning to feel warm. Anyone listening to them would think they were serious. Marriage-serious. And they hadn't even...

Evan's thoughts must have been going in the same direction. He looked up. Rose followed his gaze and saw Lucy and her friend skidding down the hill on the butts of their slippery nylon ski pants. "Can you come over tonight?" he asked quickly. "Lucy has a sleepover. June Caldwell called right before we left for sledding. It'll be Lucy's first time away overnight, but I think she'll be okay."

Rose started nodding. "Sure. Lucy said Sierra Caldwell is her best friend now."

"Then you'll come?" He reached for her hand. "No expectations. Just, you know—" he grinned engagingly "—a little grown-up time away from children and parents."

THERE WAS SOMETHING SPECIAL about the day after a blizzard. Maybe it was the gentle hush of a world muffled beneath a thick layer of snow. Or the vigor of venturing outdoors again, blood rushing against the cold, lungs inhaling the fresh, brittle air. It could be the phenomenon of starting over with a clean slate—all was white and new again.

And maybe it was simply the joy of survival.

Rose felt all of the above as she stood at the picture window in Evan's living room, watching fat flakes waft out of the pewter sky. A thin line of gold was slipping away behind the roofline of the house across the street. Soon it would be dark and she'd have to draw the curtains if she didn't want Evan's neighbors seeing her, standing in his lamp-lit living room, bold as brass, waiting for "Coach" to make love to her.

She sipped a glass of wine, feeling sophisticated, like a painting titled Woman Anticipating Lover. It took very little to make her feel sophisticated. Her experience was so limited.

Evan was kind and patient. She knew he'd accept it if she backed out. Possibly he'd even told the truth when he said he had no expectations, but he was still a man, after all, and she knew men....

Nervousness danced inside her. Better not to think of other men. Focusing on Evan was the only way to do this.

"Done," he said, coming out of the kitchen.

"That didn't take long."

"I stuck a few containers in the fridge and tossed the plates into the dishwasher." Their dinner had been another deli special—a roast chicken, salad, chunks of barbecue-flavored potatoes.

She'd gone home for a few hours to placate her mother. Evan had delivered Lucy to her friend's house. She'd called only once, so that Evan could reassure her that the clanking in the basement was an oil furnace and not a ghost with chains.

And finally they were alone, together.

"Here we are," Rose said. Alone together. Much nicer than alone apart.

"No papers to grade."

"No beer to sell."

"No kids to interrupt."

"Or complaining mothers."

"So..." Evan rubbed his hands. "What do we do now?"

Her heart hammered. She laughed a stupid, fill-the-silence laugh.

"I wasn't—" He folded his arms, as if to prove he was not intending to grab her, but the way he looked at her was so bold she felt as if she'd been touched. "We could always watch a video."

"I don't think so." Slowly, carefully, she set down her wineglass. "We've been waiting nearly five months to be alone."

Now *he* seemed nervous. "Has it been that long?"

"Uh-huh." She nodded. Walked to him, slid her hands around to the back of his neck, in full view of the window. What the hell.

"We've been alone many times."

They had. Painting, shopping, walking in the woods—but rarely alone on a date.

His eyes darkened. "What about that time, in your cottage—"

"Aborted effort. My fault. But I deserve a second chance." Her fingers played with the fringe of hair at his nape.

"Are you trying to seduce me, Mrs. Robinson?"

She gave a token smile at the quote from *The Graduate,* too tense to laugh. "I've never seduced anyone in my life."

"In that case, you're doing exceptionally well." He inched closer, linking his hands around her waist. They were joined like an infinity symbol, a continuous loop of shivery emotion and arousal. "I can't wait to see what you do next."

CHAPTER FOURTEEN

ROSE'S LASHES DROPPED before Evan could see into her eyes. He wasn't reading her that well—and he needed to. Already his body was on fire and hard as a rock, but he didn't want her thinking she was obligated. Especially considering her history, which had given him a few sleepless nights resulting in a fresh avowal to handle her like a fragile piece of crystal.

He could imagine her scoffing at that. She liked to think she was tough, and she was. But not all the time. Or all the way through.

"You don't have to wait," she said. Her eyes closed as she tilted her face toward his and found his mouth. Her lips were sweet and red with wine. He held himself very still. Afraid to move—one twitch and his control would be history.

"Come on," she said softly, cupping the back of his head. "It's okay. You can kiss me back. Unless…"

He let out a groan. "I want to."

"It really is okay," she breathed, moving her lips over his, catching and plucking at them, with her tongue brushing his teeth. He savored the moment— her warmth and curves, the scent of her hair, the sway of her bottom beneath his palms. And then he held her tighter, opening his mouth to hers so their kiss deepened into a hot, pure rush of sensation.

When they stopped, neither could breathe, let alone speak. He kept her close, dragging air into his lungs. She panted against his chest.

Eventually he let out a grated chuckle. "Whew. That was some kind of first move you've got, lady. Didn't know you had it in you."

"Only works with the right partner."

He looked into her face. "Am I the one?"

Her eyes were huge and glistening. She nodded.

"You're sure?"

She pressed her fingers to his mouth. "Yes, and don't ask again. You'll only remind me of being…not sure. I want us to do this, okay? This is your official go-ahead. You don't have to stop every other minute and ask if I'm all right."

"But—"

She kissed him with a *smack*. "I will tell you if I change my mind."

He began to relax, amazed at her confidence. He'd thought that if they ever reached this point, it would be a long, slow journey taken one step at a time. She was less inhibited than he'd expected. But that didn't mean she might not change her mind.

"One word," he said, to let her know that she could, "that's all I need."

"One word?" Her mouth curved into a sweet, sexy smile. "How about this one?" She went up on her toes to reach his ear. *"Tip-off."*

He laughed. "Tip-off?"

She unwound his arms and started toward the bedroom, tugging him behind her. "Sure. Let's play ball, coach."

FOR ALL HER REASSURANCES, he took his time and she had to admit that she was grateful. So far the nervousness inside her had transformed into an exciting electric energy, but she knew from past experiments that there was no telling when the old fear would return. A couple of times, years ago, she'd forced herself to follow through anyway, but that had always been a mistake.

With Evan, she truly believed it would be different.

Something to do with being in love.

The hardest part was supposed to be removing her clothes—the naked vulnerability. But he was so good, holding her, stroking her, making small, laughing, *distracting* comments, that the process seemed easy and natural.

Easy and natural. That was Evan.

Thank God she'd found him. Almost a miracle— Evan and Lucy and Danny, all in the same place.

And her. She was part of the world again. Their world…her world.

"You'll have to get these buttons. I can't manage."

"Oh, yeah?" Amusement bubbled through her as she leaned against him, standing between his legs while he sat on the bed. Her shirt was already hanging open. It was his own he meant—and he even leaned back on his arms, giving her space to unbutton the remaining buttons. "How do you undress yourself when I'm not around?"

"Straight off over the head."

"Lazy man." She pushed at his chest—a convenient excuse to put her hands on the satin, muscled terrain. He fell flat onto the bed, taking her with him. They kissed. She moved luxuriously against him, feeling his arousal, waiting for the debilitating anxiety, but none came. "How are you with zippers?"

"Pretty good." He reached down, and before she realized his intent he'd flipped her over and unzipped her jeans.

He dragged them off her legs and she kicked them away, laughing. "I meant your own!"

"Oh. Yeah. No problem." He shucked his jeans in two seconds flat, stretching to slide them over his feet without getting off the bed. He kissed her stomach while he was down there, and her skin felt like it rippled in one rolling wave that moved from her toes right up to her scalp.

"Your skin is hot," he said, bending over her to frame her navel with his hands. He kissed it. "Cute belly button."

She clutched at the bedcover. Her face closed into a tight scrunch. She was intensely aware of the body that she'd managed to pretty much ignore for a very long time. It was only an average body—not super-fit or toned, definitely not pampered with lotions and oils. She'd shaved her legs and put on matching underwear. That was it.

Evan's scrutiny was nearly unbearable. But in an arousing way.

He smoothed her shirt away from her torso and traced a finger along the deep V of her bra. "Rosebuds. With a tiny little bow." His other hand skimmed the waistband of her bikini panties. "And a matched set. I'm impressed."

"Glad you approve," she said, trying to sound wry. As if she hadn't bought the printed cotton undergarments especially for his eyes, knowing that expensive lace and satin would never be her style.

At least focusing on her underwear meant she didn't have to think about the fact that she was lying in bed with Evan and they were practically undressed. She wanted to look at him, but she closed her eyes instead, concentrating on the feel of his skin as he pressed closer.

She *was* hot. Shivering with a delicious fever as his hands glided over her.

Oh, man. She sucked in a shallow breath as he skinned the cup of her bra past her pointed nipple. Before she could feel self-conscious, his mouth covered the exposed flesh. He fluted his tongue against her and sucked deeply, drawing the ribbon of sensation that ran through the center of her tighter and tighter until she arched off the bed, mewing with pleasure.

Evan returned to her mouth. "Just so you know." He kissed her all over, playing with her tongue, peppering her chin, licking her throat. "I love you."

Her eyes opened wide, even though she'd guessed he did—or thought he did. He was the kind of guy who would want to be in love when he was having sex.

He kissed her again before she could respond, which was fortunate because she wasn't prepared to make a declaration. She needed to think first, and that was impossible at the moment. Her brain could absorb only one deluge at a time and right now it was the wondrous spectacle of touch, taste, pleasure.

She was lost in it.

ALTHOUGH EVAN HAD THOUGHT he was prepared to stop, as their kisses and caresses increased, he counted himself damn lucky that Rose was not shying away.

At first she'd been compliant, but restrained. So he went slowly—lavishing long minutes on her body until they were both at the breaking point and he had to pull back to let them cool off.

His lovely, blooming Rose had other ideas. As soon as she'd caught her breath, she was back, rubbing against his side with her bra open and the shirt hanging off her elbows, dragging over his stomach as she stroked down his body. Deep strokes, growing bolder with every pass. Every muscle and tendon in his body stretched taut when finally she brushed a tentative hand over his shorts. Eventually she grew even more daring and squeezed him. He inhaled sharply as she slipped her fingers beneath his waistband. His skin twitched; his muscles jumped. All of his focus was on the hot surge of arousal, begging for her touch.

Her hand withdrew. Through a haze, he saw her face appear above his, half-hidden by tousled hair. Her chin quivered. "I'm sorry," she whispered as he dazedly raised his head. "I can't."

Frustration knifed through him. He wanted to slam his head back against the pillow, but his first concern was always for her and that kept him sane. "'S'okay," he managed to say. His disembodied hand even patted her back. "Don't feel bad."

"No!" She was alarmed. "Not that. I mean, I just can't, you know, touch you. I don't know what to do. It's all so strange."

"Oh." He realized that her hesitancy wasn't only out of the twisted horror of what had happened to her—it was inexperience. "Don't worry. You don't have to do anything."

"But I want to." She was amusingly earnest. "I want

to be, well…" Her head ducked beneath the veil of black silk. "Good at this."

"This isn't your only opportunity. We can do it again. I hope so, anyway."

She exhaled, smiling a little. "Okay. I just thought that was why you stopped—so I'd, you know, uh…"

He hugged her. "I was only slowing down. We're not in a hurry."

Unless he was mistaken, her eyes glinted with mischief. "I don't know about that. I might be." She bit gently on his shoulder. "This has been a long time coming."

He slipped his hands inside the back of her pretty bikini bottoms, nudging them past the ripe curves of her buttocks. "Mm, well…if you're ready, I'm ready."

She kissed him, tasting like sweet woman and salty skin. "I'm ready." Her voice was full of an airy marvel at that. "Really, truly ready."

They lay on their sides with their arms tangled, kissing in between sliding the remainder of their clothing off. Rose kept her eyes shut most of the time, but she sighed happily, nuzzling into him when he pressed her back against the pillows and moved partially on top of her. He took a condom packet off the bedside table and moved to sheathe himself, then enfolded her, finding his place as she drew a leg up, sliding her foot along the back of his calf.

He touched her intimately, where she was made of swollen flesh and liquid warmth. Yes, she was ready. But also nervous—her fingers danced like a pianist's along his shoulders and arms. "Relax," he said, stroking her.

"I can't when you're doing *that*."

"Sorry," he said with a chuckle.

He touched her pleasure point and she hissed. "You're not sorry at all."

"No-o-o." His hands moved to her hips, sliding beneath to lift her higher. At the first nudge of his erection, her eyes flew open in alarm, then slammed shut. She gritted her teeth, preparing herself. "I don't think so," he said, and eased away.

"Evan." She gripped at his shoulders, shuddering against him. "Evan? Don't stop. I *want* you to do it."

"You looked like this was a trip to the dentist."

A long silence.

"Sorry," she said in a small voice, no longer joking.

He held her one-armed, kissed her forehead. "Maybe next time."

Now he sounded as tense as she. Was he mad? Or only frustrated? Rose peeked through her lashes at his outstretched body—fully aroused, muscles bunched like stones beneath his skin.

She lay in misery, hugging his side. How many next times would there be? Even Evan's patience would run out. And it wasn't that she didn't want him to make love to her—she was filled with longing, every sense ignited. His fragrance was a drug; she wanted to absorb him into her skin. Her fingers itched to touch him. The sight of his obvious need, even the sound of his breathing and the thunder of his heartbeat was fuel for her own desire.

So then why was she letting him stop? Was she afraid?

No. Apprehensive and awkward, yes.

That doesn't matter. Love matters.

When she moved on top of him, Evan's head came up. "Rose? What are you doing?"

She kissed a slow path up from his chest to his throat to his mouth. "Doing what comes naturally. Or used to, before I got all messed up."

He caught one of her wandering hands. "You don't have to—"

"I know that. But I want to." She laughed against his mouth, kissing him, tasting and teasing him with her tongue until he made a soft growling sound in his throat and gripped her tightly at the hips where she rode astride, her thighs squeezed around his waist.

She lifted up, bracing on her arms as he buried his face between her breasts. His mouth opened, searching, and she felt the erotic pull again and fed herself into the heat and wetness and deep, suckling pleasure.

Her hips began to rock. She slid a little lower toward the hardness pressed urgently against her, and reached for him, so consumed by the swirl of sensations that her fumbling seemed to come from haste. But still not right. She placed a hand at the center of his chest and said, "Help me."

For a second she thought he was going to say something dumb like, *"Are you sure?"* but this time his eyes were dark with hunger and apparently he was convinced.

"Just go slow," he soothed, making an adjustment that aligned their bodies with a sensual shimmy of skin against skin. Finally he was entering her and after the first shock at how big he was, she opened to him, slowly lowering herself onto his rigid length, easy, natural, gliding into the motion as his hips rose to meet her. When the bad memories tried to get in, she shut her mind to everything but Evan and herself, the crazy heat between them and the love she saw in his eyes.

HOURS LATER, they were still awake, laughing and talking in bed while they ate leftover chicken with napkins tied around their necks like bibs. Rose knew that if she stopped to think about what she was doing she'd get all self-conscious and embarrassed, so she didn't let herself stop and think. That meant all sorts of things came out of her mouth, the secrets that had been bottled up and dumb stuff, too—how she'd been fired from the best job of her life, bank teller, because she'd kneed her boss in the nuts when he got frisky; her favorite food for midnight cravings, chopped-up boiled egg and cheddar cheese on toast; the time she'd tried to ride a skateboard and had ended up with a broken wrist and a hospital bill it took more than a year to pay off; even the story of her months in the halfway house for expectant mothers and what it had been like to watch Pastor Mike and his wife walk away with her baby.

At the last, she matter-of-factly blotted her tears with the edge of the napkin and then asked Evan if he wanted the last chicken wing. "You have it," he said, suspiciously bright-eyed.

She elbowed him as she reached for the wing. "Don't cry. I'll start again."

"I'm not crying," he said, all manly bluster.

"'Course not."

"It's the pepper. I got a speck in my eye."

She munched on the wing. "This is why I don't talk about my past. All those tales of sorrow and pity. Who needs to relive it? Not me."

"I'm not asking you to relive it. Just meet with the Swansons. Make up for some of the pain and the loss."

"That's scary."

"So was making love, and look how well that turned out."

She hooted as hot blood rushed into her cheeks. The first time, she'd been happy to simply get through it without going numb and losing the sense of pleasure, but he hadn't been satisfied and had tried again, making love to every inch of her until she'd reached a stupendous climax that had left her limp, brainless and utterly blissed out. And famished, she'd discovered, rousing herself quite some time later. Hence the post-midnight snack.

"I do want to meet Danny," she said, when her flush had subsided. "But I know I'd be a disappointment to him."

"Have some faith in yourself."

"Just like that, huh?"

"Yeah. You can do wonders when you make up your mind to try. Look at—" he ripped away the napkin to reveal his bare chest and she thought he was going to get embarrassingly intimate again "—Lucy's bedroom."

Rose dropped the mangled chicken wing into the container. "I could control that. There's no telling what Danny's reaction would be."

Evan took her hand and scrubbed her fingers with his napkin, kissing each one as he finished. "You're right. No telling. He probably will be upset at first, and it might take him a while to accept you. He's got his head screwed on straight, so I think he will, but I can't say for sure. That's a chance you'll have to take."

A hundred worries and questions spun through her mind like a pinwheel. But she exhaled and said, wearied by her own stubborn resistance, "When?"

Evan looked up sharply. "As soon as possible."

"No. I—I don't want to screw up the end of your basketball season if things go wrong."

"That's my last concern."

"But—"

"Trust me." He craned his neck and kissed her. "It's going to be okay."

She put the deli container on the nightstand and slumped lower on the plumped pillows. "You say."

"I say." His hand crept under the blanket pulled to her waist.

"Maybe you should be saying something else, like—*oh*." He'd grabbed hold of the bottom edge of her napkin and given it a quick yank so it came free, baring her breasts. "Stop that," she said, batting away his fingers and covering herself with the rumpled sheet. "We were having a conversation."

"I thought it was over."

"Actually, no. I mean, we're always talking about me. I want to know more about you."

"I've told you most of it. Born and raised in a middle-class suburb of Saginaw, went to Central Michigan on a basketball scholarship, graduated and got married a month later, tried an executive trainee job to please Krissa, hated it, got my first teaching job, lost it after a couple years when there were budget cuts, was hired by Alouette…and here I am."

"I didn't ask for your résumé," she protested. "But you never told me about the executive thing. That must have been awful. I mean, you look good in a suit and all, but I'm too used to seeing you running around in sweats and fooling around with the students to imagine you stuck behind a desk."

"You don't see me in the classroom. I'm behind a desk more often than I'm in the gym."

"But it's not—" She waved a hand. "Oh, what do I know? I've been stuck in low-paying menial jobs all my life. A corporate paycheck would have been nice."

He laughed shortly. "That's what Krissa thought."

"Oh?"

"Your instincts are right. My spirit was stifled in that job. I held out for as long as possible because Lucy was on the way, but in the end…I had to quit. That was the first nail in the coffin, as far as Krissa was concerned. Moving to Alouette was the last." He folded his arms beneath his head and sighed. "You know that sign at the town limits? The one that reads: 'Welcome to Alouette. Not the end of the earth—'"

"'But we can see it from here,'" Rose completed the quote. "Sure."

"When Krissa saw that, she started crying. Tried to get me to turn the car around."

Rose leaned her head on his shoulder. "That's kinda sad."

"Yeah. I felt like Lucy's ogre, you know, forcing her to live here, away from all her friends. But there weren't many teaching positions open and I needed the job. I liked it here almost immediately. People were friendly and the outdoors lifestyle suited me. Lucy thrived, too. But Krissa—" His muscles flexed when he hunched his shoulders into a shrug. "She didn't even try to adjust."

"Not everyone can live here. The winters are brutal."

"It wasn't the move that did us in, not really."

The room became quiet. Rose wanted to know

more, but suddenly it seemed strange to her, that she was in the house—the very bed—that Evan had shared with another woman. A woman who'd died tragically young and was missed by those who'd loved her.

Eventually, Evan continued. "We wanted different lives. She realized she'd made a mistake, marrying so young and having a child. She left us to go and live in L.A., literally in search of sun and fun. She planned on taking Lucy for part of the summer, but that never happened because she found out she was sick."

"And then she came home?"

"We weren't divorced yet. She needed medical coverage. But mostly, she wanted to be with her daughter for every moment she had left. Nothing brings home the importance of family like the prospect of losing it for good. A lesson Krissa learned in the worst way possible."

Rose sat up, holding the sheet to her chest. Her head was bowed. "I know," she whispered, thinking first of her loss of Danny and then even of her own family and how wretched it was that they'd splintered apart. She resolved to show her mother more love and patience, no matter how disagreeable the woman acted.

Evan groaned. "I wasn't thinking. I didn't mean *you*."

"It's okay." Rose dragged a hand through her hair, glancing at him sidelong. "I can't imagine how difficult that was for all of you, but especially Lucy. Poor Lucy…." Any child would have been traumatized, watching a parent waste away before her eyes.

"Krissa was in the hospital for the last weeks, when the illness and pain was the worst. Lucy was too young to visit, and that was better for her. She didn't have to see—" His voice cut out. He passed a hand back and forth over his eyes, as if he could rub away the memory.

Rose frowned. "Lucy never got to say goodbye?"

"I used to take her to wave up at Krissa's window. We'd planned for them to have a final visit. But she went downhill too fast and died unexpectedly in the middle of the night. I wasn't there, either. The hospital called, but I couldn't get there in time."

"Krissa was alone when she died?"

Evan nodded. "That's one of my regrets. She'd been estranged from her parents for many years, but they'd made up at the end. They wanted to come up from Florida, but Krissa's father was ill and wasn't able to travel."

"It's like Lucy's story. Princess Kristina—exiled to her cottage, far away from the king and queen."

"Yes."

Rose pressed the back of her wrist to her nose and snuffled. "Maybe the mural wasn't such a good idea."

Evan stroked along her spine and the caring human contact felt so unexpectedly good that she went into his arms, holding onto him for all she was worth. *Holding on,* she thought. If only she'd always known how important that was. Thank God her lesson hadn't come too late.

"Don't even think that. Lucy loves the mural. I worried over her story at first, but now I see that it's helping her work through her mom's death." He fingered Rose's hair, then leaned down and planted a kiss on the top of her head. "I'm just hoping for a happy ending."

Rose closed her eyes. "Aren't we all."

CHAPTER FIFTEEN

EVAN TURNED HIS HEAD to look at Rose as they walked up to the Swansons' house on Vine Street. "Your teeth are chattering."

She clenched them. "No, they're not."

"You're not still cold." On the drive over, she'd huddled inside her coat, hat and muffler like the poor little matchstick girl. He'd turned on the heater full blast, but that didn't stop her shivers.

"I'm afraid," she admitted.

Evan wrapped an arm around her. "Lean on me."

They'd reached the doorstep. Rose stopped, taking a look at the house. It was similar to many others in Alouette—wood frame, two stories, small windows. The walk was scrupulously shoveled and salted and the shrubs were wrapped in bright orange nylon webbing to protect them from the weight of the snow. No peeling paint or loose shingles. The Swansons were good caretakers.

Rose was more certain than ever that she was out of place, despite having Evan to act as a diplomatic go-between. "I wish you'd brought your whistle. When—*if* things go wrong, you could call a foul and halt the action."

"Keep an eye out for inbound passes," he said with

a lightness that only made her butterflies increase. He was trying so hard. He must be worried, too.

"Go on," he prodded. "Press the doorbell."

A curtain had twitched in the nearest window. "Someone's watching us." Rose had no choice but to go ahead and ring the bell.

"They're as nervous as you are."

She manufactured a wry grin. "Cold comfort."

Evan gave her a squeeze for courage as the door opened. Ken Swanson stood before them, looking the same as ever—a nice, middle-class fellow with a broad smile and slightly pasty skin. He shook their hands, pumping vigorously. "Glad to have you here. Please come inside." He ushered them into a small foyer. "Alana. Company's here."

His wife appeared in the doorway to the living room. Her eyes darted to Rose. "Hello."

"Alana, this is Rose Robbin and, of course you know Evan." Ken chuckled. "Listen to me. You know Rose, too. We both do. We—"

Alana stepped in. "We've always wanted to thank you personally for your generosity and…sacrifice. Please come and sit down so we can talk."

She gestured with her hands, an offer of contact, but Rose was frozen. They were well-meaning people, doing their best to make her feel comfortable and welcomed. Not their fault that she'd turned to petrified wood, incapable of speech or common courtesy.

Only Evan's steadying hand on her shoulder kept her from fleeing.

Alana studied Rose with kind eyes. "What you did—it took a lot of courage." She was a slim, older woman, with straight dark hair cut even with her jaw and skimmed back from her face with a discreet headband. Her mouth was thin and prim, and her face was delicately lined. She was the kind of gentle person that others would call *lovely*.

A lady. Not like Rose.

"I want you to know how appreciative we are. Danny has been a blessing in our lives." Ken went over to Alana and they linked arms, making a distorted mirror image of Evan and Rose.

"Uh—" Rose cleared her throat. "You're welcome."

She cringed. What a dumb thing to say. This wasn't a tea party.

"Let me get your coats," Ken said. He lowered his voice as he helped Rose off with hers. "Danny's waiting in his room. He wants to meet you."

Rose walked stiffly to the sofa. She had to sit before she keeled over. "How did he react when you told him?" They'd decided that Danny should be told her identity beforehand, to ease the way.

"It was a surprise," Ken said carefully.

"He always knew that his birth mother was from the area," Alana explained, "but it had been so long since you lived here that we never stressed that part. It was a shock for him to learn that he already knew you."

Rose wet her lips. Her voice was scratchy. "We haven't spoken, not really."

"But he's seen you around."

"Was he disappointed that it's me?"

Alana sat beside Rose and patted the knot of her hands. "I wouldn't say that. He has questions, of course."

Rose looked into the other woman's eyes and saw that beneath the veil of good manners was an apprehension not unlike her own. Alana Swanson was saying the right things, but she was also scared spitless.

"Are *you* sorry we're doing this?"

Alana opened her mouth, then closed it, cutting off the easy platitude. Her chin quivered, and Rose's heart sank, but finally Danny's mother shook her head. "I'm not sorry. But I can't help being worried about what happens next. Danny may resent us. For keeping him from you. I don't know that he'll turn to you, Rose, and forget about me." Alana's eyes glistened.

Rose felt awful for being so self-involved. "Oh, no, that won't—"

A new voice interrupted her. "I won't do that, Mom." Danny stood in the doorway, behind Evan and his father, who'd been watching the two women on the sofa. They turned toward him, opening a path to let him through.

Danny walked into the room, his chin plastered to his chest, hands in the pockets of his baggy jeans. "You're my *real* mom."

"Oh." Alana fluttered toward him with open arms. "Thank you, Danny. That means so much to me, darling."

Rose put her head in her hands. For once, she couldn't bear to look at Danny. He might as well have come right out and said he didn't want anything to do with her. She was a pretender, not a real mom. She was fifteen years too late to make amends.

Evan sat beside her. She glanced at him, saw his concern, then had to look away. She wasn't going to cry and make a scene. That would embarrass everyone, but Danny most of all.

"Son," Ken said, putting a hand on Danny's back, "this is Rose."

The boy made a flip gesture with his chin, flicking his hair out of his eyes. They narrowed and skipped over Rose lightning-fast. "Hey."

Alana was pulling herself together, dabbing at her eyes. "Danny." Her mouth pursed. "Manners."

He sighed deeply, as only a teenager can. "Hello, Ms. Robbin. Nice to meet you." The slitted gaze moved to Evan. "Coach."

Evan nodded, then stood when Rose made a move to get up.

She was grateful he was there. A rock. Her Mr. Fix-it.

Except that no one could make Danny pleased to meet her.

Rose held out her hand. She had to be the adult, the mature one who overcame her own emotions to soothe the awkward moment. She had to *talk.* "I've wanted to meet you for a long time, Danny. I know it's strange for you. Me, too. You don't have to like me. I just want you to know who I am and that if you ever do want to—to—get together, I guess, you only have to say so and I'll be—" She faltered.

Danny still wasn't looking at her, but he took her hand and shook it briefly. The touch went through her like a thunderbolt appearing out of a clear sky.

"Yes, ma'am," he said, polite and thoroughly non-committal. Pause. "Thank you."

Ken clapped his hands together. "Ahem. We need to loosen up here. How about refreshments? Evan, Rose—can I get you something to drink?"

What Rose could have used was a shot of something

strong and alcoholic, but that was too much of a reminder of her father and her own wilder days.

"I'd like a beer," Evan said.

"A soft drink, please."

"I'll get them," Alana offered. "Please, everyone
sit. Danny, you, too."

He slouched to a reading chair in the corner of the
room, as far from Rose as he could get. She returned
to the sofa, trying to keep her eyes off him. All the
times she'd stared, wishing for this moment, and now
he was sullen and resentful. She was hopelessly
stymied.

"Take it easy," Evan said beneath his breath, covered by the bustle of Ken and Alana arranging the
drinks and choosing their seats. "Let him be for a
while. He'll relax."

"I don't know what to say to him."

"Say nothing. Just wait." He gave her a reassuring
wink, then reached for the beer Ken held out, making
a chatty comment about the weather or sports or maybe
the man in the moon, for all Rose could tell. She could
see mouths opening and closing, but her ears seemed
to be stuffed with cotton batting. The indistinct voices
came from far away. She didn't care. All that mattered
was that Danny was ignoring her and she was certain
that her heart would break.

Give him time, she thought, and it was as if Evan
had spoken the words in her ear. *Miracles don't happen overnight.*

Alana was looking expectantly at Rose.

She blinked, dragging her gaze off Danny.

"I was telling them about your artwork," Evan said.

"Uh-huh."

"I adore nature studies." Alana indicated the triple rows of identically matted and framed prints on the wall. "These are prints taken from nineteenth-century British botanical studies."

"Nice."

"I've tried my hand at pressing several varieties of ferns and autumn leaves and other flora. But I don't know what to do with the results. I'm not artistically inclined, unfortunately."

"A scrapbook," Rose suggested. "Decoupage?"

"Perhaps if I had your talent…"

"Danny's the only creative one in this house," Ken said. "He drew his own comic book last year."

The comment was meant well, but it dropped like a bomb, squelching the tentative start at a conversation. Rose closed her eyes, certain that the Swansons were thinking about how her genes were in their son. And heaven knew who else's.

It was Danny who broke the silence. "It was an illustrated novel, Dad, not a comic book."

Ken laughed with excessive good humor. "Don't know what's wrong with comic books. Wish I'd kept mine, with the prices they're fetching on eBay."

Rose pinned her gaze to the coffee table. "I once sold a couple of spot illustrations and filler art to a magazine."

"How nice," Alana said.

"You did?" Evan grinned at her. "How come you never told me?"

"It wasn't that big of a deal. It was a birder's magazine with a small circulation. I got a check for all of a hundred bucks."

Alana smiled. "Still and all, that's a professional sale."

Danny's head had cocked. He was listening.

Evan was nodding proudly. "I've been telling her she should turn pro."

"Aw, c'mon." Rose rolled her eyes. "It doesn't work the way it does with athletes. No one's hanging around, looking to sign me to a fat contract. If I work really hard at it, I might be able to sell a few drawings free-lance."

Ken became jolly again. "See there, son? You stick with the basketball team if you want to hit the big time."

"Yeah, sure," Danny said, joining in with a short laugh.

Evan exchanged an encouraging look with Rose. "There's no reason Danny can't cultivate both inter-ests. My daughter Lucy's been taking art lessons from Rose."

The elder Swansons made interested noises, but everyone was waiting for Danny's response. "Is that why you guys were always together?" he said.

It wasn't exactly clear who he was addressing, but Rose nodded. "Lucy has talent." Her hands went clammy. "I'd love to see your work too…sometime."

"Maybe." One side of Danny's mouth twitched. "Dad's just bragging. I'm not that good."

Rose held a smile, rewarded when he glanced at her, seeming more shy than hostile. She instantly knew that all the anxiety and weirdness had been worth-while.

The entire group continued chatting for a while, touching on a variety of subjects but avoiding the rea-son they were together. Once she wasn't as nervous about Danny's presence, Rose started listening. Alana had an infectious laugh that was surprisingly deep and throaty. Ken had studied microbiology in college, but was now a pencil pusher with the local utility company. They planned a spring break vacation to somewhere hot and tropical every March, and teased Danny about getting too old to hang out with his parents. They summered at a family camp on one of the many inland lakes in the area.

"What about you, Rose?" said Ken. "Doesn't your mother own that rather interesting property on the Blackbear?"

"Yes. Maxine's Cottages—we rent them. Most of our business comes during the summer and fall."

"Great potential. Particularly if you updated."

"I'm not planning to. And there's no other family left to help run the place."

"What a shame," Alana said. She sent her husband a look. "Excuse us, please. I need Ken in the other room for just a bit."

Evan stood. "May I use the bathroom?"

Rose wanted to call him back. She held her tongue. They couldn't have been more obvious, but what else could they do? She and Danny hadn't progressed past the occasional quick glance or general comment.

A physical yearning moved through her when she looked his way. She wanted so much from him. Didn't necessarily deserve it, but craved it all the same. From her hours of observation, she knew he was naturally a happy, outgoing kid. Maybe she could coax some of that out of him, if he could forget for a minute or two who she was.

Rose took a deep breath.

But Danny spoke first. "How come you didn't want me?"

She gasped.

"That's what we're supposed to talk about, isn't it?" He sprawled in the chair, crossing his arms over his chest. "So tell me."

She recognized herself in his hurt, defiant attitude. "I…ah…" She glanced at the doorway. How long did she have? Enough time to explain a situation that was so complicated even she couldn't understand?

"Danny," she said, edging forward to the lip of the sofa. Her hands shook; she clasped them between her knees. "I was barely seventeen when you were born. I'd left home, for a lot of reasons. It wasn't a good place for me to be. So I was on my own, without any support, no job or friends."

He nodded, but his eyes glared, saying, *"So?"*

"I did realize that I wanted you after you were born, but I was afraid that I couldn't raise you right, and the Swansons were already waiting for you. They loved you, too." Rose didn't know how she'd managed to say so much when the raw pain inside her was so harsh and unforgiving. Her throat kept closing up.

She put her head down and swallowed, again and again. "I knew you'd be happy and safe with them. That they'd be better parents than—" Her voice dropped to a hoarse whisper. *"Me."*

Danny didn't say anything, but he'd moved forward in the chair and when she finished he took a deep, shuddering breath. She lifted her eyes to him, hoping he could read how much she cared.

"When I've seen you around town, fooling around, or playing basketball, just being with your parents, I think I made the right choice. But in here—" she pressed a fist to her chest "—I still wish that it could have been different. And that's why I finally decided to try and get to know you. Thanks to your parents, and Coach Grant's help."

"I always wanted to know where I came from." Danny shot up and paced to the window, his hands thrust in his pockets. "But now…"

He was disappointed. She wasn't what he hoped for.

"Okay," she said. "I won't push. You don't have to see me again."

No, don't you dare give up. Hold on. Hold on.

"But please think about it." At last the words that she'd been holding back, even from herself, came pouring out. And it wasn't as painful as before. It was an absolution. "Because I do love you, Danny. I always have."

"YOUR TEETH ARE chattering again."

"Every bone in my body is chattering."

Evan hugged her. "That was hard on you."

She turned on the car seat—they were still parked outside of the Swansons' house—and tucked her face inside his open coat, where it was warm and she could feel his heartbeat.

"Just as bad for Danny," she said.

"Or as good."

She made a noise of disagreement. "Did you see his face? He could barely stand to look at me."

"He's just fifteen. He didn't know *how* to react." Evan stroked her back. "You did fine with him. He'll come around."

"I don't think so."

"Wait and see."

"There's no other choice." She closed her eyes for a minute, lulled by the vibration of the engine and the heat pouring from the vents. By Evan's embrace. "What I really wanted was to grab him and hug him so hard he'd have to know how I feel." She sighed. "But that would have made him run away even faster."

"Some people are like that."

After another minute, she realized there'd been a certain humorous irony in Evan's tone. She pulled back to see his face. "Think you're smart, do ya?"

He grinned. "I'm pretty smooth."

"You tamed the Wild Rose." She tried a smile, then had to compress her lips. Too much emotion was running around loose inside her. She was on the verge of telling Evan she loved him, but opening up to one male per day was her absolute limit.

"Nope. I didn't tame her." He leaned over for a kiss, and the loving touch eased Rose's anguish another degree. Maybe there was hope. "I nurtured her."

CHAPTER SIXTEEN

THE FOLLOWING FRIDAY, on basketball night, Rose went to the game the same as always. Yet everything was different. Almost as if she finally had a true *right* to be there. Cheering for Danny no longer felt surreptitious, even though there were no outward changes in their relationship. No declarations, public or private, had been made. To the rest of the crowd, she wasn't Danny's mother, she was just another fan.

But that didn't matter. She knew, and most importantly, he knew.

He caught her eye several times during the pregame warm-up and even at one of the time-outs, when the squad had run to the sidelines to huddle around their coach. He didn't smile, or even nod. He didn't overtly acknowledge her. But she sat a little taller, swelling with pride.

And cheered with great gusto when the Gale Storm won the nip-and-tuck game, even though Danny's play had been off. He'd had a few uncharacteristic turnovers and had missed more shots than normal. Rose wondered if that was her fault.

As usual, she and Lucy waited in the gym as the stands emptied after the conclusion of the game. Lucy skipped up and down the rows, pointing out the Valentine decorations dressing up the cement-block walls. Tomorrow was Valentine's Day and there was to be a high-school dance. Evan was a chaperon, and he'd talked Rose into being his date. She'd toyed with the idea of backing out. But ever since she'd dared to go one-on-one with Danny, a few bad memories of catty girls sniping behind her back seemed less than important.

Lucy hopped from one bleacher to the next, landing on both feet and making the metal stands vibrate. "I have *American Idol* valentines for the girls," she said, twirling stick-held pom-poms with both hands. "And dumb old *Star Wars* ones for the boys."

"Mm-hmm." Sitting several rows up from the bottom, Rose watched Gloria Kevanen go by with a couple of other women. She lifted a hand to wave.

Gloria slowed and smiled one of her fake smiles up at Rose. "Hiya, Rose. Looking good."

"Thanks." *I guess.*

Gloria nudged her pals. "I'm one of the chaperones at the Valentine's dance. Is it true that you're coming with Coach Grant?"

Rose was startled. "How did you know?"

"Then it *is* true? I was only kidding. I didn't think you'd actually dare to show up."

Damn. Rose grimaced at herself for getting caught by the woman's ploys.

One of Gloria's friends told her to get moving, but she wasn't finished. "Not the best game tonight, but at least we won. Maybe the team will do better in the play-offs."

"Hope so," Rose muttered.

"Why don't you give Coach Grant some extra

incentive?" Gloria snickered as if this was clever, and her friends dutifully joined in.

Rose felt her face darkening. She turned away, watching from the corner of her eyes as they departed, chatting and giggling. Just once, she wished she could come up with a comeback that would take Gloria down a couple of pegs.

"Rose," Lucy said from behind her. "I dropped one of my pom-poms in between the bleachers. What's 'centive?"

"Uh, it's encouragement. Like a cheer."

Lucy nodded solemnly. "Then we need my pom-pom."

"Right. Did it fall all the way to the floor?" There were open spaces between the seats and the treads.

"Uh-huh. I wanted to go get it back, but it's dark and spooky down there. I peeked."

"No problem. I'll go. You climb up to the spot where you dropped it and call for me when I tell you to. Or else I might get lost."

Lucy goggled. "Really?"

Rose ruffled her hair. "Nah. Don't worry." She climbed down to the floor and walked around the side of the bleachers, where she could step in through the metal supports. The space *was* spooky—crisscrossed with shadow and the accordion cage of metal bars. Popcorn littered the floor, along with candy wrappers, crushed paper cups, crinkled game programs and the odd cigarette butt.

"Lucy? Do you hear me?"

The girl's voice came from above. "I'm over here, Rose." She stuck a hand through the space between bleachers and waggled her fingers. "Do you see me?"

"Gotcha." Rose picked her way between the network of braces. She looked up at the stripes of light, finding Lucy's cute face peeping down. "Where's the pom-pom?"

Lucy pointed. "Over there."

Rose spotted the frill of blue-and-white streamers. The pom-poms had been handed out at the door and Lucy had appropriated Rose's so that she could wave two of them, like a cheerleader. "Okay, I've got it. You sit up now. You're so little you might fall through." She waited until Lucy disappeared, then retrieved the pom-pom and began making her way out.

She was about to slip through the side supports when she heard voices, coming from right nearby. Shifting shapes stopped at the bottom corner of the stands.

"There's Lucy." That was Danny's voice. "How come she's all alone?"

He was with his friends. Rose hesitated to step out. He might be embarrassed, especially if he'd told any of them who she *really* was.

"Yeah, where's that woman who's always hanging around? Y'know—Wild Rose."

Another young male laughed. "You mean Coach's groupie?"

"That's the one. I heard about *her.*"

"What'd you hear?"

"She's, like, a tramp. That's what they say. But not too bad-looking for an older woman. Remember that time she ran us outta the Buck Stop?"

Groans of agreement. Cocky laughter. "Mean bitch," someone said.

"At least she didn't turn you in to Coach." Danny spoke quietly. "Or you'd be off the team."

"Yeah, 'cause maybe she likes younger guys. Hell, I'd do her," boasted one of the boys.

"Coach would bust your ass."

"Not if she's a groupie. The whole team should get a piece." The boys laughed again, shuffling around, jabbing at each other. One of them started talking excitedly about how much action rock stars and athletes got.

Rose backed away slowly, crouching as she carefully stepped toward the lower end of the bleachers, where the shadows were deepest. She'd shut off her emotions. All she wanted was to escape notice until they'd gone away.

"What's with you?" said one of the boys.

"Nothing," Danny snapped. "Just keep your goddamn mouths closed. You don't know what you're talking about."

A loud thump sounded on the bleachers right near Rose's ear. She covered her face as the structure rattled. Danny had kicked or slammed a fist at it.

"Sheesh. You're acting like we insulted your mother or something."

Danny's voice was fierce. *"She's not my mother."*

"Maybe your girlfriend then." Someone made a kissing noise. "You got a thing for Wild Rose?"

"I told you to shut up."

"Okay, okay—calm down." Rose thought that was Jeremy, the team's center. "Let's get out of here before the coach starts raggin' on our asses again."

The boys moved off, just as Lucy's voice rang out. "Rose?" She was coming closer, sounding worried. "Where are you? Did you get lost?"

Rose cringed, hoping the boys had left in time.

Lucy's voice wobbled. "Rose?"

She was frightened. Rose *had* to leave her hiding spot. "I'm here, Lucy," she called. "I'm coming out. I've got your pom-pom."

She emerged from beneath the stands, her eyes darting in search of Danny and his teammates. The double doors were just swinging shut behind them and she caught a glimpse of Danny, looking over his shoulder into the gym. He was stricken—eyes making black slits in a white face. As she stared, two bright circles of color appeared high on his cheeks and he ducked his head, turning his back on her. He knew she'd overheard.

The door swung shut.

"I thought you were lost," Lucy said.

Rose handed her the pom-pom. It rustled. Her hand was shaking. "I'm not lost," she said like a robot.

Yes, she was.

Lucy's smile dropped away as she stared at Rose, sensing the mood had gone awry. Rose collapsed onto the bottom bleacher and the girl came and sat beside her, saying nothing but giving a tired little sigh as she slipped her hand inside Rose's.

Minutes later—Rose thought it was probably only minutes—Evan found them. "Hey," he said. "You two look tuckered out."

Rose roused herself. "Uh, yes." She got to her feet, feeling like a ninety-year-old with arthritis. Danny's words had pierced her to the bone. "Lucy needs to get home right away. She has school tomorrow."

"I realize that." Evan knelt and zipped up his daughter's jacket. When he stood, he gave Rose's cheek a quick, sliding kiss. "Want to come over? I'm not tired."

She stepped away. "No, I don't think so."

"It's not for *that*." He glanced down at Lucy as they walked to the doors hand-in-hand. They had agreed that Rose wouldn't stay over with Lucy in the house. He'd jokingly plotted noontime trysts in the storage room of the Buck Stop. "Just to have some time together. I haven't seen you in private since—" another glance toward Lucy "—the other day."

She sensed the heat simmering under his casualness. A heat that would melt the chunk of ice in her chest. But Danny's denial was too recent. She wanted only to get away and be alone with the hurt that made a tight knot at the center of her. She would curl up like a wounded animal and by morning maybe it wouldn't be so bad.

Not likely.

They walked into the frigid night air. Her voice was appropriately brittle when she said, "Maybe we need to cool off on that."

Evan stopped dead, forcing Lucy to stop, too. "What?"

"I don't know if it's right."

"What?"

"You have expectations to live up to. I can't meet them."

"That's nuts, Rose. What happened? Did someone make a stupid remark? I thought you said you didn't care—"

"But I do."

He was obviously confused, but her rigid expression was giving nothing away. "Even so," he said softly. "You can't be backing out now, when you've finally...you know. The worst is behind you." Lucy made a whimpering sound and pressed her face into his topcoat for warmth. He sheltered her, spreading his hands over her back, but he didn't take his eyes off Rose. "This is day-after remorse. A lot has happened in the past week. It's normal to be apprehensive."

Rose turned her face away. "Go on. Get Lucy home."

Still he hesitated. "I'll let you think about this, but I'm going to call tomorrow."

She said nothing, only hurried away across the parking lot with her arms crossed tightly over her body. Whether she was hugging herself or restraining herself, she wasn't sure.

"THAT'S THE ENTIRE sordid tale," Rose said a day later, sitting on one of the handmade rag rugs in Roxy's simple studio apartment on the top floor of the Whitakers' carriage house. She'd spilled her guts. Roxy already knew about the rape, but the rest of it was new—the adoption, her meeting with Danny and the Swansons, his subsequent rejection. Her withdrawal from Evan.

"Huh," Roxy said from on top of the bed. She put her chin on her hand. No platitudes from her.

They sat in silence for several minutes. The wind whistled against the mullion windowpanes. The carriage house was made of thick red sandstone walls with a gambrel roof. The first floor had been converted into a garage. Roxy's place was above, overfurnished with what appeared to be the entire contents of an attic placed willy-nilly around the room. Roxy was a slob, and from her seat on the floor Rose could see stray socks, an empty yogurt container, splayed magazines and thick tufts of dust under the bed.

Roxy knocked her heels together. "You haven't talked to him since?"

"Who? Danny?"

"Evan."

"Oh. Well, no. I don't have a phone, remember. He called my mom's a couple of times and left messages. She kept ringing that damn bell to get me over to her place and bug me about calling him back. But I didn't know what to say to him so I finally had to leave the house."

"You were supposed to go to that dance tonight."

"Uh-uh. I'm not going."

"But you haven't actually canceled?"

"No. But I'm sure Evan will get the idea."

"Ha! *I'm* sure that he'll show up on your doorstep right on time."

"You think?" Rose drew her knees up to her chest. She didn't know if she wanted that or not. As much as she regretted pulling away from Evan, going to the dance was sure to be painful, between dealing with bitter high-school memories and the likely chance of running into Danny. Now that she'd unfrozen and was letting herself feel again, her son's disavowal burned at the bottom of her belly like a coal.

She's not my mother.

But what had she expected? That he'd stand up in front of one and all and proclaim how thrilled he was to have Wild Rose in his life? No kid would do that, no matter how good a heart he had or how well he'd been raised.

But Evan would. He'd never shown more than a moment's doubt about her.

Rose picked up a floor pillow and squeezed it to her chest. "I made a mistake with Evan."

Roxy laughed fondly. "You think?"

"So how do I fix it?"

"Easy enough. You suck it up, call him and say he was right about your temporary attack of nerves but that now you're looking forward to the dance."

"I can't go to that dance."

"Sure you can."

"No. Gloria Kevanen is the other chaperone. She'll find a way to throw my past in my face. I don't want to be humiliated in front of Evan and Danny."

"Like they care." Roxy frowned. "Wait, that didn't come out right. You know what I mean. Evan loves you. Danny will, too, when he gets to know you." She hung her arms off the end of the bed and played with the carpet fringe. "No one cares what nasty-mouth Gloria says except *you*."

"Yeah, well, it turns out that I have feelings, too."

Roxy grinned. "And we take a major step forward in the evolution of Wild Rose."

Rose let out a dry laugh. "Stop it. This isn't a laughing matter."

"Sometimes you've gotta laugh or you'll cry." Roxy rolled over and bounced off the bed. "Gad, you've got me spouting friggin' clichés." She grabbed a pair of boots from near the door. "Get your stuff on. I know what you need."

"A piece of Emmie's chocolate cake?"

"She always makes coconut cake for Valentine's Day."

"That'll do."

"But that's not our mission."

Roxy wouldn't say more, so Rose climbed up off the floor and put on her outerwear. They walked down the creaky stairs and across the back garden, which was buried beneath feet of snow. Rose reached past the narrow path cut through the banks and touched a clean drift. It was crusted over with an icy coating that glistened with diamond flecks in the afternoon sunshine.

They didn't go in the kitchen door. "Shhh," Roxy said, tiptoeing in through the sunroom. The space was a hodgepodge of wicker furniture that had been piled up and shoved against the inside wall. "I don't want Emmie to hear us. She'll be in the kitchen, simpering over her valentine."

"*Emmie* got a valentine?"

"And a miniature box of ninety-nine-cent chocolates. A secret admirer left them on the kitchen table. Shari's having fits."

Roxy eased open the door to the hall. They scurried toward the staircase, but the housemaid's footsteps were approaching from above so they ducked into Cassia's room instead, interrupting her at the computer. Roxy motioned for quiet. "We're on an undercover mission."

The redhead spun her chair around. "Ooh. What is it? Can I go along?"

Roxy cracked the door, then immediately closed it. She put her finger to her lips. They listened to Shari Shirley clump down the stairs and through the hallway.

Roxy peeped out. "Coast is clear." She considered Cassia's wheelchair and said apologetically, "We're going upstairs."

Cassia slumped. "Then I can't come."

"If we had time, I'd get you up there, no problem."

"But why are we going upstairs in the first place?" Rose was wary. She had a terrible suspicion.

Cassia inhaled, straightening up. "I know! You're sneaking into Valentina's room."

Roxy put on a patently false "innocent" face. "Why would we do that?"

Cassia eyed Rose, who was already shaking her head. "You tell me."

"We are *not* going into Valentina's room. Besides, Rox, I thought you called the wedding prophecy one-hundred-percent bunk."

"Maybe she changed her mind after the double wedding," suggested Cassia.

Roxy flipped her ponytail. "Nah. I *don't* believe, but then again it can't hurt. Rose's love life needs an energy boost. Except we don't have time to stand around talking. We've got to get upstairs while Shari is busy downstairs." She grabbed Rose's arm. "Come on."

"But I don't want to," Rose protested as Roxy dragged her into the hall.

"I know, I know. Humor me." Roxy took a letter opener off the check-in desk and pried open a locked drawer. She removed a heavy latch key with a corded tassel. Baring her teeth in a devilish grin, she held up the key and whispered, "Here we go!"

Rose threw up her hands in defeat. Maybe Roxy was right.

With Cassia at the foot of the stairs gazing after them, the two women hurried to the second floor. Cassia hissed from below. "Get inside—Shari's coming."

Laughing silently and pushing at each other, they got the door open and tumbled into the room. Roxy closed and locked the door behind them.

Rose stopped short. "What do we do now?"

"You mean, what do *you* do." Roxy stood at the

door, swiveling her eyeballs from side to side. "I guess you walk around and let the Valentina mojo rub off on you."

Rose looked at her friend, practically wallpapered to the door. "You're chicken."

"I'm not the one who's in love."

Rose hadn't said *that* in her recitation of events, but she didn't deny it. "This is dumb," she announced, advancing into the hallowed room. A four-poster bed was made up with bridal white linens and a crocheted bedcover. The pine plank floors creaked underfoot. She stepped onto a big round rag rug near the fireplace wall, where the doomed Valentina Whitaker's bridal portrait was hung.

"She posed for it in advance," Roxy whispered, of the cool blonde's solo portrait in her wedding finery. "And even after Valentina's groom ran off before the wedding and she took a swan dive off the cliff, Ogden Whitaker insisted that the portrait should be hung. They were pompous people, not like Emmie and Toivo."

"Let's get out of here," Rose said. "Valentina gives me the creeps."

"Wait. You should lie on the bed."

"No way. And I'm not staying the night, so you might as well just forget about using wedding mojo and that dumb curse against me."

Roxy grinned. "Emmie insists it's a prophecy, not a curse."

"Yeah, according to sentimental types who believe in that kind of mumbo-jumbo. I'm surprised at you for getting sucked in." Defiantly, Rose sat on the bed and wiggled her rump around. She flung herself flat and thrust her hands and feet up in the air like a dog playing dead. "Work your magic, Valentina! Make me into the least likely bride Alouette has ever seen."

Suddenly she stopped, going limp. In spite of all her outward sarcasm, that might actually be what she wanted. Bit by bit, ever since last fall, she'd been advancing toward a place where having a husband and family wasn't as far-fetched as before. She couldn't imagine ever becoming one of the housewives who were the unheralded heart of the town with their happy families and good works and cheerful hellos.

But she didn't have to be. Evan loved her. Even when she was moody and morose, when she retreated into frozen silence, when she freaked out and told him to go away.

He was crazy to want her. Probably had gone too far with one of his fix-it fantasies.

She put her hand over her eyes. "Oh, gawd, Roxy. How do I know if Evan's for real?"

"Eh. I bet he's not."

Rose bounded off the bed. "Of course he's real."

Roxy smirked.

Rose would have explained that didn't necessarily mean that they as a couple were for real, but the maid's footsteps were clomping toward the door.

Roxy made an exaggerated face when Shari knocked. "Hallo? Who's in there?" The knob rattled. "I heard voices. I know someone's in there. Cassia? That you?"

"I'm down here, Shari," came Cassia's faint reply.

Shari grunted. The hall floor creaked. After a moment, she said, "Hey, you, in there. I can see you—standing by the door." Her voice was on a level with the floor.

Rose opened her mouth, but Roxy shushed her. They didn't move.

"I need you, Shari," called Cassia. "I've fallen and I can't get up."

"Mrrmph. I'll be keepin' my eye out," Shari muttered as she got up off the floor and stumped away. "Damn fool Valentine hijinks."

"Why can't we just walk out right in front of her?" Rose said when Shari's indistinct mumbles had joined Cassia's soprano downstairs.

Roxy shrugged. "Sure, if you want the entire town knowing that you sneaked into Valentina's room."

"God, no." Rose could imagine the indulgent looks she'd be subjected to—people would think she was trying to hook a husband.

Roxy gestured at the bed. "Then make yourself comfy. We'll have to wait until we can make a clean getaway. We've got an hour to kill, give or take. Shari gets off work at four."

Rose looked at the mussed bed. "Uh-uh. This is crazy."

"Take a nap if you want."

Rose was too aware of the portrait off to her right. She could've sworn that she actually felt Valentina's cold blue eyes following her every move.

She put up a familiar false front of bravado. "Take a *nap?* You've got to be kidding. I'd rather jump off the balcony into one of the snowdrifts."

"You may have to," Roxy said with a laugh. "Shari's a bulldog."

"Just so you know, I'm never forgetting this."

"I know." Roxy shoved her hands in her pockets. "You're welcome."

CHAPTER SEVENTEEN

"YOU'RE COMING TO the dance," Evan said to the rearview mirror. No, that was too bossy.

He watched the road, then glanced at the mirror again. "I've come to take you to the dance." Better. "Will you go to the dance with me?" But that gave her the option of saying no. "Please, will you—"

He braked hard and spun the wheel, barely making the turnoff to Maxine's Cottages. The old sign was three-fourths buried and the stone huts themselves wore white humps of snow like chef's hats. Icicles dripped from the eaves.

February 14. Valentine's Day.

He spotted Maxine's silhouette in the window and gave a toot of greeting. Before going on to Rose's cottage, he stopped in to give Maxine a dozen roses. She was so flustered by the gesture, he had to help her reach the oxygen tank. Once she was settled, she waved him on, smiling and cackling behind the mask, her lap filled with the bouquet.

The snowbanks on either side of the path to Rose's door were shoveled waist-high, the walkway deeply shadowed as the twilight faded away. A lamp with a battered metal hood shone a spotlight straight down on the doorstep. That was some comfort. She hadn't closed up and gone to bed.

But she *was* wearing a robe when she answered his knock.

"Hello, Rose," he said, the practiced lines flying out of his head at the sight of her.

She stared at the bundles in his arms. "What on earth?"

"Roses," he said, holding his arms out.

She pulled back the clouded wrappings. "We have to get these inside before they freeze! I can't believe—" she exclaimed as she accepted the crinkling bouquets. "How many did you get? This is way too extravagant!"

"Six dozen," he said, closing the door. He stamped his boots on the rug. "But I stopped and gave one of them to your mother."

Rose's mouth curved into a wry smile. "You charmer. Trying to win her to your side?"

"She's already on my side." Maxine had called his cell phone several times during the day to keep him informed of Rose's whereabouts and moods. A half hour ago, as he got ready for the school dance, she'd called to say that Rose had finished making their dinner and then gone in to take a shower, a sure sign that she was expecting— maybe even hoping—that he *would* arrive as scheduled.

"If we've got to have sides at all," he added.

Rose didn't respond, but she opened one of the bouquets wider and buried her nose among the roses. "They actually have a smell! So sweet. Like springtime." She stroked a pink blossom, her cheeks going the same color. "What kind of roses are these, you crazy lunatic?"

"Special order," he said. "I don't remember the variety, but the florist assured me that they're genuine wild roses. That's why they look kind of different—not as large and full as hothouse roses, and with the yellow stamens at the center."

"Wild roses." She breathed them in, her face going from one bundle to the next with an expression of sheer ecstasy. "Thank you. I'm totally blown away. But really—one dozen would have been enough."

"Not nearly enough. I'd give you the moon if I could."

Her gaze lifted. She shook her head in wonder, and he thought she was going to speak about last night and why she hadn't called him back, but instead she turned away and started making crooning sounds about putting the roses in warm water to ease their transition from the cold. There were so many of the flowers, she ended up sticking the stems into a plastic milk jug and the coffee can that had held her colored pencils.

Evan didn't move. He stayed by the door, watching her fuss. He still wasn't sure if she'd consent to go to the dance, and time was growing short. But he couldn't make himself hurry her. She looked so happy, padding around in her robe and slippers, turning the cottage into a perfumed garden.

Finally she stopped and looked around, her gaze eventually landing on him. She studied him up and down with obvious approval. Wanting to impress her, he'd dressed in a suit even though the dance was casual.

"I don't need the moon," she said. "I'm happy with what I have. Even if I don't deserve you."

At last he could move. He went to Rose and pulled her into his arms, kissing her thoroughly. "Don't ever say that again. You deserve the best."

She laughed almost shyly. "Oh? And is that you?"

He breathed her in. Freshly washed hair. Clean skin. Better than the hundred roses. "Probably not, but I'll try to be."

"I'll try, too," she said near his ear, hugging him with her arms around his neck.

"Promise not to run away from me without explaining, the way you did after the basketball game. I couldn't figure out what happened. If it was me, or Danny, or even Gloria…"

"Gloria! How do you know about Gloria?"

He gave a shamed shrug. "I questioned Lucy like Sherlock Holmes, trying to get a clue."

Rose stepped back, dropping her chin. "I'm sorry I did that to you." She turned away, nervous now, moving from bouquet to bouquet to rearrange the roses.

"*Was* it Gloria? I've had a few run-ins with her over team discipline, so she's not my biggest fan. If she was disrespectful—"

"Gloria's not important. She didn't say anything I haven't learned to expect from her type."

He didn't dispute that, but made a silent promise. One way or another, Gloria was going to know that she'd better watch her step around Rose or there'd be hell to pay.

"It was Danny," Rose said, with a catch in her throat.

"Danny?"

"And the boys he was with. I overheard them talking about me, and it wasn't too flattering. But I can deal with that. What hurt was when he…"

She shook her head. "It doesn't matter. I've been thinking about it ever since, and the thing is that I was expecting too much from him, too soon, even though I told myself not to. He reacted like a kid who's had his world turned upside down. In the heat of the moment I used to say things about my father that I later wished I could take back."

Evan swallowed. Danny's confusion was understandable, but he hated seeing Rose feeling so rejected. "Would it help if I talked to him?"

She shook her head with a sad smile. "Not yet. Your instincts were right—I have to give him time."

Evan approached her. "It'll get better between you two. You'll see."

She tweaked a drooping flower head. "I hope so."

"By the time the snow melts...and your own wild roses are blooming..."

"Maybe."

He put an arm around her and she leaned into him, hugging his waist. He wanted to stay like that, giving her the comfort she needed, but duty called. He thought of ditching his responsibilities, for once. The idea had immense appeal. He could imagine leading a more free-form life with Rose, one where they occasionally dropped their burdens to go hiking in the woods or paddling in the river. Lucy would be in heaven.

"You're late for the dance," Rose suddenly said.

Aw, well. It had been a nice daydream.

"*We* are," he said. "If you're still willing to go with me..." That was probably asking too much.

Her eyes were grave. "Danny will be there. That could be uncomfortable."

"You're my girl," Evan said. "He has to get used to seeing you around."

"Your girl," Rose whispered. They stared at each other for a moment, exchanging meaningful emotions through their smiles.

Eventually she raised a hand to her hair. "I have to get fixed up."

"And dressed."

"Oh. That." She looked down, untying the belt of her robe. He blinked in surprise as it fell open, until he realized what she wore underneath.

The pink dress.

"I knew you'd come," she explained, "even though I'd acted like a big baby. So I wanted to be ready."

He laughed. "You could have saved me a lot of anxiety if you'd just returned one of my phone calls."

"I intended to, sort of. Sooner or later. But then I got stuck at Bay House all afternoon and when I got home I had a special project to complete and then I had to make dinner and, well, time just got away from me."

"What were you doing at Bay House?"

She avoided his eyes. Her grin was sheepish. "Um, nothing much. Talking to Roxy."

He could see there was more to it, but he shooed her. "Go on, get ready. I'm already late. That doesn't look too good for the chaperon."

"Gloria will snipe at you!" Rose called from the bathroom. She rummaged around, running water and doing girly things, returning in five minutes with shiny black curls bouncing off her shoulders and her deep blue eyes enhanced with subtle shadings of makeup.

"You're beautiful," he said.

"Thank you." Typically bashful about the compli-

286 A FAMILY CHRISTMAS

ment, she ducked her head, zipping her legs into knee-high black boots.

Evan would have preferred spending the evening in her creaky old bed, coaxing his shy rose into full flower, but he was who he was and that included following through on his promises. Before they left, though, he liberated one of the flowers and tucked it behind Rose's ear, asking her to be his valentine. She kissed him and got a second rose for his lapel, telling him that now he was marked as belonging to Wild Rose.

They drove to the high school. The good feeling between them wasn't enough to keep out the rest of the world. He could feel Rose getting more nervous by the minute. By the time they'd gotten inside and hung their coats on the overflowing hooks near the door, he was half afraid that she would take off if he didn't keep her close.

Rose refused to dance, so he took a firm hold on her hand and began to make his rounds, saying hi to students and a few of the parents who hadn't yet been bum-rushed out the door by their mortified children.

The dance floor wasn't too crowded yet, perhaps because of the rule that no heeled shoes were allowed on the gym floor. Most of the students were in jeans and sneakers or boots. Only a few of the girls had put on dresses and heels. At some point in the evening, the kids were sure to be sliding across the floor in their stocking feet and he'd pretend not to notice for ten minutes or so before going over to break up the fun.

"I should have worn my plaid flannel," Rose said. She was scanning the youthful faces. Looking for Danny.

Even with the pounding rap music ringing in his ears, Evan heard her inhale. Or maybe he only felt it as her shoulders stiffened and she caught her lip between her teeth. Her eyes went wide. "There's Danny."

The boy was one of a group of athletes lounging on the bleachers, trying to look cool. Girls walked back and forth in front of them, chatting animatedly. Danny sat with his knees wide, hunched inside his school jacket, his usual happy-go-lucky personality vanished. He wasn't moving, not even an eyelash. There was no way of telling if he'd seen Rose.

Evan squeezed her hand. He could imagine what had been said, and she might have claimed to have brushed off the hurt—or buried it—but *he* wasn't having it. Hot blood thundered through his veins at the mere idea of Rose being hurt. He'd always had the animal instinct to defend Lucy by all means possible and even impossible, but now that feeling extended to Rose. Goddamn if he wouldn't roar like a lion for her.

That went beyond the urge to care for and fix things. Beyond duty, pity, sympathy.

Had to be love.

He inclined his head to speak near her ear. "Want me to go and talk to him? I can set him straight."

Rose considered the offer. It was terribly tempting to let Evan ride in on his white horse and slay her dragons. But how would Danny feel? He wouldn't go against anything Evan might say. Danny had respect for him, as a coach and teacher and friend.

She wanted just a little of that for herself. But a forced reconciliation would be bittersweet at best.

"No," she said, reaching across to grip Evan's sleeve. "Don't talk to him. Don't try to fix it." She turned her face toward his, silently pleading with him to understand that she had to stand strong. If not all by herself, then at least beside him. "Not this time, okay?"

He sighed. "Okay."

Relief washed into Rose. She'd find her own way to prove to Danny that she loved him. Someday, somehow. Being with Evan had given her that confidence.

The conviction started to crumble at the edges when she saw Gloria Kevanen bearing down on them, bedecked in an oversize flocked red sweater, black leggings long out of style and the smile of a shark.

"Uh, Evan?" Rose pointed discreetly. "If you want a problem to solve, there she is. *I'll* be in the ladies' room."

She escaped the dance out a side door and walked down the empty school corridor to find a washroom. Her time here had rarely been enjoyable. She'd always felt out of place. And being back for a high-school dance was the worst, making her remember the turning point in her life—the night she'd run away and into the backseat of Rick Lindstrom's convertible.

Water under the bridge. Currents in the river. All right, so she'd drifted in the wrong direction and had been swept up in turbulent events that had just about been the end of her. But she'd resurfaced. And the past months were proof that it was never too late to change course.

The washroom was unoccupied. Rose went into a stall for an extremely short tinkle. Nerves. They gamboled inside her belly with skittery claws.

She came out and washed her hands, then peered into the mirror and fluffed her hair. Her rare application of lipstick had already been gnawed off, and she hadn't thought of bringing a purse. Normally she shoved a few necessary items in the pocket of her jeans and headed out the door.

"There you are!" Gloria barged into the room. "I saw you with Evan, but you snuck off."

"Mmm."

"He was late."

"My fault."

Gloria quirked a brow. "Oh?"

Rose wiped a pinkie under her eye. "He was waiting while I did my makeup. I'm not very adept with eyeliner or mascara." Ha. Two swipes and she'd called it good.

"Come into my shop. I'll give you makeup tips." Gloria widened her lashes, pulling at the skin beneath one eye. "I got my eyeliner tattooed on. See?"

"That must have hurt."

"Beauty is pain." Gloria tilted her head toward the mirror and inspected her roots. Her eyes swiveled to Rose. "You look funny in a dress."

Rose blinked. "Funny ha-ha or funny peculiar?"

"Aw, you know I didn't mean anything. It's just strange seeing you in anything except grunge. But, you know, no one wears dresses to these things anymore. For prom, sure, but this is just a run-of-the-mill Valentine's dance."

Rose let the "advice" roll right off her. She didn't need Gloria's approval. The woman was an aphid and always had been, attempting to chew holes in Rose's self-esteem.

"I never did have the correct fashion sense," she said, but not as if she cared. If the layouts in the women's magazines were proof, no one wore clingy leggings that showed every lump and bump, either.

"That's true." Gloria's gaze was pinned to the flower in Rose's hair. Her mouth pinched. "You and Evan, huh? It's a serious thing?"

"Serious enough."

"Then you'd better get back out there. It was ladies' choice when I left and Evan was getting mobbed by teenage cuties."

"No problem. I'm secure."

Gloria narrowed her eyes. "Well, aren't we having delusions of grandeur?"

Rose turned a serene smile upon the woman. "I'll leave that for you, Gloria. If you'll excuse me."

It wasn't a flip remark or a smart putdown, but Rose felt satisfied as she returned to the dance. The negative energy of people like Gloria, or her parents—and herself for many years, if she was honest—took too much effort. Loving others, and allowing herself to be happy, was surprisingly easy once she was started. And becoming easier every day.

The DJ was announcing that the next dance was men's choice when Rose arrived. She spotted Evan on the dance floor, where he really *was* surrounded by teenage girls. He broke away and headed toward her with a smile of definite intent.

She could always count on him. Intending to accept the dance, she sat on a bottom bleacher and unzipped her boots. Her socks were awful—purple and fuzzy, with a hole in the toe. Totally embarrassing.

She was fumbling with the sock, trying to slide the hole beneath her foot, when she felt a presence. A low male voice said, "Want to dance?"

Rose straightened. Athletic socks and jeans. A Gale Storm jacket with a big block *A*. One nervous face, reddening to match her own.

Danny.

"Me?" she squeaked.

His head twitched. "Yeah."

"You want—to dance—" she couldn't breathe "—with me?"

Danny nodded.

Suddenly Evan was there beside her, giving her an arm so she was able to stand. "Looks like Danny beat me to it."

She threw Evan a glance. "Did you set this up?"

He said, "Nope," and grinned, prodding her at the small of her back. "Go on and dance with the kid. I'll get the next one."

Rose found herself out on the gym floor with Danny. The dance was slow. She didn't know where to look or put her hands. It was too strange.

Danny took her right hand. She glanced at him and rested her other hand on his upper arm. They began to move—not really dancing, just swaying and sliding their feet a little. Almost immediately, she could feel her big toe poking out of the sock.

Why hadn't she changed her socks?

Wait. Why was she thinking about socks?

"I…uh…thank you for asking me to dance."

"That's all right," Danny said. He didn't seem to know where to look, either.

"Your friends—they'll probably tease you."

"That's okay. They're idiots."

She almost smiled. "But still your friends."

"Yeah." There was a long silence. Danny's eyes flickered at her. "Sorry about what they said."

"Not your fault."

He cleared his throat. "Sorry about…what *I* said." He was in misery, but she couldn't tell if he was sincere or if this was just something he was compelled to do out of good manners. "About how you're not my mother."

"I'm not, I guess."

"I didn't mean to hurt your feelings."

"And I didn't mean to eavesdrop."

Danny exhaled. He removed his hand and wiped the palm on his jeans, then took her hand again. They swayed in a small circle. Rose glimpsed Evan's face over the crowd, encouraging her.

She licked her lips. "Maybe we can just forget about that and start again."

"Okay. But…"

She waited, her heart in her throat.

"You are my mother," he said. "It's just, y'know, weird."

With great effort, she resisted the urge to grab on to him in a giant bear hug. Instead she smiled and moved her hand up to his shoulder, moving close enough that it was almost like a hug. A long-lost mother deserved to make some kind of gesture. "Yeah, it's strange. But we'll get used to it."

"So, like, I can come over to your house sometime?"

"*Any*time."

He relaxed a little, nodding. "Good." But he still seemed doubtful.

She sensed the questions that he must have, about her decision to give him up, the circumstances of her pregnancy. His father.

His father. She didn't want Danny to know. And yet…starting off their relationship with a lie was wrong. Could she fudge the explanation, evade the details? When the time came that he demanded to know, she'd pray for wisdom. Evan would help.

For now, she and Danny needed to become acquainted with each other.

"I'll show you the river," she said, latching on to the good in her life. "And my drawings. You'll have to meet my mother, and in the spring we can have a bonfire and—" Roast hot dogs. Go fishing. Play Scrabble. Eat birthday cake. Look at photos. Meet family. Stay up late to talk. Get into fights. Celebrate. Laugh, scream, cry.

Live and love like a real family.

She wanted all of it, with Evan and Lucy, too.

But for now, she had this—her son, smiling—and that was plenty.

ROSE AND EVAN DANCED once more, toward the end of the evening. The floor was almost deserted, the strings of heart decorations drooped, the lights turned low. Danny and his friends had left an hour ago, but her heart was still full with the pleasure of hearing him say, *"You are my mother."*

"Looks like we're closing down the sock hop," Evan said.

Her head rested on his shoulder. "Mm-hmm."

"The baby-sitter's probably wondering when I'll get home."

"Let her wait a little while longer."

He kissed the top of her ear. "It was a good Valentine's Day."

"One I'll always remember."

"Me, too. Even though the only Valentine I got was one from Lucy with Chewbacca on it."

Rose's head came up. "Oh! I completely forgot." She took his hand. "Come with me."

"Are we going to make out in the stairwell?"

"No, I need my coat."

"I'll get your boots." Evan went running across the gym floor, throwing up his hands halfway across and sliding in his socks all the way to the bleachers. He whooped like a little kid, making Rose laugh out loud.

A minute later, they met beneath the basketball hoop. "Where's your coat?" he said.

"I only wanted this." She handed him an envelope.

He dropped her boots to take it. "Ah. You didn't forget me after all." He tore open the flap and pulled out her hand-painted valentine. Hearts and roses—no great work of art, but painted with a sincere sentiment and all the love she could muster.

He opened the card, probably expecting the usual *Be My Valentine* inscription.

She'd written other words—the ones she'd never used with him even though they'd been waiting to be expressed for a long time now.

When he looked at her, she said them at last. "I love you, Evan."

A cocky, charming grin slid onto his face. "I knew

you did." He took her into his arms and kissed her, blanketing her in the warmth and kindness that had healed her jagged edges. "I was just waiting for you to say it so I could finally ask you to marry me."

"*Marry you?* B-but that's not— I'm not— You can't—"

He kissed her again, quieting her fears. "Marry me, Rose."

She wanted to say yes, but there was still a doubt. Maybe he thought that she was so messed up she was a lifelong project.

"I don't want to be another Krissa," she said softly.

"I don't want you to be, either."

"But aren't you worried that I might be?"

"No. Because you're here to stay. You've stopped running."

"Then this isn't about fixing my problems?"

"What problems?" he said with a typical air of cheekiness.

She smiled. She still had the problems, of course. Dealing with her lingering anxieties, her mother, money troubles, the rocky road ahead with Danny. Guiding Lucy to her own happy ending…

Evan put his forehead on hers. Their noses rubbed. "We're already a team," he said. "So go ahead—tell me you'll marry me."

A team. Yes, they were a team, one that included Lucy and Danny and even her mother.

With a sigh of pleasure, Rose went up on tiptoe and touched her lips to his. "Okay, coach, you got it. I'll marry you. How can I resist? It's not every girl who gets proposed to under a basketball hoop with a gigantic hole in her fuzzy purple sock."

Evan looked down, looked up, looked deep into her eyes. "Some women get mistletoe…"

She threw her arms around his neck, smiling hugely. "I'd rather have you."

For the rest of their lives.

HARLEQUIN *Super* ROMANCE

A six-book series from Harlequin Superromance.

WOMEN *in Blue*

Six female cops battling crime and corruption on the streets of Houston. Together they can fight the blue wall of silence. But divided, will they fall?

Coming in December 2004,
The Witness by Linda Style
(Harlequin Superromance #1243)

She had vowed never to return to Houston's crime-riddled east end. But Detective Crista Santiago's promotion to the Chicano Squad put her right back in the violence of the barrio. Overcoming demons from her past, and with somebody in the department who wants her gone, she must race the clock to find out who shot Alex Del Rio's daughter.

Coming in January 2005,
Her Little Secret by Anna Adams
(Harlequin Superromance #1248)

Abby Carlton was willing to give up her career for Thomas Riley, but then she realized she'd always come second to his duty to his country. She went home and rejoined the police force, aware that her pursuit of love had left a black mark on her file. Now Thomas is back, needing help only she can give.

Also in the series:
The Partner by Kay David (#1230, October 2004)
The Children's Cop by Sherry Lewis (#1237, November 2004)

And watch for:
She Walks the Line by Roz Denny Fox (#1254, February 2005)
A Mother's Vow by K.N. Casper (#1260, March 2005)

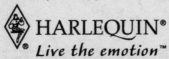

HARLEQUIN®
Live the emotion™

HARLEQUIN®

AMERICAN *Romance*®

A COWBOY AND A KISS

by Dianne Castell

Sunny Kelly wants to save the old saloon
that her aunt left her in a small Texas town.

But Sunny isn't really Sunny.
She's Sophie Addison, a Reno attorney,
and she's got amnesia.

That's not about to stop cowboy
Gray McBride, who's running hard for
mayor on a promise to clean up the town—
until he runs into some mighty strong
feelings for the gorgeous blonde.

*On sale starting December 2004—
wherever Harlequin books are sold.*

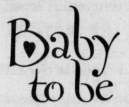

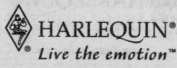

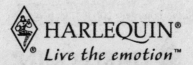

HARLEQUIN *Super*ROMANCE®

YOU, ME & THE KIDS

Along Came Zoe

by Janice Macdonald

Superromance #1244
On sale December 2004

Zoe McCann doesn't like doctors. They let people
die while they're off playing golf. Actually, she knows
that's not true, but her anger helps relieve some of
the pain she feels at the death of her best friend's
daughter. Then she confronts Dr. Phillip Barry—the
neurosurgeon who wasn't available when Jenny was
brought to the E.R.—and learns that doctors
don't have all the answers. Even where
their own children are concerned.

Available wherever Harlequin books are sold.

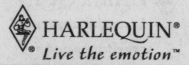

HARLEQUIN®
Live the emotion™